HOSTILE MAKEOVER

Reba Koll leapt at Sabatini. Their merged bodies became a single, seething mass of amorphous flesh; it writhed and wrinkled like some great monster, and slowly a form began building out of the center.

At first it was a head, humanoid but hardly human, with bloated, puffy flesh and no hair or features. Then the torso started to emerge, then the waist, and finally thick, sturdy legs. Subtly the skin texture and muscle tone changed, becoming flatter, harder, and more natural. Very slowly but steadily the rest of the detailing came in.

The figure shuddered, then breathed deeply. The eyes opened, and the new Sabatini looked at them.

By Jack L. Chalker
Published by Ballantine Books:

THE WEB OF THE CHOZEN

AND THE DEVIL WILL DRAG YOU UNDER

A JUNGLE OF STARS

DANCERS IN THE AFTERGLOW

THE SAGA OF THE WELL WORLD
Volume 1: *Midnight at the Well of Souls*
Volume 2: *Exiles at the Well of Souls*
Volume 3: *Quest for the Well of Souls*
Volume 4: *The Return of Nathan Brazil*
Volume 5: *Twilight at the Well of Souls:*
          The Legacy of Nathan Brazil

THE FOUR LORDS OF THE DIAMOND
Book One: *Lilith: A Snake in the Grass*
Book Two: *Cerberus: A Wolf in the Fold*
Book Three: *Charon: A Dragon at the Gate*
Book Four: *Medusa: A Tiger by the Tail*

THE DANCING GODS
Book One: *The River of Dancing Gods*
Book Two: *Demons of the Dancing Gods*
Book Three: *Vengeance of the Dancing Gods*

THE RINGS OF THE MASTER
Book One: *Lords of the Middle Dark*
Book Two: *Pirates of the Thunder*
Book Three: *Warriors of the Storm*
Book Four: *Masks of the Martyrs*

Book Two of *The Rings of the Master*

PIRATES
OF THE
THUNDER

Jack L. Chalker

A Del Rey Book

BALLANTINE BOOKS ● NEW YORK

A Del Rey Book
Published by Ballantine Books

Copyright © 1987 by Jack L. Chalker

Library of Congress Catalog Card Number: 86-91384

ISBN 0-345-32561-3

Manufactured in the United States of America

First Edition: March 1987
Fourth Printing: February 1988

Cover Art by Darrell K. Sweet

For Judy-Lynn del Rey,
a unique giant in a field
dominated by pygmies,
for all that I am today.
I wish you'd stuck around for the climax.

TABLE OF CONTENTS

PROLOGUE

NINE HAD DIED IN THE FIGHT, NINE GOOD FRIENDS AND family members. From her haven in the small hollow escape pod attached to the great tree, she stared out into the rain, but she could see little more than water and mist. The tears began to flow as a dark shape seemed to move in the grayness outside. She raised the pistol but did not fire; the shape paused a moment, then moved on past the tree.

She knew that it had somehow still missed her, but it was heading for the nearby compound where twenty more would be taken by surprise as her party had been—and possibly slaughtered for not telling the thing what they did not know.

Its pause between her escape and its pursuit certainly meant that it had beamed a full account of the progress to date to its master module, in orbit somewhere above. Its programmers would make certain she never left this cursed world, and if she destroyed it they'd send another Val, and another, until they got her—no matter what the cost.

How many lives, both human and Sakanian, was she worth? How many would be massacred for her? And for what? Sooner or later they would get her, and even if she could elude them indefinitely in this mess of a world she could do no more useful work.

With a sigh, she crawled out of the pod and into the rain. The thing had not gone far and was easy to track, and she was amazed at her sudden calmness. Sensing it was being followed, it stopped and waited, a large, hulking, obsidianlike humanoid that was plastic enough to become whatever it needed, and now needed to be nothing more than itself.

She stepped into the clearing and faced the Val from a distance of five meters or so, her pistol still pointed at it.

"I have been waiting for you, Ngoriki," the Val said in a voice that sounded somewhat like her own, but full of stoic self-confidence.

"I know. I can't let you kill any more innocent people."

"Yes. Inside me is a record of you, you know. I fully understood what the action would do to you. I very much regret having to do it, but there seemed no other way. I had tried the traditional approaches and nothing else seemed sure."

She felt suddenly furious, and her grip on the pistol tightened. "You *regret*! How dare you! How can you regret? You are a machine, a soulless monstrosity! You don't *feel*. You don't know what that did to me! You're nothing but a machine carrying out your programming, no matter what the cost!"

"You are both right and wrong," the machine said. "It is true that I am a construct, carrying out my master programming instructions—but so are you. I am made of different stuff, in a different way, than you, and, unlike you, I know my creator and my engineers. Human beings are programmed by their biochemistry more than you would like to believe. I think—and that makes me an individual. I am not free, but neither is humanity."

"Yes. That's what you'll do to me, isn't it? Reprogram me. Perhaps that is what sets us apart, then. I have a yearning to be free, and you see that yearning as only a flaw in my own genetics."

"No," the Val responded. "We have a disagreement, that is all. This is not a good, let alone perfect, system we have, I grant that. It is merely a better system than the alternatives. It saved the race of humankind and many other races from inevitable self-extinction. Having saved them from their demise at their own hands, it now saves them from extinction at the hands of others. Survival outweighs all other considerations. If one survives, one has opportunity and hope at some point for changes for the better. If one does not survive, nothing else matters."

"Damn it!" she screamed at him. "You have everything I was inside you! *Everything!* You *know* I am innocent of what I was charged!"

The Val almost seemed to sigh. "Yes. I know. That more than anything has made this so difficult for me. We hate to get the rare innocent to track, yet we must. Do you know why we are called Vals? After a character in ancient Earth literature, one Jean Valjean. He stole a loaf of bread to feed his starving family and received life at slave labor as his punishment. He escaped, became great, and did only great things for others, yet he was hunted relentlessly and brought down all the same. The name is that of the victim, not the pursuer. The greater good for the greater number requires that the system work. An individual injustice here and there is inevitable, but so long as the trial is fair and the conviction proper, the system must be served, for otherwise there is chaos and disorder, and the masses will suffer. Better one than the many, as painful as that may be."

"You bastard! Where does justice and mercy fit into all this?"

"Is it mercy to spare one so that a thousand be killed? The system ensures survival. Without survival, justice and mercy are irrelevant, as well. Therefore, they are irrelevant here."

The pistol dipped down, and she felt the tears returning. "But—without justice and mercy, why survive at all?" she asked.

She suddenly raised the pistol, ready to fire, but the Val had anticipated her and was quicker. A snakelike tentacle suddenly shot from its midsection and struck her once, hard, on the side of her head. She cried out, then crumpled. It retracted the tentacle, then went over to her and gave her a quick examination. She was out cold.

"We *are* different," the Val said aloud. "I have often wished, in circumstances such as this, that I, too, could cry."

It lifted her gently in its huge arms and carefully made its way back to the compound and, eventually, the ship.

Absolution was a destruction of memory that left a Val in some way impaired, missing a part of itself. Rarely did a Val crave Absolution—but this one did. The girl had been so beautiful, so innocent, yet the Val had been forced by the logic of its system to destroy her. Reprogramming a human brain was not death, of course; the system demanded some mercy. Still, she would cease to exist as a separate entity who had been born, raised, and molded by the world of her birth. She would become someone entirely different, someone totally artificial, and she would never even suspect that she had changed. She would be a character in Master System's grand play, no more a true and natural sentient creature than, well, than the Val itself.

Absolution would erase all knowledge and memory of her, of the hunt for her, along with the traces of guilt and doubt that such operations always induced. In a personal sense, the Val would welcome the relief, but in another sense it would not. By now those memories that were hers existed only in its own data banks; when they were gone, she would be truly dead.

How many others had been like her? How many of the thousands it had chased and brought to justice—or destroyed, when that had been the only alternative—had been in fact not the system's enemies but its victims? It would never know, but that very thought was treason and disturbing down to its core; Absolution was a necessity, and must be done as soon as possible.

Vals had at their constant disposal a reading of all the memories, all the personality factors, of their object. To catch someone, the hunter had to know the quarry more intimately than the quarry knew itself. Even such people as murderers and traitors might be viewed with sympathy if all that they were was seen with detachment.

No, that was getting even worse. Perhaps this Val was defective. Perhaps this time there would be no awakening from Absolution.

The Val went to its cubicle and plugged in its receptors. The complete data was first read out into Master System's files; there, at least, the information and the personality files would always reside. Then all data in the auxiliary banks and the core was erased, so that the Val was as virginal and ignorant—and as nonfunctional—as when it was built.

Master System then reprogrammed the core as a new unit updated with all the newest findings, the newest technology, and the newest tricks of the trade. The Val did not feel, did not wonder, did not doubt. It was merely a machine.

But it was a machine with the *capacity* for all those things, for if it were not it could never comprehend its quarry, never second-guess them and trap them. Without Absolution, the Vals were in serious danger of becoming somewhat human.

Now came the assignment.

Master System was the greatest computer ever built. All data ever on a computer network was inside it from the start; it knew all there was to know, the sum total of human knowledge and experience. Designed as a last link in a massive defense against impending nuclear war, its sole purpose were the preservation of the human race and its knowledge, and the quest for new knowledge.

It had done its job; and having prevented holocaust, it had set about to carry out its dictates that would prevent even the remotest possibility of such a horror ever happening again. It seized command of the world, all weapons and powers, and tied all computer systems into a master system of its own design. It selected examples in doubting and resisting countries, and certain cities along with their teeming populations ceased to exist—and so did resistance to Master System.

But its basic programming still reigned: *The human race must never be permitted to die out.* So robotic scouts were sent out to find worlds for humanity. And such worlds were found. Colonists specially tailored for survival on those not-quite-Earthlike worlds were brought to their new homes by great universe ships. Earth was left not with billions, but a mere five hundred thousand, who could be reprogrammed and resettled.

The great cities were leveled and traces of modern civilization were all but wiped out. The survivors were confined to isolated reservations whose cultures were modeled after more primitive periods of history. Humanity became its own living museum, not with great accuracy but with great effect.

Only a few human beings knew the facts. These were the elite, the brightest from each of the indigenous people, the chosen administrators who kept their own people in primitive darkness as the price of their own luxury and privilege.

Giving knowledge to those who ran humanity was not without price to Master System. Putting the best and brightest together and allowing them access to tools and history resulted in the development of a hidden subculture that had discovered how to beat the system. They had learned to edit their own memories, eliminating any forbidden knowledge that might be detected in the periodic recordings made of their minds. They did their own research and played their own power games beyond the reach of Master System. The great computer tolerated a certain measure of such activities, but was eternally vigilant to any that threatened the system itself or its own near-total control. Those who overstepped the bounds had the Vals sent after them—and the Vals rarely failed.

Now a Val was being informed of a new element, one that might be the greatest threat of all times to Master System. For the great computer was vulnerable. It had taken all the measures it thought it could to hide that fact, but the vulnerability remained, having been built into it by its creators: An overriding command could suspend all existing programming imperatives of Master System and make it subject to new compulsive orders. It was also compelled to allow anyone actually attempting this to do so. For the attempt to succeed, however, the cancellation codes had to be read into Master System's core memory. The codes were hidden on tiny microchips disguised as five individually designed elaborate and ornate golden rings. Anyone inserting all five into their corresponding interface slots in the correct order would in effect be the master of Master System. The rings themselves, Master System's programming demanded, had to be at all times in the possession of humans with authority. If a ring were lost or destroyed, another must be fashioned to replace it. Altering any such imperatives in its programming would destroy Master System.

So it had scattered the rings, leaving one on Earth and sending the other four into the trackless void of the involuntary interstellar colonists. It had wiped out all references it could find to the rings, their function and their use—and even to the very location where the rings had to be used.

But somewhere, somehow, possibly in ancient archives uncovered by Center archaeologists, some record of the rings, and all they implied, survived the centuries. After nine hundred years of static life in darkness, there were humans who knew. Already a few technological underground cells had discovered how to command and reprogram Master System's computer-piloted spaceships. Some such groups as the freebooters, who were occasionally useful, were even allowed to exist as a sort of Center in space, so long as they remained selfish and did not threaten the system.

But now a small group of renegades had all the information it needed to start out. They knew of the rings. They knew how to command the ships. They did not know where the rings were, nor where to use them, but there was a strong possibility that they could discover these things in time. They were on the loose, and they were dedicated— with nothing to lose.

Although the group seemed insignificant, and its chances of doing anything more than providing a minor nuisance were billions to one against them, Master System was tremendously concerned. It claimed it was fighting a bitter and stalemated war—although even its own Vals were not told whom it was fighting, or where, or why— and that if Master System were to be in any way disabled, defeat would be inevitable, with consequences horrible for all. The mere fact that information on the rings had survived and gotten out beyond Earth was unsettling to it. It felt so threatened it was actually considering a new mass reprogramming of humanity, the destruction of all the Centers, and the imposing of a new limit where even the concept of agriculture or of a language capable of expressing complex and abstract ideas would be forbidden by computers that would be worshipped and obeyed as tangible gods. But it would take a very long time to do this.

The capture of the rebel band was given overriding priority to the Vals. There were ten individuals to find, but there were recordings for only a small number of those. What information they did have was provided by Doctor Isaac Clayben of Melchior, the penal colony in the asteroids from which all the renegades had escaped.

The Val absorbed the available information, then was fed the mindprint of the band's leader, Hawks. The historian was a fascinating individual, a man of some brilliance and accomplishment literally torn between his tribal and Center worlds. Though he was not a rebel or an adventurer, nor a man of action in spite of some romantic fantasies, it was clear that once Hawks had the documents in his possession he would have felt compelled to read them out of sheer curiosity and a hunger to know—and that he no doubt understood them and their implications.

Recent events not included in the mindprint showed that he was capable of much adaptation, capable of killing if need be, and capable of living in and out of the wild as well. The Val was convinced that in a hopeless position Hawks would kill himself rather than surrender. He would not, however, desert his own people, particularly the women, unless forced to do so by circumstances or necessity. As a result, if Hawks could be located, so might most or all of the rest.

They will go after the rings, the Val noted. *Although it is unlikely, we cannot assume they do not already know their location. Vals must cover all four rings.*

Agreed, Master System responded. *But you will not be posted there. They will need ships other than what they have. They will need contacts among the freebooters and others. The Koll Val is working on this end. You will assist. If any are sighted, trace them. So long as they do not possess all five rings, it is imperative that they be taken alive, so that we may find how many others share the forbidden knowledge. However, once they possess all five rings, if they ever do, then no limitations will be imposed.*

But surely there is no danger of them ever obtaining all five! They must run our gauntlet in each case!

*It is always possible. I see a hidden hand in this, one
who has selected most of these for just this purpose. It is
this hidden hand I want most of all. It is possible our great
enemy is behind this. If so, then they are dangerous indeed. We can take no chances. Also, time is not necessarily
on our side. If they do not succeed, but escape, we might
well face their grandchildren. Go. You are programmed
and assigned.*

The Val disconnected. The entire process, from Absolution through reprogramming, had taken just a few seconds.
The Val, who thought often in computer time but func-
tioned in human time, could not help but note this fact
alone.

How could they possibly win?

1. THE WORLD THAT MOVES THROUGH STARS

IT WAS A SPACESHIP—AND IT WAS MORE THAN THAT.

It was a starship, a ship designed to go to places even the eye could not follow and to go distances beyond the grasp of human minds—but it was more than that.

It looked very much like a great tube, flattened a bit on top and bottom and rounded at both ends, with protuberances that were bays for the scout ships that clung to their mother in special recesses, and sensors, and communications devices—and much, much more.

The ship itself—one of the hundreds that circled great Jupiter in silence, shut down, but preserved and ready for reactivation if their service should ever be needed—was a bit over fourteen kilometers long. The ship had a brain and massive amounts of stored knowledge and skills that had not been needed in a very long while.

"I wonder if it is bothered by that," Cloud Dancer said, more to herself than to the others who were gazing at the viewing screen of their relatively small interplanetary freighter.

"Huh?" Walks With the Night Hawks, her husband and co-conspirator, looked at her. "Who is bothered by what?"

12

"The ship. It has a mind, a soul, as this one does. Its spirit is dedicated to work, to a great task, and it has been told to do nothing since it did that task. I wonder if it minds, sitting there idle, without hope or opportunity to do its task, to be itself, for all this time."

"It sure fought like hell to keep *us* out," came the gravelly voice of the Crow Agency man, Raven. Not long before they had been the targets of some of those fighters nestled inside the great ships; only deciphering the clearance code in time and some fancy maneuvering had saved them from being blown from the sky.

"That was its duty," the Hyiakutt Indian woman responded. She was quite smart, but having been raised in a primitive culture, she saw the universe from a perspective as alien to the others as they were to the computer brain of the great ship they now approached. "Now it receives us. I wonder if it is eager, or if it is waiting to devour us?"

"Neither," an odd voice said through the ship's intercom. When Star Eagle, as they had named the computer pilot of the ship, spoke on his own, it was in a pleasant male voice, but when China was interfaced into the ship's system, forming a human-computer synthesis, the voice sounded strange, neither male nor female, but somehow both at once. "There is no command module on any of these ships. It was removed when they were placed in storage here. These ships have many brains, as it were, since even the tiny fractions of a second it might take to relay an order might cause needless risk, but the only ones there now are automatic maintenance and ship's security. The tech cult that discovered the human interfaces intended to fly the ship themselves, without a command module."

Hawks frowned. "Is that possible?"

"Yes, but not efficient or practical. They did not think beyond that point, since even attaining that much was highly improbable. All plans were based on the escape, not what came next. Just like us."

Yes, but we're at least better off than they would have been. We have Koll, who's been out there, and information from Raven and Warlock. We are not going completely blind. He frowned, wondering if that was really true or if he was just trying to reassure himself.

Still, he had no doubt they would get away. No mystical sense informed him, and he knew of no particular edge on their part, but even though they'd had to fight every step of the way to this point, he couldn't shake the feeling that somehow they were being *led*.

Most of this crew had been selected, somehow, by Lazlo Chen, the ambitious chief administrator of the central Asian district and discoverer of the information that five gold rings could, if found and used properly, deactivate or control Master System. Chen owned the only one of the rings remaining on Earth, and was determined that this group secure the others for him. The stakes were quite high—nothing less than godhood for the one who found all the rings and brought them together.

But even Chen was subject to Master System; even Chen had severe limits on his knowledge and power. Chen's reach extended over the whole of the Earth and even beyond, but it did not reach as far out as Jupiter. Since their escape from the asteroid penal colony, Melchior, Hawks had been convinced that another player was also on the scene, one who also wanted them to succeed and whose reach *did* extend farther out. Who or what this player was could not be known now; nor could they guess whether *it* was using Chen for its own ends, or whether Chen was using it.

This was a strange band to pick for such a mission. Hawks was a Hyiakutt Amerind historian, a student of rebels and warriors, not one himself. Cloud Dancer had been born and raised in the Plains culture, a primitive suddenly thrust into a world of what to her was magic. The Chow sisters came out of an equally primitive society in China, but as personal servants to Center personnel they'd had more experience with technology; they had an uncanny ability to pick even computer-encoded locks, though they were otherwise ignorant. Raven, the Crow security man built like a boulder, and his associate Manka Warlock, the Jamaican beauty with the cold personality and a liking for killing people, seemed more obvious choices, but neither of them had ever before left Earth. Out here in space they were as ignorant and helpless as he was. The selection of China, too, made some sense—originally known as Song Ching, she was the daughter of the chief administrator of China and the product of a breeding experiment to produce a subrace that was physically perfect and mentally so advanced it was hoped to be a match for the computer system—but she, too, had never been off Earth, and thanks to the cruel experimentation of the scientists on Melchior she was hardly a perfect choice now. Blind and compulsively pregnant, her true value was only in her ability to use the human interface to become one with the mind of the ship's computer pilot, as she was doing now.

That, too, was a mystery. Why did these ships have interfaces for humans at all? Master System alone could build them, in far-off, wholly automated factories among the stars. Why was there a bridge, with connections to the vital parts and operations of the ships, as if humans and computers were supposed to work together? It was this absolute control of space that made Master System unbeatable, and it had been perhaps nine hundred years since any humans had traveled on spaceships as anything other than passengers. It would have been simple to build these ships so that no one could ever control or tamper with the command modules, the computer brains. Why hadn't that been done?

Even the huge interstellar vessel they were now approaching had positions for humans, and more than one bridge, yet these ships had not been built until after Master System had taken total control of humanity. These ships had been designed not for human use but to carry the bulk of humanity against its will to captivity among the stars. Why, then, were there a bridge and interfaces for humans, since without those they would have no escape, no opportunity to flee, at all?

And then there was Reba Koll, the essential one, the only one who'd been out there before, and the only one who herself had used the interfaces illegally to pilot a spaceship. They had a lot riding on the memories and long-unused skills of the strange old woman with the tail, and she was quite mad—who wouldn't have been after enduring ten years of experimentation on Melchior? She claimed not to be Reba Koll but someone—or something —else she would not now reveal. Even the security forces who had pursued them from Melchior claimed the same, and that worried Hawks. He didn't think she was some sort of inhuman monstrosity, but he wondered if she was something very dangerous such as the carrier of a dread disease.

The final two in the party had been unexpected additions to the mission. Silent Woman, a product of years of slavery and degradation in the primitive culture of North America, her tongue cut out, her body covered with colorful tattoos, was almost childlike, and there was little or no way to communicate with her on more than a rudimentary basis. She understood none of the languages the others used commonly—though Hawks had used a mindprint machine to give her basic English—and she seemed to live in a world all her own.

Sabatini, the cruel captain from whom they'd taken this ship, was here involuntarily, a prisoner. They could neither trust him nor let him go; sooner or later, Hawks knew, they would have to face his disposal.

There was nothing left to see on the viewscreen; Star Eagle was now so close to the massive interstellar ship that the vast bulk blotted everything out.

"Strap in and prepare for a set of big jolts," the ship warned them. "My reverse thrusters are shot thanks to the battle, and that means, in effect, no brakes. I've done as much as I can, but now we will have to be caught and halted by tractor beam and that's going to be a pretty big shock. Helmets on and switch to internal air supply. I have no idea if we can maintain pressurization."

They were already all strapped in, both here and in the lounge and up on the bridge, yet each checked his own straps and webbing to make certain they were secure. The ship then activated the restraint system, pulling them back and holding them so firmly that it was hard to breathe. All were wearing pressure suits and helmets now, and they could only wait.

Suddenly there was a massive jolt, a tremor that shook the whole ship, followed by another, then another. The ship seemed to lurch, moving in all directions at once, and all around were creaks and groans of metal in distress. Loud hissing sounds punctuated the moaning and groaning of fatigued metal. The sense of motion and the shocks stopped quickly; the noises did not.

"What's happening?" Warlock asked nervously. "We're not going to die just on the edge of victory!"

The speakers sputtered, hissed, and crackled. "I—released China—to her," came the pilot's normal voice. "Ship—break up. Suits on, hold tight—I—"

"You're breaking up!" Hawks said through his suit radio. "If I understand correctly the ship is breaking up in the tractor. Will you be all right?"

"You—get in—soon as bays close. Decompressing . . . mand module—no serious danger to—China—"

Suddenly there was silence except for the faint buzz of the carrier in the suit radio. The lights blinked, then went off, leaving the passengers for a moment in darkness and then in an eerie semilight as their helmet and small body locator lights came on.

"Is the ship dead?" Cloud Dancer asked, awed by the idea. "Has Star Eagle now soared to the otherworld?"

"I—I don't know," Hawks responded. "The *body* of the ship is dead, that's for sure, but those computers have their own power supplies and sources of energy. It's possible he's still alive and we can rescue him. I hope so."

There was a sudden and unexpected jarring and the whole ship shuddered, then seemed to roll over slightly on its side, as the big ship's tractor mechanism pulled them in, controlled by the automatic maintenance and defense systems.

"We're in!" Raven called. "Damn it, we're inside the thing!"

Hawks was suddenly galvanized into action. "Warlock, go forward and see to China and Reba Koll and bring them back here."

"No need" came Koll's sharp, raspy voice over the radio. "We're all right and coming back now."

"The command module," China said in her own soft, high voice. "Have you seen to it?"

"Huh?" Hawks frowned. "Where is it?"

"Aft, in the first cargo hold. There's a big round plate in the floor secured by nine recessed bolts and an electronic combination. You throw two long switches to reveal the lock."

Hawks looked around. "Okay, Chow sisters. That sounds like it's in your department."

"No need," China told him. "I know the combination and it can be set and timed to blow the bolts. I come as quick as I can. Someone get a measuring tool and meet us there."

"Do we have to do it now?" Warlock asked irritably. "It's a damned machine. It'll wait."

"It is one with us," Cloud Dancer responded in a bitter, almost menacing tone. "It comes with us."

China was there now, being led by Reba Koll. Hawks shrugged as he was handed an electronic measure from Sabatini's kit and went back with them. "Nobody leaves yet," he cautioned. "You don't want to go into that kind of place without backup."

"How long's the air last in these things?" Raven muttered.

"Better than sixty hours," Koll told him. "There's time."

"Yeah." The Crow security man sighed. "There's time, but is there air out there?"

Hawks wasn't quite sure what China had in mind, but he was willing to go along with her. She was a strange sort, but she knew these machines like nobody else did, and in a real sense the whole group was dependent on the blind girl.

The plate was not easy to find in the dark; even under normal conditions they might have missed it. Recessed into the deck were two long mechanical rods that took some effort just to get lifted up a bit; they were almost as difficult to raise the rest of the way, eventually requiring the combined weight of Hawks and Raven. Finally, though, both rods were pulled up and then pushed over as far as they could go, and a center plate popped out revealing a dirt-caked touchpad. When they'd cleaned it off as best they could, China gave them the combination that she had learned from Star Eagle.

Hawks nervously keyed it in, then they all stepped back, well away of the plate, and waited. There was no sound in the airless ship, but a sudden series of flashes burst around the plate and the bolts all seemed to leap out of their sockets. Moving quickly now, they pried the plate up and put it out of the way, revealing a cavity perhaps half a meter deep in which sat three small rectangular objects.

"Pull up the center one carefully—very carefully," China instructed. "Then measure its dimensions and tell me of its connectors."

Doing so carefully was a chore; magnetism or some other force kept the device seated well, and breaking that grip was tough. Finally, though, they got it up, measured it, and checked it over. The connectors, smoothly polished and brass-colored, seemed etched into the sides and bottom of the box; there were a lot of them in numerous patterns. Hawks did his best to describe them to China.

She nodded. "For now, put it back so that it can continue to draw on its emergency power reserves," she instructed. "Now we must go into the big ship."

"Just what *is* that, lady?" Raven asked, irritated that this didn't seem to have much point after all that work.

"That is the command module—the brain—of Star Eagle," she told them. "The other two are management modules. They can live far longer there than we can in these suits, so we must hurry. We need to discover the equivalent place on the big ship and check it out as well."

Hawks understood. "You're thinking of moving Star Eagle from this ship into command of the big one. Is that possible? Surely the design of the command modules will be different for a massive interstellar craft than for an interplanetary freighter. The operations will be far more complex."

"Not really," she told him. "Most of it appears standardized so that they can be reprogrammed easily at any point. Master System doesn't want any computer *too* sophisticated running these things, and particularly not one that can't be reprogrammed on the fly. There is no guarantee; the size might be right but the connectors different, for example."

"What if it is?" Hawks asked her. "What if it's impossible? How do we fly this monster?"

"The way the tech cult who discovered the plans for these intended to do it. Direct interface, human mind to machine. Or minds, in this case. I suspect it will take several to manage it."

"You know where this thing's supposed to go in?" Raven asked.

"Yes—more or less. It should be obvious once we're

there. The trouble is, I have no idea where we are in this ship except that we are on an outer deck."

"You realize how *big* this mother is?" Raven asked her. "It could take days, weeks, to find our way around, with nothing much working. There's limited water in these suits, even more limited air, no food, and no road map. It's impossible!"

"So was getting this far," Hawks snapped, trying to break the mood. "First, two of us go out and find out where we are—some landmark, something, that'll give China a clue. Then we get her and Captain Koll up to that bridge to start doing things the hard way while others of us try and find the interface. I assume, China lady, that you have some sort of map of this thing in your head if we can find landmarks."

"I have a schematic imprinted there, the memory of which was further enhanced by Star Eagle, but it is not of the detail I would like. The bridge should be easy, and we'll take it from there. At least if I can find the bridge and establish some sort of interconnect we ought to be able to get some life-support systems operating."

Hawks sighed. "Well, Crow—you feeling up to a walk in the dark with me?"

"Anything to get moving," Raven responded.

There was something ironic about moving around in a strange, dark, eerie environment using a blind woman for eyes. The compartment they were in was enormous, far too large for their lights to illuminate even a wall. The freighter they had just left was close to three hundred meters in length and it didn't even crowd the place. The first step, then, was finding a wall, and that took almost forty minutes.

With gravity their task might have been impossible; there were few objects that could be used as ladders or footholds. In zero gee, however, they were able to explore more efficiently. Eventually they found hatchs on an inner wall and studied one. It was locked electronically, of course, but they found the manual override and opened it.

They moved through the hatch and were startled when a small string of lights came on along both sides of the corridor near the floor.

"Motion sensing," China explained through the radio from back inside the freighter's remains. "That is a break for us."

"I'm not sure about that break business," Raven noted sourly. "There are corridors leading to corridors leading to corridors."

"I have a marker here from the ship's kit," Hawks tried to reassure him, although he wasn't feeling very secure himself. "I'm making a mark every ten floor lights or so, and I will indicate direction at every intersection. That's the best we can do."

They went on for what seemed like a long time without hitting any landmark that China could use to place them. The corridors seemed to go off in all directions into eternity.

"Hey, Chief? You noticed we ain't come on no big rooms, no lines of rooms? No offices, dormitories, or camp meeting places, for that matter. Just access ways for equipment and service. We got to be in the service corridors and not the main halls. I mean, this was built as a cargo ship and its cargo was people. Lots and lots of people. Where in hell did they *put* them?"

Hawks didn't reply, but he was getting a bad feeling

about all this. As a historian, he knew of these ships and
what they'd done—although he'd never dreamed that they
still existed—and he had always imagined them as great
inverted worlds, with gardens and dense apartmentlike
clusters, like an immense floating and self-sufficient city.
This, however, was sterile, spartan, cold, and lifeless.
Raven was right. A ship this size might be expected to
transport and support thousands of people. Where? And
how?

And, quite suddenly, through one more hatch, they
found the answer.

They must be, Hawks guessed, in the belly of the ship,
yet it was crowded and went off in all directions. Their
helmet lights and the lights on what had now become a
wide catwalk revealed only a tiny part of it, but there was
the sense that this, too, went on forever.

"Jeez! It's like some kinda monster honeycomb," Raven
remarked. The many catwalks divided an enormous section
that extended above and below as far as the light carried.
They could see down past some half-dozen levels of
chambers before the honeycomb was swallowed in darkness.

Hawks turned and studied the way the catwalk was fas-
tened to the inner hull wall. "Rails," he noted, pointing.
"The walks move up and down. See the stops there? Each
walk would service, I would say, five rows of these holes
or chambers up, and perhaps five down. They were
probably not marched in. It would be too messy. Most
likely the people were placed in some sort of drug-induced
coma, probably in large groups by gas, then hauled in here
and loaded automatically by equipment designed for that
purpose. You said it, Raven—cargo." He leaned over and

felt just inside the nearest chamber. "Some sort of soft synthetic lining. See? Each one is large enough for one human adult. You can see small vents, and that tiny box looks as if it contains tentacular tubing. They put them in, then the tubing attached itself where necessary, and they were sustained for the journey."

"Yeah," Raven said dryly. "Gives you the shakes. I suppose they kept a mixture of the gas and pure oxygen in here to keep 'em out, or maybe these things can be sealed and separately flooded. Gives you the creeps, though."

"Until now this was only an academic thing for me," Hawks told him, his voice strained. "In its own way it was even somewhat romantic. Whole human civilizations being carted off to the stars to found new colonies. It does not seem very romantic now. This is the true face of Master System, Raven, the one we served and even believed in to a great degree when we were younger. Even this expedition, this rebellion, was, I admit, as much a romance to me, a chance to live beyond the confines, to experience rather than merely study—but no more. I have lost an innocence here I did not know I retained, and I am filled with revulsion. These weren't humans to Master System and its machines, Raven. Not their makers, not their charges. Just digits. Binary ones and zeros. Quantity this. Not even the dignity of zoo animals or pets. Carrion. No—live meat in its despicable deep freeze."

"Sorry to interrupt," China's voice broke in, "but can you get any real landmark on the central cargo bay? You've got a lot of people back here who are getting hungry and will also need air."

Hawks resented her intrusion, and also her tone. She *must* have heard them. When she saw—but, no, she wouldn't see. She couldn't. She could be standing right here and it could only be described to her as it might be read by him from some book or computer printout. At times that strange girl seemed more machine than human, anyway. She might very well stand here, even if she could see, and explain the cold and efficient logic behind the system from a computer's point of view. She probably would.

"The corridor we entered on has to be one that services this level, running parallel to it," Raven responded. "Best we might do is pick a direction and follow it until it ends."

Hawks tore himself away from his reverie. "No. If we're near one end of the chamber and go the wrong way it might be ten kilometers to reach an end, and it might be an end with nothing worth the trouble. We must split up. You walk one way, I, the other, until the first one of us comes to an end or some other recognizable feature. Remain parallel to the hatches leading to the walks. If we are not in the center, and the odds are against it, then one of us should reach something useful in a short time."

"Fair enough. I'll go left and if I junction I'll continue to always take the left fork. You do the same on the right, taking the right fork. We have to get cracking on this. History can wait, as usual."

After about another thirty or forty minutes, Raven called out. "I've gotten to the end! There's another catwalk out here, but also ones leading up to hatches all along the wall."

"Any distinguishing features on the wall?" China asked him.

"Hard to see with the light we got. There's five hatches makin' kind of a triangle goin' up one side to a center one and then back down. Lemme haul myself up there and see what's what." There was a pause filled with some intermittent grunts. Then Raven spoke again. "It's recessed in the whole area. Triangle shape, and right up top is a whole bunch of what looks like pipes that come together in a neat line and go into the wall. That help?"

"Yes. I know exactly where you are. Look carefully down from the center hatch, perhaps centered in the middle. A round plate of some kind, possibly secured by rivets."

"Ugh! No handholds down there, and I ain't got this no-gravity stuff down yet, if I ever will. Let's see . . . Yeah! It's here. Looks like it was designed to turn if you had a handle, but I don't see one."

"A strong magnet would do it. I think we can find something here. It is probably not locked. That is a service tunnel going down to the core room. The center hatch above should lead to the bridge. Hawks?"

"Yeah?"

"Stop going where you've been walking. You're walking aft and you'd be a long time getting to anyplace useful. Best you return here and get the rest of us. We must take Star Eagle's core and the two support modules and see if we can make them fit in there. If we can, we will be masters of this ship."

"Uh huh," Raven grunted. "And if we can't?"

"Then we will have to work around it. Let's try the other first. Master System is almost maniacal about standardization. It's one reason we have been able to beat the system so often. The interplanetary ships were designed as precursors to these, and there is no evidence that they have ever been significantly changed in their basic design and specifications. You remain there and let Hawks and the rest of us come to you."

"Yeah, I'll just sit here all nice and comfy," the Crow responded. "Sorta like hangin' around the mausoleum."

When they finally succeeded in removing the bulky plate, they revealed a round cavity large enough for a human in a pressure suit to enter. Hawks and Raven were again the first inside, the latter pushing the three modules from their crippled interplanetary craft.

The tube angled down for perhaps twenty meters, then opened into a large bubblelike chamber. Around the wall in a band were drawerlike module compartments, all filled, and in the center was a raised squared-off pedestal with four rectangular cavities laid out in a cross. All were vacant.

"Well, we have the right place, but which goes where?" Hawks asked China through the suit intercom. "All four look exactly the same, and there aren't exactly instruction sheets printed on them. Also, we have four holes and only three modules."

"That won't matter much, I don't think," China assured him. "The core had a unique set of contacts. Those contacts should match only one of the sockets. Are the sizes right?"

"Look right," Raven told her. "We'll see when we try. There's a million of these tiny nipples in this gold leaf, though. Hard to tell which is which by just looking at them. Maybe *you* could see a difference but I sure as hell can't."

"I wish I *could* see it," the Chinese girl responded. "Well, there is only one core socket; the others are data modules. The data modules aren't socket specific, only the core, or brain. If there is no other way, then place the two support modules in any two sockets and then attempt to load the core in one of the remaining sockets. Be careful not to damage or scrape any part of it. If it fits, fine, but don't force it. If it doesn't fit, try the other. Then switch."

"Be easier if we just tried the core first," Hawks noted.

"No! The core is its brain but the storage modules are its basic memories. If it connects with this ship but does not immediately have access to its memory modules it will not know where it is or who we are or what this is all about. The core is still the basic Master System core; it is the modules that were altered to allow it freedom. Activating the core without the modules will simply deliver us into the hands of a slave of Master System."

"Uh, yeah. Uh huh." They turned and carefully selected one of the storage modules, then studied the cavities.

"I'd say let's put these in the right and left cavities as seen from the hatch and try the core with the vertical," Hawks suggested. Raven shrugged.

The first one slid easily and seemed to be firmly seated. "So far so good," Raven noted, sweating. They inserted the other, which went in just as easily. "Best guess is that one of the two remaining is in fact the brains."

"I had only a partial schematic," China told them. "I'm not certain what the fourth one would be. Possibly additional memory to help manage a ship this size, or possibly a subsidiary brain, one handling the ship and the other the cargo life support. It is possible it might fit both places. Try it and see. We have no choice."

"Top one," Hawks guessed. "Seems silly, but it's closest to the actual bridge above."

"Yeah, by about a meter and a half," Raven responded, but they carefully maneuvered the core and then fitted it into the cavity. Nothing happened. "Seems to be sitting just a little higher than the others. Want to try the bottom one?"

"We couldn't get it *all* right first time," Hawks said. "All right—use the small magnets and pull."

They lifted the module out, then maneuvered it slowly to the lower cavity, checked its position, and lowered it into place. Again, it didn't seem to go in quite all the way. "We're either wrong on the others or we're gonna have to risk pushing on the thing," Raven noted.

"Careful!" China warned them. "They are tough but not *too* tough. It is why they are shielded."

There was a tiny bit of play, and they tried moving the module first this way, then that, pushing down slightly as they did so. They were just beginning to decide that perhaps they had the wrong one, after all, when Raven accidentally jiggled the top as he shifted position, and the module sank down just a bit in the socket and seated itself firmly.

"Hey! It's in!" the Crow shouted, staring in wonder at the thing. "But nothin's happening!"

Suddenly there were strange clicking, whirring, and beeping sounds through their intercom sets.

"It's on all frequencies! Radios off for now!" China yelled over the din. "Count to a hundred and check each hundred until it's quiet again!"

It was eerie enough to be in the ghostly dark bowels of the strange ship, but in silence it was even worse. Hawks took some comfort from seeing Raven and Raven's light, but he couldn't help wondering about China. Deaf and dumb because of this, like the others, she was also blind and now completely cut off.

At each check the horrible sounds were so painful that none could stand to keep his or her radio on for more than the briefest moment. The number of hundred counts seemed to go on forever.

Outside the hatch, China waited in a world of silent darkness, hand in hand with Cloud Dancer and Silent Woman on either side of her, that touch the only reality she had other than the breathing sounds from her suit. She had never felt so totally helpless, and her complete dependence on the others was only now being driven home to her. She didn't like the feeling at all. Worse, she could not understand what was happening, or why. Nobody, not even the researchers who'd theorized all this, had actually touched one of these ships. Nine centuries had passed since humans had been even cargo on this ship; no human being had ever set foot in here as an independent agent.

Suddenly a million possibilities presented themselves to her mind. A power mismatch. Inverted circuitry that would cause a loop and ultimately a burnout. Or, perhaps, the great ship and its complexities was simply too much for Star Eagle to handle or comprehend, much as his mind was actually alien to hers.

Keeping hold of China's left hand, Cloud Dancer turned to look back into the darkness of the immense cavity. Suddenly she gasped and squeezed that hand tighter, then tried to poke one of the others. Koll, finally, turned and saw what Cloud Dancer saw.

Behind them a snake of lights was growing, writhing, twisting, going ever outward, upward, downward. It took them a moment to realize what was happening.

All the floor lights on the catwalks were being illuminated, section by section. The ancient cavity that had transported uncounted thousands or perhaps millions was soon lit up like a festival, dimly but beautifully, as far as any eye could see.

They tried their radios. There was still a lot of static and odd background noise, but the sounds were no longer unbearable.

"Anybody on?" Reba Koll called. Her voice crackled a bit, but it carried all right.

"I'm in!" Hawks's voice sounded even worse.

"We are here!" the Chow sisters chimed in. "Is it not beautiful?"

"All of us are going to die," Carlo Sabatini wailed.

Cloud Dancer kept nudging China until the girl finally let go and activated her radio. One by one they all checked in.

"Still nothing much down here," Raven reported worriedly. Cloud Dancer told them about the lights.

"Nothing like that here, but I'm feeling something. A low vibaration," Hawks told them. "What about up there?"

"Faint. Very faint," China responded in a voice that sounded curiously unlike her. The sharp edge, the confidence, was gone, Hawks thought. *She's been badly scared.* It was almost a relief to discover that she was human after all.

A strange voice cut them all off. It was quite high at first, then went down a scale as if it was testing each note to find one it liked. Finally it stopped.

"Do I have communication?" the voice asked at last. It sounded a bit less than human, like a man's voice played at a speed slightly too slow and irregular. The effect was eerie.

"You have it," China responded. "Is that you, Star Eagle?"

"Star Eagle . . . Yes, I identify with that. It is . . . difficult. There is so much, so much at once. It keeps coming at me, but it is far too much to absorb. I am grown *enormous*! It is . . . difficult . . . to focus my primary consciousness, to limit it. Somehow this must be partitioned."

"We require entry to the bridge, then the establishment of power and life support there," she told it. "Can you handle that?"

"Proceed up to the bridge. It is essential that the capping locks be placed on my modules and then the hatch resealed before we can proceed. I can then activate the isolation circuitry that will keep the core bay suspended and vacuum insulated from shocks and vibrations."

"You heard the man, Chief," Raven noted. "See what he's talking about?"

"Now I do," Hawks responded. "We've been walking on it."

They had taken the one flatter area on the floor of the bubble as some sort of ramp. Now they stepped off it, then lifted it up and into place. "No fasteners, though," Hawks added.

"Stand back. I will activate the locking mechanism," the ship told them. A series of clamps came up through the bolt holes and flatted out, then the entire metal surface seemed to buckle slightly inward. Hawks assumed it to be some sort of magnetic and vacuum seal.

They made their way back out, then managed, not without difficulty, to get the round giant screw part of the way back in. Again the ship warned them to step aside, and the plate screwed itself in the rest of the way, sealing itself shut.

"The topmost hatch," China told them. "We must head for the bridge."

They had to walk through more corridor for a long way, then up railed ramps. Finally, though, they reached a ceiling hatch that led to an air lock, which opened onto the bridge.

Star Eagle had turned on the bridge lights, but the resulting red glow was barely adequate to illuminate the room of gun-black metal. It was perhaps twenty by thirty meters, a big semicircular room with stations at instrument clusters lining the walls and more stations in three banks of boxy machinery front to back. The station chairs, of black metallic mesh, looked uncomfortable: They had swivels, but they were low-backed, armless, and were solidly fixed to the floor.

"We'll have to shift some of the more comfortable stuff from the old ship to here," Cloud Dancer remarked. "This is not very comfortable."

"Most of 'em's pretty spare," Reba Koll commented. "Big mother, but no privacy at all."

"I do not notice a kitchen or a bathroom," Manka Warlock noted. "This will not be a pleasant place."

"I am going to pressurize the bridge," Star Eagle informed them. "It will be very oxygen-rich and quite dry, but it will be serviceable. Until I can gain better mastery of what is here and how it all works, I will have to make do and so will you. Later on I can give more comfort. The transmuters here have enormous capabilities, I think, but they are *huge*. A more suitable interface to the bridge area will have to be arranged. I will order Maintenance to see to it. I am afraid the fare will not be very good right now, but I believe I can arrange some basic food and water needs. My food service programs are for the small transmuter aboard the old ship and won't be much use here. Your suit mechanisms will take care of liquid wastes; I fear you must improvise on solid waste until something can be worked out. In all this ship, the only bathroom is the one back on the old ship."

"What did he mean by 'transmuter'?" one of the Chows asked.

"A ship this size needs spare parts always, and spare everything," China explained. "Also, it could never carry sufficient water and air and the rest to support the number of people it carried. It is sufficient that the master computer contain the plans and schematics for everything required, from computer consoles and circuitry to basic water, and be able to make them. For this it uses a device called a transmuter. All of the food that we consumed on the old ship was made that way. It takes something solid or some energy and it converts it to whatever is needed. The salad you ate a day ago might well have been worn-out parts from the ship once, or spare exhaust gases from the propulsion system. Nothing is wasted, you see. Very small transmuters were even used on me back on Melchior, to speed what they wished to make of me. Shortcuts to surgery, to create—or to destroy. We have all had it, to a degree. The tattoos on our faces—this is why they seem so much a part of us and do not wear out."

All of them who had been prisoners on Melchior had the tattoos on their faces. Those of Hawks, Silent Woman, Cloud Dancer, the Chows, and Reba Koll were silver; China's was a metallic crimson. Each was an abstract design, ranging from a solid ball near the corners of the mouth and spreading up, tendrillike, to the side of the eyes and ears. The markings were slightly indented and quite smooth, but they had sensation like that of the surrounding skin—the tattoos were, indeed, the prisoners' own skin. No prisoner could ever fake not being a prisoner, and the color of the tattoo indicated the levels to which one had access, so one could not even sneak away. It was the indelible mark of Melchior. Only Raven, Warlock, and Sabatini lacked tattoos; they had not been prisoners.

"Someday these designs will be marks of honor," Hawks said, more to himself than the others.

"This transmuter, then—it can make food? And water? And air?" Chow Mai asked. "It is the magic of the gods."

"It is only technology, nothing more," China responded. "A machine, like the others, but an essential one—for us. This ship was never designed to carry humans such as we."

Cloud Dancer looked around at the chairs on the bridge. "Then how do you explain *this*?" she asked.

"If we could explain this, then perhaps we could explain Master System," Hawks noted dryly.

"Pressurization complete," Star Eagle reported. "It is safe to take off your suits. The air temperature at introduction is well within the comfort zone. Avoid all flames and sparks, since it is mostly oxygen. You might feel some slight dizziness or intoxication, and slight changes in voice, as well, so be prepared."

They had been in the suits for many hours, and in close quarters for far longer than that, so they were happy to remove their suits and stretch out on the floor. They were tired, sweaty, and now mostly helpless, dependent on a computer that was trying to learn how to run the ship. Even Sabatini seemed to have had all the fight taken out of him. None of the others trusted him, but under the circumstances there was little he could do to harm the party as a whole, and if he tried to hurt an individual member, the others were more than willing to take care of him, a fact he understood well.

The metal walls and decking were still cold, but Hawks didn't care. His wives, Cloud Dancer and Silent Woman, came over to sit beside him, and he put one arm around each of them. *What a strange, motley crew of revolutionaries*, he thought. Silent Woman, with her garish multicolored tattoos from the shoulders down; the Chows, with skin grafts to heal their once badly mutilated bodies in place but discolored, giving them a camouflagelike complexion; Reba Koll, a little old lady with a thin tail; and China, her exquisite body very visibly pregnant. He could only wonder if the child would survive all this, and, if so, what they would do with it.

How the hell were they going to do anything? Damn it, out here even such as he and Raven were as primitive and ignorant as Silent Woman. He was hungry, and thirsty—they all were—but he had endured such before. He—and they—could only wait. But for what?

More than fifty thousand kilometers out from the graveyard of ancient generation ships, just outside the activation limit of the automatic defense system but within scanning and sensor range of the mothball fleet, was another ship. It was not a large ship, not by the standards of that ghost fleet or even by the standards of the freighter they'd chased, but it was far sleeker and, locally, within stellar systems, far faster.

Arnold Nagy, Chief of Melchior Security, sat in his usual padded chair, half reclining, only casually looking at the screens. He was bored and depressed at the same time, a man who had failed at his job and who did not dare to go home. In a sense, he was as much a wanted fugitive as the party he was chasing, only more comfortable.

An older man came up from below and settled into the next chair. Even Master System, the all-powerful, nearly omnipotent master of the known universe, would have been shocked to see him there, since he was simultaneously captive back on Val-occupied Melchior.

Doctor Isaac Clayben had not gotten as far as he had without being clever. For more than three decades he had fooled Master System and maintained a combination prison colony and research station to probe the Forbidden Knowledge, the proscribed and hidden knowledge of Master System and its technological wizardry. To such a man, creating a physical duplicate who appeared to be the real thing with his mind erased was child's play. Yet now he, too, was a fugitive, a man who did not even exist. Were Master System to get even a hint that he was not only alive and in full possession of his mind and skills, but that he had with him the data banks representing tremendous advances into things humans were not supposed to know, would cause a hunt as great or greater than that now being organized to chase Hawks and his group of rebels. Thanks to them, he also knew about the five gold rings. In many ways, he was better equipped technologically to obtain them, but he had no idea where they were. He assumed that the renegades knew where in the tractless universe to find the rings and quite possibly the names of their owners. The obvious solution would be to make a deal, but not so long as they were partially led by China and Reba Koll. China had reason to despise him—more reason than she now knew. And Koll—well, that was a special case.

"No signs of any activity after all this time?" the scientist asked. "I would think, by now, if something were possible it would have been done. It will only be a few more days until Master System's own fleet of Vals and who knows what else will be here. Be pretty hard to miss a target like that."

"There's a lot of 'ifs,'" Nagy agreed. "That ship was banged up pretty bad. They got it aboard, but who knows how much of that was automated? Air, food, water—and how the hell you gonna drive one of them hanging cities, anyway? I think maybe we oughta be thinking about our own skins. I figure sixty hours more is it, and that's pushin' the safety margin. Master System doesn't hav'ta allow for the survival of human beings, you know."

"They'll do it, Arnold. I *know* they will. China will get it moving, somehow, and Koll will get them out of there. If we aren't right with them, if we lose them, we also lose any chance at the rings. And, Arnold, unless we have the rings we're goners. We're too hot. The freebooters won't shield us, we have no large transmuter capable of integrating with one of the other populations nor the knowledge and contacts with them to use it to any advantage, and we have no place else to go."

Nagy sighed. "Yeah. In a way, they're better off than we are. Seven women and only three guys. Pick a nice planet and let your kids do the rebellion."

"*Six* woman, Arnold. Six women, three men, and a monster."

"Yeah, well, six to three is still better than none to two. What do you think, Doc? Is Koll gonna kill 'em and go after the rings herself, or what?"

"I doubt it. Not most of them, anyway. She'll use them. So long as it is not a choice of her survival or theirs and so long as she thinks she can get her hands on the rings, she'll play along with them." He sighed. "This is deep, Arnold. Deep and complex. So many sides, so many players."

"Yeah, well, I—" Nagy broke off suddenly and sat up in his chair, his attention drawn by data on one of his screens. "They've got power! Damn me to hell, but they got power on that big bastard! That sucker's charging its energy banks!"

Clayben stared at the screen. "Yes, you're right. Well, I guess that answers your question, anyway. They are alive, they are in control of that ship, and if they can build up sufficient energy they are going to move."

"We'll be ready for them. This is one express we ain't gonna miss."

2. THE PIRATES OF THE THUNDER

S TAR EAGLE HAD BEEN AS ACCOMMODATING AS POSSI-
ble under the circumstances. The ship had a host of maintenance robots, most of which were quite specialized and of
no practical use to the current crew, but a few could be
turned into convenience mechanisms in a pinch. One, a
spindly thing with a clamp and tray, was most useful: It
was able to bring some blankets and other such luxuries
from the remains of the old ship, as well as some more
important items. An old casing with a medium-sized hole
in the top became a portable toilet; it was smelly and not
really built for human comfort and convenience, but it
worked for now—if their little robot took it out at least
every twelve hours or so to clean and sanitize it.

Water was no problem; the huge holding tanks on the
ship contained all that was needed and could create more
out of by-products if need be, all distilled pure. Food was
much more critical; Star Eagle had to improvise with what
was handy, and the result was a large cube of sickly green
with the consistency of cake icing and a taste that was a
cross between dead grass and library paste. It went down,
however, did not upset, and provided the minimum neces-

41

sary to sustain them. Later they could have more amenities; now they had to move, which meant that Star Eagle had to learn how to drive the ship. The information was there, but it was far more complicated than what a computer programmed and designed to run an interplanetary freighter was used to. The sheer bulk of data was the problem. All, even Star Eagle, knew their clock was ticking, however. Even now Master System would be closing in on them with heavily armed ships that knew exactly what they were up against.

The big ship was hardly defenseless; it had an enormous range of real and potential weapons at its disposal, suggesting that in the old days Master System was not at all confident of what it would find out in the farther reaches of space even though it knew where it was going and had scouted the routes. Had there been resistance? Had there been opposing interstellar civilizations? There was no way to know.

It took more than three days to power up the systems and check them out as best the computer could. Communication with the computer pilot was still awkward, however. It could flash a message on the bridge screens to let the humans know that it wanted to talk, but only the helmet radios allowed good two-way conversation. Still, it was now confident that it could at least get them out of there— but to where?

"Initially it doesn't matter," Hawks told it. "Just— away. Far away, and off the beaten track, as it were."

"The fact that the existing star charts are nine centuries old doesn't matter much," Reba Koll assured them. "There is some shift, but not a lot and nothing that can't easily be allowed for." She worked with Star Eagle, who had figured out how to put star charts and grids up on the bridge screens without much trouble.

"I ain't got time to explain how this drive works," she told them, "if, of course, I knew how it did anyways. Best idea I can give you is if you take this here piece of cloth and make it hump up—curve. That's how space is, really. Shortest distance ain't across the top but straight through. You punch a hole here and you come out there. Course there's lotsa other shit involved. There's black holes and gravity curvatures and all the rest. Don't look at me that way—I only fly 'em, I don't hav'ta understand 'em. Net result is you tell it you wanta go *there* and if figures the route and trajectory and gets you there in days or weeks instead of years or centuries like it would the usual way. You let the pilot do the figures and time the jumps and energy and speed. Now, I suggested some routes to Star Eagle, but he's got reservations."

"The region she suggests is not well charted," the pilot explained. "Oh, the stars are charted well enough, but there's no detail. It was not part of the pattern of resettlement. Also, to get there we will have to make a large number of punches and this will intersect for the first half of the journey with the routings to and from the remote colonies. We must cross known shipping lanes."

"Bah! That's no worry!" Koll snorted. "The odds of actually hitting within sensor range of any ship is practically nil, but even if we did we could deal with those freighters and supply ships. There's little or no armament on them. What's to fight when you're in Master System's territory?"

"I was thinking more of monitors and navigational stations," Star Eagle responded. "They could chart us without us even knowing about it. We could be traced. This interstellar punching is all straight-line routing. To change direction, course, or speed you have to come out, readjust, then punch in again. The amount of energy expended on the punch determines how far you go before you come out again. Just measure the energy level at the punch and note the course, direction, and speed, and it wouldn't take a computer to figure the destination."

"You're not devious enough, pilot!" Koll told it. "I'll explain misdirection to you. A series of small punches whenever we're in a dangerous area. Each small punch increases the number of possible courses, directions, and speeds. Not even Master System has the resources to track down that many variables."

"That will take time, though," the computer pointed out. "There will be frequent recharges necessary. If we took a more or less direct route to the region you suggest it would take twenty-seven standard days. To do as you suggest would take three to five times as long."

"But we'd get there," she noted. "And we'd get there unknown and undetected. Maybe we'll even have this stinkhole livable by then. Plot your course with the minimum number of exponential variables to get us there and get any possible snoopers hopelessly lost and confused. If we don't get away clean, what difference did all this make?"

They took a vote—Sabatini excepted—and all agreed to her plan.

"My energy is sufficient," Star Eagle told them. "Let's do it."

The vibrations, which had been growing throughout their tenure on the big vessel, grew much stronger now, more intense. The throbbing and pulsing sensation that at first had been difficult to get used to but had become merely background noise was in the background no longer.

"Everybody just lie on the floor as comfortably as you can and grab hold of something solid—a chair or something like that," Koll instructed. "Once we're completely up to speed and out we'll be able to regain some movement."

Forty thousand kilometers away and on station, Arnold Nagy jumped in his seat and then sat up straight. "She's moving, Doc! They're underway!"

"Strap in!" Clayben shouted back from below. "Punch in the codes and maintain distance and monitoring! We don't want to lose them!"

The great ship came to life on the outside, as well. Red and green lights flashed on along the length and breadth of the ship, and in the rear huge engines flared into brilliance.

Quite slowly at first, but very clearly, the big ship turned and began to pull away from its siblings in orbit around Jupiter. On the bridge, loose objects floated toward the back wall and the vibration grew intense, joined now by yet another strange sound.

"Thunder," Cloud Dancer whispered. "It sounds like the approach of a great storm across the prairie. This is truly a mighty ship. Does it have a name?"

"None that means anything anymore, I suspect," her husband replied.

"Then it should be the *Thunder*," she said. "That is the awe that it inspires, and that is its sound and being, its soul."

"What about it, everyone? Star Eagle? Shall this ship henceforth be the *Thunder*?"

"It is an appropriate and mighty name," China responded.

"And easy to remember," Chow Dai added.

The computer was agreeable. "Then we are the *Thunder*. I think it is a good name."

"I think I'm gonna puke," Carlo Sabatini said.

For something so huge, the ship's acceleration rate was startling. Within two hours it had cleared the grip of mighty Jupiter and was heading in a great arc that would take it first away, then back toward the mighty giant at tremendous speed. It would use this combination of speed and the gravity of the mighty planet to build up massive acceleration very quickly.

As the speed grew, the more pronounced the sounds of thunder became, as if just outside and all around them raged a great storm.

For those on the bridge, the long hours of getting underway and the limitations it placed on them was simultaneously exciting, somewhat frightening, and extremely boring. Finally, however, the rate smoothed out, and they could move about easily again. But some of the vibration and noise remained, giving them a constant feeling of motion, even though inside the ship all was calm and still.

"We're being followed," Star Eagle reported. "A single ship. Small. Unfamiliar design. I have searched all database patterns and can find nothing close to it. Great power. It might well be interstellar capable."

Reba Koll frowned. "Master System? A Val?"

"It is somewhat like their ships, but it is not one of them. Besides, my sensors show a life-support system activated aboard it. Not certain, but it is probably a rogue ship, like us."

China thought that over. "It's possible that Melchior had something in reserve. Those fighters it tried to use against us were pretty impressive overall and also of a unique design. They were using a sister ship of our old ship to give chase. *Star of Islam*, I believe. Could the *Star* have carried it?"

"Not inside," the pilot told her, "but piggybacked on the exterior it would be no problem at all. It contains weapons systems that might be close to what their fighters had, but those fighters were not manned. Any action recommended?"

China talked it over with Reba Koll and the others. "No," she finally replied. "If we hail it, they'll know we know about them and possibly make it harder for us to keep track of them. If we slow to bring them in range of our weapons it will also cause great delay in us getting out of here, which is the first priority. Are you certain there is only one? No more?"

"Yes. One."

"Then let it follow. If it gets within weapons range, hail it and order it to stand down and be boarded or destroy it. If it attacks, defend. Otherwise, do nothing until we are well away from this stellar system. Even if they are of Melchior they are in an illegal ship engaged in prohibited activity. My guess is that they did not think we could do what we have done, but now that we have they want what we want but for themselves. We will deal with them when we can."

"Acknowledged. I am now receiving faint stop orders on both superspace and subspace command frequencies. Master System knows about the *Thunder*."

"To be expected," Raven commented. "We're hotter

than a burial fire right now. What's the odds of us being intercepted by any force that could do us any real harm?"

"Very slim. Negligible. They might get a ship in before I can make the punch but nothing that could handle these systems. They really don't make weapons ships like that. A Val ship would have the most firepower, and that would be little more than that of the fighters Melchior sent against us. The security computer informs me that this ship is able to take virtually any known system of its own day, and they were far more heavily armed then than now. Our worst enemy would be another ship like this one, and it is unlikely that such would be set against us. Too easy to avoid. Security believes it most likely that Master System will order ships constructed specifically to exploit our weaknesses and take us out, but that will take considerable time. If we can get lost the first time, and if we are careful, it is unlikely even they will find us when they can surprise us and take us."

"Then they won't try to take us aboard," Raven surmised. "We're no real threat or problem cooped up in this monster. If they can't trace us now, they'll put out all the alarms and wait for us to move."

Hawks sighed. "Yeah. If *we* know where three of the rings are, good old Master System knows where all of them are, I bet, and has a pretty good eye out for them. Unlike those bastards from Melchior back there, it doesn't really have to chase us. It just has to wait, and we must come to them."

"Infinite patience is one of the hallmarks of computers," China noted darkly.

Hawks scratched his chin. "Don't get too downcast. Maybe it *is* impossible. So is what we have done so far."

A few hours later the pilot reported, "I have attained sufficient speed for a punch and we are sufficiently clear of Jupiter's gravitational pull that I can compensate for it. There should not be any untoward effects, but I cannot predict for certain, never having done it before."

"Won't be nothin'," Reba Koll assured them. "Might sound like the whole ship's breakin' apart, but don't let that worry you none. Once it's done, it'll be still and quiet as death until we come out the other side. You might get some funny feelings inside or even some hallucinations, but they'll only last a real short while, and it's a good idea to sit or lie down 'cause most everybody gets a little dizzy, but it all passes pretty fast and each time you do it the effects will be less and less. Just relax and don't let it scare you."

They waited, nervous in spite of Koll's assurances, and the punch came.

First there was tremendous vibration that continued to build with a supporting roaring sound until it seemed to engulf them. At that moment the lights blinked and the sound seemed to fade as if swallowed up in some huge drain; the vibration, too, settled down to a level far lower than that produced by the regular space drive. There was a wave of dizziness, and some nausea, and each one of them found his or her attention fixed on something—an object, a reflection, even another person—unable to tear away that gaze. Even China, who could see nothing, appeared to be staring at something specific in her world of darkness.

Hawks stared involuntarily at the blind girl and she seemed to shimmer, taking on a wraithlike appearance of stunning beauty. She seemed to float up and come toward him, then change again into a horrible, skeletal monster, jaws open, coming for him—

He screamed, and suddenly everything was back to normal. He found himself sweating and shaken, breathing hard, and it took a few moments for him to get hold of himself and look around and reaffirm reality. The others had varying degrees of reaction, but all of them clearly had seen *something*, something uniquely their own. Sabatini looked scared to death, and the Chows were shivering. Sooner or later, Hawks decided, he would find out what each had seen, but for now he just noted the differences. Of them all, Raven and Warlock looked the least affected and the least concerned.

The thunder was quiet now; there was nothing but a very low steady vibration through the deck and walls, quite distant. None of them, except perhaps Koll, understood what had just happened, but Hawks grasped at least the basics. Somehow, they were no longer in the universe at all. Somehow, now, they were in another medium, *somewhere else*, traveling across a ripple in space–time by the shortest available route.

It was a frightening, awesome concept, yet it meant one thing above all.

"Well, I'll be damned," Raven commented aloud to no one in particular. "We actually got away."

Spanning hundreds, perhaps thousands, of light-years by the punch method was incredible, but it still took time.

Some of that time was spent in attaining a more livable, civilized environment. Star Eagle now had a reasonable command of the ship's systems and how they worked. The maintenance computer subsystem was employed creating and then using an army of spindly robots that were able to turn chambers in the bow of the *Thunder* into reasonably private rooms. Much of the old ship was dismantled, its essential parts modified and duplicated by the *Thunder*'s transmuters. A square meter of passenger-lounge carpeting was sufficient for the transmuters to create a carpeted floor for the new rooms and for the bridge. The old ship's toilets were modified and duplicated, as well, and tied into new piping using the vast support system of the *Thunder*. The old ship's transmuter-driven automated galley was reinstalled with some modifications, allowing the old menus to be used. The bridge chairs were replaced with copies of the more practical and comfortable passenger lounge chairs. Since the *Thunder* wasted nothing and recycled everything, even a shower chamber was possible, although in the zero gravity it had to be a more or less sealed system and strictly a one-at-a-time affair.

Of equal importance were the interfaces that had to be designed and installed between the passengers and the pilot and master of the *Thunder*: a central amplifier and communications system that might eventually extend to the whole of the ship; a way of specifying human-supplied designs for the transmuters to work with, to create things like furnishings for the new cabins and some basic clothing. The women chose robes with soft linings and rope ties; the men got flimsy versions of Sabatini's usual shirt and pants. Only Manka Warlock broke the pattern by insisting on the shirt and pants for herself.

China and Reba Koll worked on installing the interface helmets on the bridge. China was anxious to see if they would work here as on the old, smaller ship. The idea of interfacing with Star Eagle and becoming one with *this* ship excited her.

Some tubular lighting was arranged, but it was still kept

low and indirect. In normal space there was no power problem, but during a punch the ship was the only reality; there was nothing at all outside, according to the pilot. Nothing. That meant that all transmuting—all power consumption—was accomplished using materials within the ship, and particularly with all the modifications and construction going on it was a drain. There was a consensus not to start cannibalizing the ship for luxuries until they knew their limits and understood their new environment.

They also began exploring the ship.

There were over twenty thousand pods in the transport bay. There had been a hundred ships like this one, and an Earth population of possibly six billion, when the grand project had begun. That meant that each ship had made hundreds of round trips over the two or more centuries of interstellar colonization. The time frame was not clear in the records, but the evidence here was clear enough. The *Thunder* was a veteran indeed.

Slave ship, Hawks couldn't help thinking.

"How many worlds are charted as being part of the settlement?" he asked Star Eagle.

"Four hundred and forty-seven," was the reply. "But it might not be complete. The region spans over forty thousand light-years."

He tried doing some quick math in his head. That was only about thirteen or fourteen million a world!

"The initial populations were not large," the computer agreed. "Nor was Mars, the prototype, if you remember. There are almost two hundred million Martians now, and they have a relatively slow birth rate. You forget that Earth was limited in its reproductive rates and carefully regulated, but that this does not necessarily hold true for these worlds. It is entirely possible that we could find planets with billions on them—or planets with few, if any, survivors. How would we know?"

"Four hundred forty-seven," Raven commented. "Minimum. Good thing we know where three of the rings are."

"Ever the optimist," Hawks retorted. "We know the *worlds* where they are, but nothing about those worlds and nothing about how many possible leaders could have them. And that leaves us with just four hundred and forty-four other worlds in which to find the last ring. Perhaps our grandchildren or great-grandchildren might find it."

"Don't you worry, Chief. We'll find it. We didn't come this far to fail in that. *Stealin'* it, and the others, will be the tough job."

"Please pardon the intrusion," Chow Dai put in, "but might I be permitted to ask why, if this Master System knows that we know, it will not just collect or hide all four, perhaps all five, from us before we can even try for them?"

It was a good question. "There's no easy answer to that," Hawks told her. "It remains a possibility, but I think not for several reasons. First, those rings are the only avenue to us. It knows we're going after them, and so it will be waiting for us. Second, there's something very odd going on here. There's more than just us in this. Maybe you should ask Raven about that."

The Crow's eyebrows went up. "Don't know what you mean, Chief. I told you the straight stuff. Chen's the only one I know behind all this. Word of honor."

Hawks privately doubted that Raven's honor was worth very much, but he knew it was fruitless to press the point. It was even possible that the former security man was telling the truth. Why would Chen select this crew—particularly *this* group—and think they had a snowball's chance in hell of succeeding? He'd asked himself that a thousand times and had no answer, yet Chen was a wily, even brilliant man. Did Chen, and perhaps Raven, know something that might explain it, and might also explain how they had been able in the first place to pull this off under a system that had some cracks but no chasms? They had walked through the Grand Canyon of cracks in Master System's rule, and they should not have been able to do so.

In many ways, the *Thunder* proved something of a disappointment in that beyond its transport bays and incredible lengths of corridors and catwalks there was little else with any use for humans. In spite of the mysteries of the bridge and its interfaces, the ship had never been built with humans in mind for anything except cargo. Much of the romance engendered by the mere sight and thought of such a ship was gone in the sterile metals and plastics of the reality. Star Eagle could show them more than they could see themselves on the screens of the bridge—another anomaly. If the ship was run by a remote computer brain directly connected to service and security subbrains and to the mobile machines they controlled, why were there viewing screens on the bridge?

The star drive was actually forward and well shielded against any type of prying. It appeared that "punch" was indeed as good a word as any for what it did; it appeared to focus forward, open up some sort of hole in space–time, and allow the ship through, encased somewhat in an energy field to protect it from whatever forces were out there now. The massive rear drives were strictly for in-system movement and docking, and were not used in interstellar flight at all.

The top of the ship, as oriented from the bridge, consisted of massive tanks of gases, fuels, and all else needed both to sustain the human cargo and to provide whatever was necessary to the ship's systems. If the *Thunder* had a weak point, this was it, but the tanks were armored to an amazing degree and atop them were complexes of defensive weapons. If a potential attacker somehow got past the fourteen small automated fighters that provided the ship's primary defense, there would still be no easy taking of the main ship.

Below were the four massive cargo bays, in one of which sat the remains of the interplanetary ship that had brought them from Melchior. Each of the bays had extensive equipment for moving and reaching almost any point in the cavities, and independent medium-sized transmuters.

"One thing I haven't figured out," Raven said, "is how they got all those people in here and back out again. There's no docking piers for support ships."

"This ship could never land anywhere," China explained. "The transmuter is the heart of Master System's whole scheme. It is the heart of everything that also makes the rest possible. Some are used simply to manufacture spare parts, repairs, and to recycle everything that can no longer be used. The corps of robots Star Eagle is using were nothing but plans in the ship's data banks, fed to transmuters along with something of necessary mass—exhaust gases, waste products, debris, garbage. The mass is transformed into energy and then reformed as whatever solid matter the ship might need. There are transmuters in the bow which can literally scoop up space debris—rock, dust, gases—and feed them into the storage tanks above us in compressed form. When we're inside a punch, as now,

the ship uses this stored material to keep itself and everything else going. These were very low when we moved
out, but in the transit of Jupiter the ship picked up enough
to fill those holding tanks.''

"Yeah, but—people?"

"In the same way that the things can change one form of
matter or energy into another, it can also maintain a specific object. All of it is catalogued when it is picked up, so
if necessary it could be reformed as itself. We could put
you in a transmuter, reduce you to energy, then beam that
energy to a receiving transmuter along with that pattern.
You would then be converted back into yourself. The process would take only as long as light required to travel the
distance."

"Space travel without spaceships," Hawks commented.
"Incredible."

"But very limited. First, there must be a matching
transmuter at the destination. Second, the signal must be
very powerful to retain its full consistency from station to
station, which limits its range. Third, it is strictly line of
sight, and conditions must be perfect. In the old days, initial setup ships must have been sent to all the new worlds
and transmuter receiving stations established at various
points on each planet's surface. Then, when the passengers
came along, they could be beamed serially—one at a time
—to the receiving stations. What you send from here is
precisely what you get down there. There is a mobile
transmuter system in the main cargo area that seems almost
like a gun; it is designed to move along guides on the
catwalks and line up to each cargo cavity. It is connected to
the external system, so we know that the people were put
to sleep on Earth, then beamed up to here and inserted

sequentially into the holding modules. Upon arrival at the new world, the process was reversed. They probably never even knew about all this. They went to sleep on Earth and woke up on a strange world."

"But not necessarily the way they left," Raven noted. "I saw a Martian once. They came from human stock but there's no way they're human like us."

China nodded. "That was the primary function of the missing fourth module in the core. It was preprogrammed with certain necessary biological information. The cargo bay mobile transmuter made a new pass after all were aboard and the ship was underway. Each human occupant was once more dissolved to energy and then reformed as something else—a human able to live and survive on the target world. Otherwise, it would have taken thousands of years to change those worlds into places fit for human habitation. The transmuting of individual humans must be extremely precise and exacting, requiring a second core module and probably supporting data banks to get it right. Many human beings certainly died each time a new form was attempted before the computers got it right. Then they sent a small colony to the new world to see if they could and would survive there. Only then did mass transmutations and movements of large numbers of people begin. It was the only logical way such a plan could be carried out, but the cost in lives must have been quite high."

"Even when they got there," Hawks put in, a bit awed and more than a little frightened by all this, "this would change the body, but not the mind, a mind used to thinking in human terms, to seeing things according to human standards, even themselves. They had to *learn* to be alien creatures. Many would be unable to do so. Many more would go mad."

"That's true," she agreed. "Although I suspect that the mindprinters were used to minimize it. Take data and information from the early colonists who survived and adapted, and feed it to the newcomers when they come down. The mindprinter taught most of us the English we are using, and made some of this possible. It could teach the basics."

Hawks had a sudden, uneasy thought. "You say it takes a receiving station to work as a transport mechanism? Then how will we get to wherever it is Koll is taking us? How will we get down there? And, when we go after the rings, how will we get to the target planet? Assuming the stations on the planets are still operational, we can't use them. It would be like a thief walking up to the front door, knocking, and announcing himself to the intended victim."

"Getting to the surface of a world not in the system should be possible," she told him. "Star Eagle assures me he can duplicate the necessary receiving station and get it down using one of the fighters, although I suspect it's more complex than that. Getting into the other worlds will be much tougher. For one thing, the *Thunder* is going to be rather obvious in a stellar system controlled by Master System. We will have to work on that."

"Bah!" Raven snorted. "We are like children in this! The technology is so beyond us that we are no less ignorant than Cloud Dancer! We might as well be villagers faced with great magic!"

"So?" China responded. "What difference does that make? Back at the Center where you lived and worked, did you really understand why and how the light came on when you touched the wall switch? Did you understand the process by which your food arrived, or did you just take it for granted and eat it? The same for the heating and the air conditioning and all the rest. I can fly a skimmer, but I have only a vague idea of how it works. I can use powerful computers, yet I do not truly understand how they think and the intricacies of their work. One does not have to know how something works to use it. Many people have been killed by guns wielded by gunmen who have not the slightest idea of the physics involved. Even Star Eagle does not understand some of that which he is doing. He was never intended to run a ship of this type and complexity. He does, however, have access to the operating instructions and can run them."

"Point taken," Hawks replied. "All right, so we savages can manage this thing. I think the time has come to have a council meeting and decide just what the hell we are really going to do."

They sat in a circle on the bridge, relaxed but interested, not all of them understanding what this more formal meeting was for.

"I called this meeting, but that may be a temporary usurpation of authority," Hawks began. "Among my people, this would be a tribal council convened to create rules, objectives, and policies for all. We come from different places and different backgrounds. We think in different tongues, and some of us have less in common with one another than even we might think. However, we come here with a common bond. We are all fugitives. We all live under a death sentence or even worse. We also share a secret, of sorts. We know that there is a way to beat Master System. We know that there is a way to totally destroy the dictatorship of the machine. We are all here, together, with no others to share our bond, and we are, in a sense, stuck with each other, like it or not. We are all escaping now, but not to a specific place or a specific set of objectives. Before we can discuss the future and set those objectives, we must have someone in charge, not as dictator or chief but as chairman, as it were, of a collective."

"You're doin' fine, Chief," Raven said. "I'm content to let you chair the meetings and bang the drums. Some of us know about the different parts of humanity and some of us know a lot about machines but you're the one person here with the education to see the big picture. Any objections?"

There were some nervous glances from side to side, but nobody seemed to be unhappy with that.

"Very well, I assume the leadership, but when a majority of you is dissatisfied with it, I will step down. I will appoint our China, here, second in command and with full authority. I think the two of us are better at planning than in direct action. Very well. We then proceed to the first really important item on the agenda. Captain Koll, just where are we heading?"

"In the bush, sir. A region two punches off any known interstellar routes. It was crudely scouted in the old days by Master System and there were some early experiments on some planets there, but none proved out. There are several stellar systems there that show some promise and might possibly sustain a land base with the support of the *Thunder*. We can't be expected to live in this can indefinitely. It's not healthy and it's a sitting duck. If we're tied to it absolutely we'll just have to accept a life of constantly being on the run, or heading this thing out and just punching until we're so far away even we couldn't find our way back. If we're gonna stay close enough to Master System to do some damage, then we can't ever have all our eggs in one basket. Somebody's gotta survive, with the information on the rings and the story of all this."

"I find the ship more than adequate," China responded. "It can be modified to support many more of us, and it gives us mobility. We do not seem a likely group for survival on a hostile world."

There were several nods, but Hawks understood what Koll was saying.

"This is not and cannot be a passive vessel," he told them. "We are going to have to get what we cannot make for ourselves. The interstellar shipping system is totally automated and runs that way. Right now it is vulnerable, perhaps wide open to us. We need smaller, more practical interstellar vessels. We need backups to our systems. We will also need information channels, and that will mean direct contact with freebooters and the like, those who live outside the system. We will need to pillage and plunder, as it were, and also to reconnoiter our target systems without advertising our presence to Master System. Everyone, even the freebooters themselves, might be our enemy. The captain is correct. If we are to be pirates, we must have a place to study and bury our loot. We will eventually require more people, perhaps as allies. And, finally, these confines are no place to raise children, and we will have children, won't we, China?"

She nodded somberly. "Yes. Star Eagle was checking out the transmuter system and eventually required a human. It—tickles. All over. Nothing more. You are not even aware that it is done until it is over. In so doing, he also had to make a molecule-by-molecule memory map of me in order to reconstruct me. I was aware that a transmuter was used upon me by Clayben's staff on Melchior. I was not aware until now of the extent." Her voice was dry, hollow, as if that tough exterior was about to fragment into a million pieces.

Star Eagle broke in. "She has been thoroughly transmuted," the computer pilot reported, "although the changes are not so obvious. I had hoped to be able to restore her to some semblance of normalcy with my devices, but that is impossible. Perhaps Master System could restore her, but I cannot. There is a certain—instability—inherent in a full transmutation. I knew that just from the small transmuters on the old ship. There are some minor losses each time something is actually changed—no loss if absolutely reconstructed. That was why a separate core was needed to transmute the human cargo of this ship. There is literally no tolerance for errors. The losses she suffered at the hands of Melchior are negligible, but to do it again would compound those losses. Reassembly might well kill or cripple her. There is some indication that this is actually built into the system when dealing with complex organic life forms. Master System wanted to make certain that none of those it created could change themselves back. It wanted permanency, and it designed it into the system."

"I was—am—a genetic experiment," China explained. "My father worked to create me. My extreme beauty—I am not saying that to be egotistical—and my very high intelligence were part of it. I was part of a larger project to breed a race of superior intellects, intellects that might do more than simply cheat on the system. I was but stage one, however; that race was to be bred, and it was my purpose to be one of those who would bear the next generation that might be the rebels. It was to escape this life as a breeding factory that I fled. I saw my father as unfeeling, as even evil, and I ran into the hands of Clayben, who was far more unfeeling and evil than my father ever dreamed of being. Melchior was Clayben's playpen, possibly the only place in the known universe where such vast knowledge and power could be wielded without restraint by human beings. He examined me, discovered my background, and decided my father was correct."

"But you escaped from him, as well," Chow Dai noted.

"Not soon enough. They analyzed what my father's geneticists and biochemists had done and made improvements on it in computer models, but as you know such modifications would not be inheritable if induced, unlike my father's more direct approach with laboratory eggs and sperm. They were also aware of all that I had accomplished in escaping my father, Center, and even Earth. They wanted my mind *and* my body—in that, at least, their ideas were better than my father's—but they wanted me secure, particularly if I was to work with their best computers and data bases. Melchior was originally established as a research station by Master System to create the Martians. It has a small but very workable transmuter. They use it for many experiments. Captain Koll's tail is a good example."

"I'm more familiar with it than you know, dearie," Koll said enigmatically.

"At any rate, they modified me. All of me. Incorporated their genetic changes to be inheritable, building on my father's work. Star Eagle can tell you the rest."

"They wanted to make certain she couldn't pull a fast one on them," the pilot told them. "That was how they hit on the blindness. She is not merely blind—she does not even have the processing inputs for visual images. The entire interconnection system simply isn't there as it is in you. This is not a genetic modification; her children will see. There may be devices that bypass all of that that might just work, but I have no knowledge of them. She is also what might only be called a baby factory. Brain and body chemistry is set up for that. Her natural and normal condition is pregnancy. When she is not pregnant she will have almost no self-control. She will become increasingly frenzied until that condition is restored, after which she will again be as she is now. The combination of genetic work and Melchior's modifications is astonishing. She is resistant to much of what inflicts others. She will age very slowly and heal very quickly. Her defensive and regenerative powers are enormous and automatic. She could very easily remain youthful and sexually functional for sixty or seventy years."

That got them all. *Sixty or seventy years with pregnancy a natural condition . . .*

"Even in my day there was ways to beat that," Reba Koll noted. "Fool the body into thinkin' it's pregnant, or, hell, take out the equipment if you can't shut it off."

"Not here. Her body would treat any control method I might be able to come up with as if it were a disease and destroy it or render it ineffective. The same would go for psychochemicals. Surgical alteration would be repaired and healed quickly by the body and in the interim she would still be possessed of the lust and frenzy, which is induced by chemicals made in her own body. They knew she had used mindprinters before to her advantage, along with psychochemical alterations, and they wanted to be certain she could not do so again. To remove her reproductive organs would be far worse. It would drive her horribly and irreparably mad. A bullet in the brain would be kinder, and quicker. No, they fed her mindprint into their computers and their computers came up with an absolute system. I am not certain what Clayben intended—breed his own super race, perhaps. In the meantime, so long as she was pregnant, he had the complete services of her mind and abilities."

That stunned those who hadn't already known about it, but Hawks had a different point to this information. "Understand this well, then. We need her mind and her skills; therefore, she will receive what she needs when she requires it. If we are to have a substantial second generation, then it might fall to them eventually to get the last of the rings. We require a colony."

"There's darker stuff here, Chief," Raven put in. "More than that problem. I been listenin' to all this and, as you know, I followed it when we was still researching the whole thing, and when I first heard about these transmuters I figured our problem on getting into our target world was solved. We could change ourselves into what was needed. Now I see that's not gonna happen. For one thing, old Star Eagle don't have the codes and genetic shit to do it to any of us. For another, even if he did, it's a one-way trip. There's no way I'm gonna be changed into a monster for good, or, even if it was something I didn't mind bein', wind up bein' left forever on some world while somebody else sticks them rings in Master System's ass."

"A good point," Hawks agreed. "I'm afraid we might have to face the transmuter to accomplish our goals, at least at the start, but while that sacrifice might have to be made by some or even all of us, I could not ask anyone to place him- or herself in the position of having to remain behind. I am personally prepared to make any sacrifice, including death or mutilation, to end the tyranny, but only if it means something. I would not shed an eyelash if it meant that an Isaac Clayben or a Lazlo Chen, who is much the same sort, would wind up our masters. I know enough history to understand that achieving a revolution is not the same as winning it. I am as dedicated to our revolution as I can be, but I am equally dedicated to not replacing Master System with a human monster."

"I'm afraid I shall have to insist on a planetary base," Star Eagle interjected. "I will need time to convert this ship into something more practical, and I will require independence and mobility."

"All right, so we're agreed that far," Raven said. "So we go out there and we build a base, more than a colony. Then what?"

"As I said, piracy. We need mobility. We have the only active colony ship in the known universe. We need another ship, preferably more than one. Their data banks alone might tell us of other targets worth hitting and the schedules we need. We outfit them. Either Star Eagle converts them to our side or we learn to fly them without a core. Outfit them. Weapons. Sensors. Our own communications and codes. Then it will be time for some of us to make contact with the freebooters. By that time we'll have something of a mysterious reputation. We need information. We need to know about these worlds we're going to be going to. Who are the people there? What's the culture, the language, the physical and biological problems? Who's in charge and who runs what? Which leader wears a large gold ring with a design in it? Does anyone know of another that we do not? Step by step, a bit at a time, with infinite patience and dedication."

"It sounds impossible," China commented.

"It's not. Difficult, yes. Dangerous, yes. Certain? By no means. I would say the odds are against us overwhelmingly. But impossible it certainly is not. I have thought it through and thought it through until my head burst, but I think I have it now. What Raven and Warlock, there, and Chen as well, knew from the start." He looked at the Crow and the Jamaican beauty. "It *can't* be impossible, can it? It is *required* to be at least possible."

The Crow grinned. "You got it, Chief. You're smarter than I thought. I would have explained it, sooner or later, but why bother now?"

"I do not understand this," Cloud Dancer commented. "Pardon my ignorance, but I must have much of this explained. The evil lord I understand, and his great power, and the use of the talismans to break his power, but—*required*?"

"Don't feel bad," China said. "They just lost me, too."

"Think about the story," Hawks urged them. "Master System is incredibly powerful, but it is a computer. A computer designed by humans. All this, all this subjugation of humanity, the reduction of Earth to primitivism, the diaspora that scattered and somewhat dehumanized the vast bulk of humanity, all was simply an interpretation by that computer of its creators' command. Think about that. *Command*. It was *commanded* to find a way so that humanity could never destroy itself completely. It was *commanded* to find a way so humanity could never use its terrible weapons of mass destruction nor spread them. It was a classic deal-with-a-demon fable. Out of fear, or desperation, or whatever, those people raised a great demon and they offered it absolute power over them and their dominions in exchange for safety. They tried as best they could to build into their wish every safeguard, to close every loophole, but the demon, being a demon, was far too clever for even the most brilliant of mere mortals and found the loopholes anyway. It granted their wish—and took away the souls of their children and grandchildren unto the last generation and swept away all their works. But we're safe—from everything except the demon."

"But they must still have suspected or they wouldn't have created the rings in the first place," China pointed out.

"Indeed. I think, perhaps, it was simply part of the bargain. The demon, as all great legends have it, *must* fulfill the wishes as stated. It is compelled to do so. One safeguard was the rings—the magic talismans, as my wife referred to them—and what went with them. A guarantee of some access. The rings must be in human hands—humans with authority. If any are lost or destroyed, duplicates must be made and provided to said leaders. The other part of the bargain must be a *guarantee of access*. We have a *right* to go after the rings, to gather them together, and to make our way with them to Master System and use them. A *right*, guaranteed as part of the bargain—the core program of Master System itself, a core that could not be altered. Another part of the bargain."

China nodded, and even Cloud Dancer, Reba Koll, and the Chows seemed to get the idea. Sabatini sulked off in a corner in silence, and Silent Woman was as impassive as ever.

"It could scatter them among the stars, because there

were now humans out there with authority of sorts," China said in wonder. "It could try to stamp out all knowledge of the rings and their purpose and use. But it could not violate the basics. It just made it damned near impossible for anybody to actually do it."

"Perhaps not as impossible as you think," Raven responded. "We never really thought it was an accident that the data on the rings survived all these centuries, or that it was discovered now. See, there's a real indication that Master System is gonna radically change people, even on Earth. Wipe out civilization and knowledge, push us back to the start, make us little better than apes with clubs. But, see, that really *would* make it impossible. Old Master System slipped up. By merely making that decision it forced itself into a vulnerable position. Ten to one it's pulled back now from doing that, thanks to us, because otherwise it might make a lot more teams like us 'cause it *has* to. But before it fully understood what it was doing, we got out—and maybe others. We might not be the only ones who know and got away, you know. We might not even be the only ones Chen arranged for. There's that ship that was following us, for example."

That was a sobering thought.

"In the light of first things first, what should we do about that ship?" Hawks asked them.

"Blow 'em out of the skies," Reba Koll replied. "You can't give any quarter in this and expect to succeed."

"That *would* solve the problem," Hawks admitted, "but I don't see any reason right now to do so. If we must, we must, but I just can't see any direct purpose to indiscriminate killing. If it was a Val ship, it's be different, but it's definitely got humans on board."

"You got the question wrong, Chief," Raven interjected. "It's *why* is it following us? It can't take us, but it's taking a big risk that we'll take it. If they wanted to join up, they'd have called us by now. If it was Master System, there wouldn't be people on board for any reason. They'd just get in the way. Figure it's this Nagy fellow and maybe others from Melchior. They know about the rings thanks to the mindprints they took from you, but they don't know where to look. We could really use that ship but we have to destroy it or lose it unless they give it to us. They're just on our tail 'cause they don't know where to go and they're otherwise as lost as we are. I say we try to lose 'em. Can you shake them, Star Eagle?"

"The problem would be in the energy required for quick punches in and out," the computer reported. "Yes, I could lose them. It is not that difficult, but it would leave us without punch power for quite some time and exposed while we're still in the shipping lanes. There is a low, but definite, probability that we might be sensed or spotted by Master System."

Hawks sighed. "All right, then. When we punch out, we'll give them one chance and a warning. If nothing else, it might reveal just who they are and whether they are acting alone. If we can't cut a deal and they won't talk to us, then we will take some sort of drastic action. Before I will kill or expose us to needless risk, though, I would like to know who it is I am killing and why."

"Ship still back there, Star Eagle?"
"Yes. It has dropped back but is still within range."
Hawks sighed. "Open up communications and patch me through, then."

"Channels are open. You are on the three most common frequencies. I will narrow it when and if they reply. We are exposed in this position although I sense nothing nearby or in range. Even so, I would rather not make broad-band broadcasts. The signals will travel, and it might be one more way of being traced."

"This is Jon Nighthawk aboard the *Thunder* to the ship in our wake. Respond, please."

There was no reply.

"This is Hawks aboard the *Thunder*. I would rather talk but I cannot risk this sort of broadcast for long, If I receive no response from you I will have no choice but to determine you a hostile ship and order fighters to launch and commence action against you. You have one minute."

He paused, then said, "Fifty seconds," and counted down every ten seconds. He was not bluffing, but if he launched he would have to recover those fighters, as well, and that would be needless delay in the middle of a shipping lane. "Ten . . . nine . . . eight . . . seven . . ."

"All right, damn it! We're here," came a gruff male voice through the speakers. "I suppose this was inevitable anyway."

"*You* are following *us*," Hawks noted, "not the other way around. You must have thought it through—that if you were close enough to keep us on your sensors the reverse was also true."

"We assumed nothing of the sort. Who would have believed you could attain mastery of a ship like that in so short a time? Very well, let's talk. You're in trouble, and so are we."

"We are not nearly in the same predicament as you are. If we are all on the same side here, why follow? Why not hail us and join us?"

There was a pause. "Because it would be my death at the least if I were to fall into your hands, and a very unpleasant one, that's why."

"I'd know that voice anywhere," Reba Koll muttered. "That's Clayben! Shoot him, damn it! *Rip his guts out!*"

Hawks was startled by the outburst, but ignored it. "I can see your point from the reaction here, Doctor. Captain Koll considers just your existence in my sights to be sufficient grounds to blow you to hell."

"That is not Captain Koll. Koll's dead, been dead almost two years now. That is an inhuman, terrifying monstrosity, a horror. It's the thing that killed Koll and assumed her identity. I should know. I created the damned thing."

"Stand by," Hawks said. That uneasy chill he felt only when danger lurked close at hand was creeping into him. He turned and looked at Koll. "Isn't it about time you explained this, or should I ask him?"

"He told you true," she admitted unhesitatingly. "At least about the fact I ain't Koll and that I'm not human and that he's responsible for it. I kinda object to the horror and monstrosity parts, though. I ain't such a bad sort. I only kill at all 'cause he made it so I have to. I got choices, though. I got a conscience. I don't kill none who don't deserve it unless it's them or me. You gotta believe that."

Hawks felt his throat going dry, and he licked his lips nervously. "We were depending on you to take us someplace safe. If you're not Koll, then even if the rest of what you say is true, how am I to trust you?"

"'Cause I got all of Koll's memories, you idiot! I'm a damned near perfect imitation—absolutely perfect when I wanna be!"

"Doctor? You want to explain all this?"

There was a pause on the radio. "It was a grand experiment," Clayben said finally. "Melchior, all of it, was devoted to just one ultimate goal: Beating the system. Cheating it. Eventually, hopefully, destroying it. I was taking up the work of my predecessors, that's all. We—our computers and our experts in security and biology—thought we had a part of the answer. A weapon, as it were, in human form. A being who could beat the system at will. Become anyone it wished. Sail through security ports, passing every test—memory, retinal prints, even blood and tissue samples. Gain the full knowledge of whomever it imitated and therefore have full access to anyplace human beings could go. The first of a race, an army, that would collapse the whole control system. We used the transmuter for the final prototype. It worked, but it worked too well. The—thing—saw no difference between humans and computers. It hated us all. It killed half the station before we found a way to incapacitate it and stabilize it. We could have killed it—absolute incineration or transmutation to gas or energy would have done it—but we could not. It was so close. It *almost* worked. We kept it—stabilized. In human form. With the chemical compounds we used, it would remain stable for two, three years. Then it would have to have another template, another form. We used prisoners for whom we had no other use."

"Like Koll."

"Like Koll. But the next time it—feeds—and changes, there won't be any compound. No chemicals. It will be free to do it at will. It will kill all of you and absorb your knowledge, your memories. It wants the rings for itself. God will be an insane monster!"

Hawks stared at the frail-looking Reba Koll.

"Bullshit," she said. "I don't know what sane is, but I sure as hell ain't hankerin' to eat the lot of you. It's true what he says—right at the start I *was* nothin' much but an animal, a killer, but the more people I become, the more memories I got, the more ways I had to behave, the more *human*, I guess, I got. I got all them memories, all that knowledge up *here* in my head and all over my body, I guess. I don't even know how it works. The only thing I don't have is who I was to start with. Only *he* knows that. You think I liked killin' Koll, or the others? I didn't pick 'em—*he* did. Just to keep me alive so he could study and figure out how to make a ton more of me he could control. His own Vals, in spades. I want the rings, sure, but not alone. Nobody should have that power alone, not even me. You need me to get 'em, Chief. I can go down to them worlds no matter how much they're monsters there, and I can become one of 'em and know all the rules right off, and I can waltz right in and take them rings off the fingers or whatever them leaders have. You can't."

"I doubt if it will be that easy, even for you," Clayben replied. "But you see why this is as close as I can approach. You haven't the power to keep her from me, Hawks, and I would fight to the death before I would allow that."

Hawks stared at Reba Koll. He had expected to have to make some very tough decisions as the leader but he hadn't expected something like this at all, and certainly not right off.

"All right, Captain, or whatever you are. You really have the biggest problem. I can't stop you from killing us all, but you can't take this ship and run it and you know it. It's Star Eagle's ship. But whether you are friend or foe, and whether I have to die, along with others here, making certain our mission fails at the start, depends on you. It's Clayben—or a shot at the rings. China?"

"The gods who might be, if any, know that I have only hatred and contempt for this man, yet if it is the choice of the rings or him, I will kneel to him and lick his behind before I would throw away the rings."

"This ain't fair!" Koll grumped. "I spent ten years dreamin' of nothin' but gettin' that bastard in a position where I could torture him to death real slow. I wouldn't eat him. I wouldn't want to *be* him, and I wouldn't *never* be in the position of understanding him. Now you got him and you're tellin' me to kiss and make up."

Hawks was beginning to see the larger picture in all this. He just wished he knew who was drawing it. "It's why you're here, Koll, or whatever you are. It's the reason you're here and not back on Melchior with Master System in control of it and you. You say you can take anyone. I have no reason to doubt you on that, but can you become a Val? A computer?"

"Of course not, idiot!"

"Master System wouldn't care how many people you killed. It would study you and analyze you and then melt you down for the final analysis, and it would be perfectly willing to incinerate all life forms on Melchior if it thought it needed to dispose of you. You're not here by accident. Your name was on Raven's list. You're here because you can do what you say—go down and get very close to those who have the rings without penalty. But it's still a group effort. You think it over. You're no use to me if you have no self-control." Hawks turned back to the communications set.

"Clayben, I don't like you very much, and I don't trust you at all, but I'm willing to deal you in if you have something to offer me. I can really use that ship of yours, but I don't *require* it. Nobody here will shed a tear if I order you blown to bits. You are a problem and a luxury for me. Tell me why I can afford you."

"My knowledge, my skill, my experience," the scientist replied. "You have computer people and security people there but not one good experimental scientist. I have aboard this ship the backup copies of all the essentials of two decades plus of research done on Melchior. The data is unique and priceless. It is also coded only to me. Then there is the ship, as you mentioned, and Mr. Nagy's not inconsiderable background and contacts. He's been out here before. He knows the freebooters—who can be trusted and who can't. I don't think you can afford to pass us up, sir, or I wouldn't have chased you."

Hawks turned to the others. "Mute the communications link for a moment, Star Eagle."

"Muted. We are here far too long, Hawks. We should move."

"The risk might be worth it. It isn't the worst we've taken and it won't be the worst we take in the future. Now, listen, all of you. I want to hear it from everyone. Clayben's right. He has the data we need, and Nagy the contacts. They have a ship we could use that we don't have to convert from Master System control. Can we trust men like this? No. Their record speaks for itself. They aren't so much demonic as they are uncaring about human beings or anything except themselves. They'll be trouble. Raven?"

"Bring 'em on, Chief. We'll take care of them if they get out of line. I kinda think they'll be real cooperative, real team players, until push comes to shove. Besides, it's a great way to get the ship. If they get nasty later we can always eliminate them."

Warlock snickered. "We are of Security, Hawks. This is our job and we are good at it. We can handle them."

"Chows?"

"They are no worse than any of the others we have always faced. If they can do us some good, then it is about time they served someone else," Chow Dai said. Her twin nodded.

"Cloud Dancer?"

"Whatever you decide I will accept," she replied. "I am not certain that such evil men can ever be turned to a good purpose, but if we lose to them we deserve it."

"Star Eagle?"

"By all means let them come aboard. My core defenses are extensive and there is nothing they can do aboard the *Thunder* without my knowledge. In order for Clayben to use his data he will have to interface with my data banks. Anything he decrypts I will also learn."

Hawks sighed. "It's up to you, then, Koll. Think of it this way. For once Clayben will be under our authority rather than we under his. He might try something, but if he does I'll give him to you, no strings attached. The moment he betrays any one of us, he is yours."

She seemed to have already made up her mind. "All right—but keep him away from the bridge. Quarantine him. On the ground he'll be on my turf, as it were, and I think I can handle him if he can handle me. But not here. Not on the *Thunder*."

"Communications open," Hawks ordered. "All right, Doctor, you're invited aboard by unanimous consent, although our one real dissenter here insists that you be kept isolated from the bridge while on this ship. If that is agreeable, approach at moderate speed and prepare for instructions from our pilot. We will punch as soon as we have you securely aboard, so remain in your ship with full life support until we tell you otherwise."

"Understand. Acknowledge. You won't regret this."

"Maybe. Maybe not. But you might," Hawks muttered under his breath.

It took almost an hour to get the *Star* into an outer hold, but Star Eagle knew his job and was now fully master of the big ship's systems.

The pilot didn't hesitate once all was ready, though. The *Thunder*'s great engines roared into life, raising the massive sonic storm, and within minutes they punched.

The sensation was still very unpleasant, but this time there were no hallucinations and only relief that they were out of there.

"You handled that right well, Chief," Raven commented.

"Perhaps. Perhaps I'm handling this on gut instinct, Crow. Instinct and educated hunches. But they'll be a time bomb once aboard and you know it. I want no quarter given. The slightest wrong move and, well, they are expendable."

"No!!" China said sharply. "Use your head, Hawks. We need them—but on *our* side. That man has played whatever games he wanted with people at his mercy using mindprinters and transmuters. *We* have transmuters and when we are finished cannibalizing the old ship *we* will have a mindprinter."

"But that one's too limited to be of real use," he pointed out.

"Perhaps, but I will wager that Clayben had that ship of his outfitted as a fully equipped fast escape ship from the planning stages on. The fact that all data from the Melchior master computers was automatically transmitted to it in encoded form shows that. I'll wager that aboard that thing he has a small transmuter and a state-of-the-art mindprinter. Possibly even a psychogenetics minilab. That ship, I will wager, is a one-or two-person Melchior in miniature. By the time Star Eagle's maintenance robots and probes get through with it, I think we'll be able to do to the doctor whatever we wish—before he does it to us."

3. AN ISLAND IN THE WILDERNESS

She was sheer power, able to see in many directions at once, to have all things background monitored and brought to her notice, if need be. A mere thought brought access to more data on more subjects than her mind could handle; in some ways, it was too much for her, yet she could not get enough of it. While she was the ship, she was a goddess, and it was no fantasy, no wish fulfillment—it was real.

But she was also a small, fragile thing lying there in a command chair on the bridge, wearing a huge padded helmet from which specialized cables extended into the front panel. Star Eagle understood that the small form there was her primary reality, the one that made the rest possible, so he limited the duration of her stays in his mighty realm, while giving her absolute freedom while she was there.

She sped along the hundreds of thousands of kilometers of communications and monitoring circuitry and enjoyed it as her own private sort of peep show. Of particular interest was the large, rectangular module in Cargo Bay Four that had been constructed by Maintenance and endowed with full life-support and comfort facilities. Hawks referred to it as the Leper Colony, although he alone aboard knew what a leper was. They had built it for Clayben and Nagy, and then sent Sabatini down there as well, if only to get him out from underfoot.

Since Star Eagle had designed and constructed the module, it was hardly private, in spite of assurances to the occupants that their space was secure. Every move, every spoken word, every pulse beat was monitored and recorded, and it was all carefully scrutinized by Raven and Warlock, who knew just what to look for.

Clayben looked about fifty, with thin white hair, blue eyes, and a ruddy complexion. He appeared fat and chubby-faced, but he was in remarkably good shape and worked to keep it. He had a deep, pleasant, throaty baritone that always sounded confident and secure, the voice of a family physician or top salesman. He certainly had one of the best minds of his or any other generation, the sort of mind that could work on a dozen problems at once and master virtually any discipline it wished. That was both his greatness and his curse. He had run a torture chamber, yet never once had he thought of it that way. To him, the entire universe and all the creatures in it were merely props, put there for his convenience. His was total egocentrism, but, unlike most such conceited people, he really *was* superior to most other human beings. The only other he recognized and truly feared was Master System, and it would never have occurred to him that he and the great hidden computer were mortal enemies—primarily because they were so much alike.

The best way to describe Arnold Nagy physically was to think of a wide-angle photograph of a man in which the sides were compressed, making him a distorted stick figure. His head was very long and narrow, and it sat on a long neck attached to a body that was also very tall, very angular, and very thin. His tremendous hawklike nose and lantern jaw, narrow eyes, and very small mouth only accented his peculiar appearance. He was very dark complected, with deep-brown eyes and long jet-black hair, and it was impossible to guess his age.

This was the man who had been trusted with Melchior's security by both Clayben and Master System—he was formidable and dangerous. So far he seemed to speak and understand about every language he'd come across. He had long and often involved discussions with Sabatini in the latter's native Italian, and he even had the dialect and the slang right. One could not use Mandarin, for example, to comment privately where he might overhear, and Cloud Dancer couldn't even be certain Nagy didn't know Kyiakutt. Clearly Nagy was a natural linguist. Languages could be learned by mindprinter, to a point, as many of them had learned English and were still perfecting it by listening to those who spoke it naturally, but dialects and slang were not so easy to impart.

"*Boring.*" Nagy sighed, settling down in a chair. "Sitting watch on the patient monitors was a thrill a minute compared to this."

"Patience, Arnold," Clayben responded. "Doubtless by now they've gone over the ship almost molecule by molecule, and they're sorting out all their data and trying to break the encryption on the data-bank records. Our active time will come. Great goals require great patience. Would you rather put on a pressure suit and go up and say hello to Reba Koll? She's going to *have* to eat someone, you know, sooner or later, and there aren't many likely candidates around."

Nagy looked suddenly uncomfortable. "Sacrificial goat no matter what, huh, Doc? Is that why you wanted me transferred from the *Star*? For this?"

"No, Arnold, I did not. The last thing I imagined was being in a secondary role on this ship with that *thing* aboard and running free. I actually intended us to get to the freebooters and establish a new working base somewhere from which to build an organization and obtain the rings. It would be very difficult to find them on our own, but not impossible. They are quite distinctive. Someone, some-place, must have noticed them. Then, when it became clear that these people might get this ship started, it was worth the risk of improvising and following. I had no idea that such people could get something of this size and complex-ity running so smoothly at all, let alone this quickly. I would be willing to work with most of these people, but I shall never be comfortable while that creature is loose. I should have destroyed it ten years ago, when I had the chance. It is my greatest mistake."

He sighed and patted Nagy on his shoulder. "Don't worry, my boy. They need you. They need *us*. We just have to watch our backs, contribute, and bide our time. If, somehow, that creature can be controlled when it is free of constraint, we are where we want to be, aren't we?"

Sabatini had entered the compartment and had just stood there, listening to all this. "Yeah, well, that's all well and good for you two, but I'm dead meat to them. I lost my ship, I lost my pilot, and the inmates are running the asy-lum. I just want *out*. Failing that, I could die happy if I could just push them Chink bitches out some air lock like they did me."

Nagy turned to stare at Sabatini. "You know, Captain,

I'd listen to the Doc here and stop all that talk. Cooperate, go along with them, make yourself useful, even friendly—and survive. They can't carry much excess baggage even if they do have a ship as big as a small city. Watch you don't get dumped."

That was enough spying for now. *Analysis—Reba Koll.* The response was almost instantaneous. *Insufficient information. Input provided by subject and Clayben consistent with possibilities inherent in transmuter and psychogenetic technology. No more. Scans do not show her in any way different than would be expected for a human female her age.*

The analysis of Clayben's ship was more productive. As China had guessed, it was almost a miniature state-of-the-art laboratory, as well as a zone of comfort and an interstellar spacecraft. It was a larger and more elaborate variation of the Melchior fighter design, and it contained full and rather impressive armaments, not sufficient to do more than minor damage to the *Thunder* if it penetrated the fighter screen at all, but sufficient to do a lot of damage to lesser craft.

Also aboard was a reference computer system of unfamiliar design, possibly developed by Clayben personally. The information in it could be gleaned by a normal type of computer interface, but it was stored in a highly compressed and coded system. The decryption method was unclear; it might be hardware or special codes or a combination of the two, but it was quite sophisticated. The ship did not contain a practical transmuter, although it had one that it used for its interstellar drive fuel and maintenance; it did, however, have a single-unit, fully functioning mindprinter, attached to a psychochemical unit. While they were tied into and run by the encrypted data computer system rather than the ship's computer, the design and operation was straightforward. Star Eagle was working on duplicating the system and creating his own, tying it into his own banks for operation. Such a system might be very handy indeed.

Unfortunately, the smaller ship was still too large for the *Thunder*'s transmuters to duplicate, but it could be flown, at least. The pilot had a cold, neuter persona, but would obey anyone who had the control codes to activate it.

China and Star Eagle continued to explore, spy, probe, and hypothesize as the *Thunder* sped on through the nothingness.

"There," Star Eagle told them. "The second planet out." Not much was clear from the images on the screens; they were computer graphics and not true pictures in any event, and showed a huge sun and some small, bright dots that represented planets.

"Won't it be too hot that close to the sun?" Chow Mai asked worriedly.

"Perhaps," the pilot responded. "No way to know for certain until we take a close look at it." It was the third one in the region they had checked out. The first had been far too cold; the second had an atmosphere that would prevent them from living any more freely than in the *Thunder*. "The distance from the sun *is* important, but only within a very broad range. Planets two, three, and four, here, and possibly five are all in that range, but even my long-range scanners indicate that only two has an atmosphere dense enough to have potential. It is also the only one showing any readings indicating early terraforming."

They were not blind, even in this poorly charted region. Master System had been here long before them. The area was better termed "unused" than "unexplored." For one reason or another, the worlds here that Master System had attempted to change had either taken too long to develop or developed wrong. Although those worlds had been abandoned when more suitable planets elsewhere were developed, the processes put in motion were not halted. No one had ever found a paradise in this sector, but a number of the worlds, given many centuries to develop and mature, were at least usable and useful. And the sheer size of the sector ensured against accidental discovery of the *Thunder* by either freebooters or Master System.

"I'm getting promising readings," Star Eagle reported. "A very thick ozone layer and a high water content. We will have to see what the surface temperatures are like, though; it's impossible to guess anything except the fact that this will be a very humid place and certainly warmer on the average than Earth. Let's see."

One of the robot fighters had launched itself from the *Thunder* hours before and was now, under the firm control of Star Eagle, approaching the planet. This fighter had been modified by Maintenance for much more than defense and was capable of a soft landing if need be.

"Initial readings aren't optimistic," Star Eagle told them. "The world has an axial tilt of less than eight degrees, which means little seasonal variation, and the equatorial surface temperature appears close to sixty-five degrees Celsius. Tremendous, vast water bodies, with very odd landmasses. No continents as such, just islands, none incredibly large so far. The average water depth must be very deep to account for this. Lots of islands, all with rugged topography, but not much else. Some of the volcanoes are active although there is no sign of massive eruption to the atmosphere. I would guess that these are not the major explosion type, but rather the slow, steady erupters with dense lava."

"What's that mean?" Warlock asked, in an uncharacteristically chatty manner.

"It means that there won't be constant dust and soot in the air that would cause things to be too hot or block so much sun that it'd be freezing cold," Hawks told her. "But it also means you have a chance of having liquid rock wash into your house almost anywhere, and probably frequent earthquakes. Not very appetizing."

"Interestingly, the most comfortable surface temperature would be in the polar regions," Star Eagle said, "but there's not a lot of promise there in surface area. The best compromise would be about thirty degrees north or south. Lots of island masses in clusters there, and a surface temperature estimated at perhaps thirty to forty degrees. I am sending the remote ship down to that latitude north for a ground scan. If I find something promising I will let you know."

The others looked at Hawks quizzically. "Hot," he told them. "Days hotter than the worst summer days of America or China and nights as hot as hot summer days in Europe, with very little difference over a year. We could live there, though, if the air has the kind of makeup to block the worst and most damaging rays of the sun. Even so, those of us with the darkest skin will have the best protection. It won't do anything for comfort, though."

"Atmosphere is quite good," the pilot reported. "The trace gases are quite different and the water vapor is extremely high, but the oxygen-nitrogen balance is very close to nominal. The difference can be attributed almost certainly to the level of volcanic activity. Still, you can tell by how close it is that this is induced rather than natural. There might be some odors, but you could breathe the air unaided without harm."

"What about vegetation?" Hawks asked. "Any sign of life down there?"

"Considerable, although it's not possible to tell its full nature from here. Many of the islands appear to be almost junglelike, and I get some minor animal readings, as well, possibly insects or birds or something like that. The seas also contain much life, although I doubt that there are any deep-water creatures. The plant layer is thick enough that it probably blocks most or all light farther down. There is definitely animal life on or near the surface, though. Not an enormous amount, but it's there."

Hawks frowned. "Should it be? Would this have gotten far enough to be seeded with fish or something?"

"Mostly mammalian, by the spectrography. It's possible. It's possible this one got far enough along to be a full test."

"If it got that far, then why wasn't it used?" China asked, fascinated.

"Probably because of the slow development of the pattern and the heavy growth of algae or funguslike plants on the water," Star Eagle guessed. "I suspect it was a prototype rather than a finished product. Ah! A cluster of islands that includes one very large one with a volcano at each end and perhaps forty kilometers of flat land twenty or thirty meters at most above sea level. The flats are ancient lava flows that ran together. Both volcanoes appear dormant; there is no sign of very recent lava flows into the flats, at any rate."

A huge map appeared on the bridge screens showing a somewhat crescent-shaped island with two enormous high peaks, one at each end. The center area was relatively flat but uneven, thin in the middle—perhaps only a kilometer across—and thicker as it approached each of its two parents, perhaps as much as ten or twelve kilometers at those points. One of those jagged parent peaks was over two thousand meters high, the other slightly lower than that. Both had enormous craters inside that were hundreds of meters deep. There were several other single-peaked islands nearby, but none showed a promising landing site.

The small fighter set down on a rise in the flats region and went right to work taking samples and testing. Air temperature: Thirty-six degrees C. Humidity: Ninety-seven percent. The rock was basically basalt, its chemistry containing nothing odd or unusual. Radioactivity was fairly low, considering the volcanism. The outcrop showed extreme weathering, indicating the passage of frequent storms and high winds, a pattern confirmed by the early orbital survey. The ultraviolet reaching the surface was within the range of human tolerance, but might pose a long-term hazard to lighter-skinned people who allowed themselves to become over exposed. There were airborne spores and micro-organisms; the ship captured some in its filter and found them to be variations of Earth organisms. While this indicated that Master System had adapted readily available materials to create its balance, it also indicated that this was a very early experiment, with no assurance that such organisms would be harmless to Earth-humans.

"I should not like to come this far only to be wiped out

by some virus." Hawks sighed. "But we must also face facts. Anyplace we are likely to find that can support us will have these risks. These are, after all, the prototypes, the throwaways, the leftovers. Any world in this sector that might be better and more comfortable and safer certainly is used by the freebooters. In fact, that is the one thing that worries me about this world. It is no paradise, but it is good enough. Why *aren't* there freebooters here? Koll, if you knew about this, then so must they."

"Most likely," she agreed. "I can't answer that. Maybe it *is* an out-of-control disease. Why don't we send Clayben down there to live awhile and do research and tell us?"

That brought a chuckle from almost everyone, but Hawks shook his head. "How long do we wait? A day? A week? A month? Star Eagle, what are the odds of us surviving normally down there as of right now? I understand all the variables—an educated guess."

"I could be dangerously wrong, but I would suspect that there is nothing down there more hazardous than you would find on Earth, and a good likelihood that there is less, since there would have been mutation and adaptation as well as the initial alteration made by Master System. As to why it has not already been used, though, the most probable reason I can think of is that the native life forms, whatever they are, might be dangerous. If other alternatives were available, and many other worlds were, why would the freebooters go to that extreme? But I would not go down unarmed, and I would create an effective defensive perimeter and watch system. There is also the possibility that the region is occasionally patrolled. Measures will have to be taken to maintain the *Thunder* well away from here and ready for an instant getaway, coming in only as necessary."

Hawks thought about that. "That would mean *Lightning*, as well," he said, referring to Clayben's ship by their new name for it. "The camp would, in effect, be land-locked there. I'm not sure I like that."

"Of necessity, no matter where we settle. If a patrol came in close enough that it punched within a day or so of the planet, it would be impossible to pack everyone aboard and take off without being sensed, tracked, and quite possibly destroyed. We will establish a subordinate computer net down there and an effective communications system. There will be a substantial time lag, but I will be able to monitor you, and we can still contact one another. In a tight pinch, *Lightning* can be dispatched to take on and flank a patrol ship, but I would suspect that the best defense is to simply ignore it and it will go away."

"But wouldn't any patrol craft spot us down there?" China asked, worried. She didn't like the idea of being separated from Star Eagle for that long.

"Unless you become a population of thousands, I would suspect not. It will be looking for indications of a space-ship and communications and transmuter-powered equipment. It's not going to do a survey, only a patrol. You would show up in such a patrol in the same way as those life forms down there now, nothing more, nothing less, so long as you cut power. It is not going to spend a year on the suspicion that someone minus ship might just be hiding out down there."

Hawks nodded. "All right, then. I'll still feel better if a couple of people go ahead to scout out the place first. We'll need someone with good reflexes and skills with a gun. Any volunteers?"

"I'll go," Raven said. "Warlock can handle things here.

And I think maybe it should be Clayben who goes with me. I'll handle the firepower and he can handle the science. If we get in over our heads, then, Manka, you and Nagy come after us with all the firepower you got."

Isaac Clayben was not exactly thrilled with the assignment, but he could not argue that he was not best qualified for the job. It also got him off that damned ship for the first time in countless dull weeks, and that was almost worth it.

The modified fighter had established a small one-at-a-time transmuter station, which Star Eagle used once the *Thunder* was in a stable geosynchronous orbit over the chosen position. It was agreed that, as a first step, Raven and Clayben both would use the fairly comfortable pressure suits in spite of the planet's clean bill of health.

Neither Clayben nor Raven had ever before traveled by transmuter. In spite of his worldly cynicism and modern knowledge, the Crow had some deep reservations about this mode of travel that had nothing to do with its safety. For the life of him, he couldn't see how this differed from being killed and having a duplicate manufactured elsewhere.

"It is possible to look at it that way," Star Eagle admitted, "although the energy matrix created here is isolated, unique, and self-contained. What I convert is what I transmit and all I use to reconstruct below. In other words, you actually physically go, just in a different form. In a sense, I almost wish it were the way you imagine. Then it wouldn't matter what was transmuted; since everything would be a duplicate, I could change anything and anyone an infinite number of times at will. But I am not transmitting a formula. I am transmitting *you*."

Somehow that made Raven feel better.

The *Thunder*'s transmuters—it carried one in each of the four cargo bays—were huge, but the receiver below, modification of a maintenance transmuter, was strictly a one-person affair. Raven, as security, had to go first.

The transmuter was a circular disk that looked almost as if it were made of a solid piece of red brick, and a second disk above coated with some very shiny, black reflective material. Raven looked at it, hesitated, then took a deep breath, stepped onto the circle, and walked to the center. He had his pressure suit on, helmet and all, since the energy expense was too great to justify pressurizing an entire cargo bay.

He stared nervously back at the others—most of the group had come down to see the volunteers off, with the exception of China, who was currently interfaced with Star Eagle, Silent Woman, who had no understanding or interest, and Reba Koll, who stayed away out of a sense of caution. There was no sensation, nothing. He felt something vibrate, and inside his suit he heard what could only be described as *click*! Suddenly he was alone in the dark someplace, and he felt as heavy as lead, so heavy that he almost buckled under his own weight. It disturbed him. What the hell?

A hatch opened automatically in front of him and he looked out on a strange landscape. He drew his pistol and walked away and into it, frowning. "That's *it*?" he said, mostly to himself. "*Click* and you're someplace else?"

"I had no idea it was that efficient." Star Eagle's unusual tenor came to him over his suit radio, as clear as if he were still aboard the ship. "That is very good to know. Any problems?"

Raven was still a little shaken by his experience, but he was a pro. He looked around. He was standing on black rock with some whitish streaks in it; here and there it was interrupted by a small patch of growth in cracks or a moss-like plant in small dabs where the rock seemed to have been roughened. The surface was very uneven, but he had no trouble with his footing. About ten meters away the real growth started—a dense forest. The sky was mostly cloudy, but the exposed parts were blue—a slightly different blue than he was used to, but not enough to cause real alarm or disorientation.

"Better tell Doc to bring an umbrella. I think it might rain."

Less than a minute later, the hatch opened again behind him, and the orange-suited figure of Isaac Clayben emerged holding a carrying case of some sort. He walked slowly, somewhat bent over, dragging his case as if it weighed a ton. "That—that is simply amazing," said the scientist, who wasn't amazed by very much. "With a sufficient number of those things each in line of sight you could have a near-instantaneous transport system covering the whole world."

"I wouldn't like to try a system that big, Doc," Raven replied. "Sooner or later one of 'em would hav'ta go wrong."

"I have more equipment coming. We'll wait for it, then I'll need some help setting up." He looked around. "It's actually quite attractive. I have lived the past twenty years cooped up inside a giant rock or in the bowels of space-ships. I had almost forgotten what it's like to have a sky, and greenery, clouds, and weather. It's almost—disorienting. I didn't expect this. I'm feeling somewhat phobic about wide open spaces."

Raven shrugged. "Better get used to it. You're supposed to be the superior one, above all these weaknesses we mortals suffer, Doc. I think the rest of your stuff's here. Let's get it and get cracking. *Jeez*! I feel tired as hell. I'm havin' trouble just walkin'."

"I, too. I'm in worse shape than you, I suspect. I haven't been under more than six-tenths of a gee since before Melchior. I—I'm dizzy. I'm going to have to sit down for a moment." He settled down on the rock and sighed. "Stupid of me. I never really considered this. I was too busy worrying about the transport."

Raven sat, too. He felt like he'd been working for two straight days at hard labor and he had only walked four meters away from the modified fighter sitting there on its leg struts on the rock just behind them. "Well, maybe we ain't gonna do a whole hell of a lot real fast, Doc, but we can do something while sitting. Who wants the honor of being the first to breathe the new air?"

"Be my guest," Clayben responded.

Raven sighed, adjusted his suit control to "maintenance mode," then touched the fastener plates and cautiously removed his helmet. He took a breath, then relaxed and hooked the helmet on his neck strap. "*Whew!* Like gettin' hit by a soakin' wet wool blanket! *Boy*, is this hot! Crazy feeling. The suit's still got some air conditioning and insulation, but my face is hot as hell. I'm sweating like a stuck pig."

"The air—smells—all right?"

"As a matter of fact, it doesn't. There's an undercurrent of something—a mixture of things—that smells a little putrid. Not enough to make you sick or anything. I guess I can get used to it. Figure it's from being on mostly oxygen?"

Clayben wearily unfastened his helmet and took it off, then took a deep breath and wrinkled his nose. "I see what you mean. No, it's not that. That is clearly salt water over there—you cannot imagine how long it has been since I've smelled that smell—and it's mixing with the smells of the jungle." He sighed. "Well, all I want to do is sleep for a week, but I think we'd better get things set up here and take our preliminary measurements. Then I think we should encamp and sleep in shifts until our bodies adjust to this gravity before exploring very much—if mine ever *does* adjust."

"I think they *are* birds, but they never come close enough to really tell." Raven was clad now in an improvised loincloth, which consisted of two towels draped, one front and one rear, over his gunbelt.

"We must go into the jungle at some point," Clayben said. He was wearing a pair of shorts, a pullover T-shirt, and rubber-soled shoes. He was still terribly uncomfortable and very slow, and beginning to wonder if he'd spent too much time in low gravity to ever get used to full weight again, but he was still fascinated and excited about being on a new and remote world. Even during the night, agonized by muscle cramps, he still found it impossible not to stare up through holes in the clouds to a star field that was much denser than the one he'd known. "We will need more than these spore and insect samples, fascinating as they are. From my analysis, I suspect that those birds—or whatever they are—are not quite what we expect at all."

Terraforming was an incredibly complex science and one that Master System had had to learn from scratch. Mars had been far easier than planets like this one; there the process had involved mostly adding or transmuting to water, planting dense growth, and letting things take their course. But even there a complex chain of interdependent species of plants and animals had had to be modified and stabilized so that the ecosystem would remain in balance.

Not a single one of the flying and crawling insects they'd managed to trap here was familiar, but they seemed to fill the same not-always-obvious roles that their Earth ancestors had back on the home world. Unfortunately, some of them bit, and of those some had defensive or offensive toxins causing itching, but none of the bites suffered by Clayben and Raven had been more than minor nuisances.

The heat and humidity were still hard to take, and the gravity was murder, but at least they had grown used to the alien smells in the air and hardly noticed them anymore. Raven was certainly delighted about one thing: Finally he could smoke his cigars again without worry. His endless supply of half-smoked cigars had baffled Hawks until the latter had heard about and understood enough about the transmuters. Raven had a way of making the things duplicate his cigars, but the only model he'd had was the last half of one brought from Earth. He had a huge supply made from that half a cigar—and all were duplicates of it. He hoped that the others would never discover that he was using the food transmuters to make cigars, or that they wouldn't mind if they *did* find out.

By the end of the second day, Raven felt well enough to do some exploring, but it was clear that Clayben simply wasn't up to it. He might, in time, adapt to a gravitational pull that was actually very slightly less than the Earth on which he'd been born, but that was by no means certain

and definitely not imminent. Unwilling to trust Clayben
alone with the fighter and all his gear, Raven called for
reinforcements. "I want Warlock and Nagy down here as
quickly as possible," he told them. "We need to get moving."

The newcomers, who arrived with fresh supplies,
seemed to do a lot better with the sudden weight than the
first two had. Nagy explained that in light of the problems,
Star Eagle had induced a spin that gave some measure of
gravity to the ship. Warlock and Nagy still felt some strain,
but after a good night's sleep in the makeshift tent, they
seemed to be in as good shape as Raven was.

It was a bright, sunny day. They had actually watched
rainstorms in the distance over the water, but so far none of
the clouds had given the interior more than a few drops.
Raven opened up a security case and surprised Nagy by
giving the spindly man a pistol.

"You might need it to save one or both of our necks,"
the Crow told him. "You'll need a good knife, too. I had
Star Eagle duplicate my best." He handed him a huge flat
blade and a gunbelt that had a notch for the knife.

Nagy looked at the dense jungle. "I think a broadsword
might be better, considering that stuff." He hefted the
knife, put it in the belt, then drew and aimed the pistol at
the trees. "I—uh—guess this is some kind of test."

Manka Warlock's stern expression did not change. "No
test," she said. "If Raven doesn't come back, first I kill the
doctor here and then I come for you."

Nagy shrugged and gave a *"Who, me?"* sort of look,
then turned back to Raven. "Now's as good a time as any, I
guess. I'm not too thrilled about this, but it has to be done
if we're gonna stick around this hothouse."

Raven checked a small communicator that had been removed from one of the pressure suits and slipped into a special casing. "*Thunder*, are you reading me?"

"Perfectly," Star Eagle's voice responded. "I have you on intercom as well. Doctor?"

"No problems." Clayben looked at the others. "Bring me back some specimens. Plants, insects, sea water, even one of those birds or whatever they are. And Arnold? Be certain you *both* return."

Nagy shrugged again. "Which way, O intrepid explorer?"

"That way," Raven said, pointing with his knife at a spot almost exactly between the two huge cloud-shrouded volcanic peaks. "It's the shortest route to the sea if the map we saw was right."

They made their way carefully down to where the foliage met the rocky outcrop of ancient lava. "I don't expect that there will be any really dangerous plants and animals in there," the Crow said, "but you never know what a computer might throw into a prototype. Still, its mission was to preserve people, not get rid of them."

It was rough going almost from the start. The lava did not stop as it met the greenery, but there it had been more severely weathered, partly broken up, and overgrown with moss and vines. Much of the growth masked cracks and fissures in the ground that seemed designed to twist ankles and trip the unwary. The men used their knives as best they could and were thankful that they'd decided to wear the thick, heavy boots from their pressure suits.

When they finally hit much older rock covered with humus the footing became soft and spongy. Their passage seemed to disturb the insect population; the air was thick with tiny flying things and a few very large, angry buzzing ones. "If Clayben wants his damned insect collection let him come and get 'em," Raven shouted angrily, swatting the air.

After a while they came to a short but fairly steep drop, perhaps two meters, at which point the thick vegetation stopped and they found themselves on smooth, flat, and pretty solid gray-black sand cut with chasms. There was a great deal of driftwood on the beach, as well. Now, for the first time, they could see as well as hear the pounding waves and look out upon the ocean.

"First time I ever seen a bloody red ocean," Raven commented.

Nagy walked toward the edge of the water perhaps fifty or sixty meters away, then knelt and looked at the water. "Not blood and not red. Not the ocean, anyway. It's a thin layer of some kind of plant or animal stuff. Plant, I'd say. Some kind of modified plankton, maybe. Stuff must cover a lot of ocean. Ten to one the only reason it doesn't cover all of it is the wind and storms. Only small tides here, what with no big moon."

Raven stared at him. "You a scientist?"

"Naw, I'm like you. I pick up stuff. You never know when something's gonna come up useful."

Raven stared at him. In occupation—and somewhat in personality—he and Nagy were twins, yet the Crow was far cruder in his approach, and Nagy far more intellectual. Raven suspected that in the jungle or in the bush, Nagy would be dead meat, but that in any sort of civilization Nagy might be even more dangerous than Clayben.

"Nagy—I know why I'm here, but why are you?"

"Maybe we ought to trade information," the tall, thin

man replied. "Fact is, I was about to ask you the same question. For me it's simple—survival. We went to the same training schools. Survival is the first priority of an effective operative. I blew Melchior—thanks to you. The administrators don't like that. The escape brought Master System down on us, as I knew it had to, which is why I personally directed the chase. I didn't want to be there when the Vals crashed in the locks. The board, now, it can lay all the illegal stuff on Clayben and me. I was in a meat grinder. The way to get out is to run out—and the stars were the only place to run. So when Clayben pulled up in that souped-up custom interstellar job and took me off the *Star*, I was only too willing. Now, that's simple enough. It's *you* I don't get. What was it? The lure of power? Those rings can get anybody sick with the god disease."

"No," Raven said quietly. "I didn't fail and I didn't turn traitor and I didn't run out. I'm just doing my job."

"Huh? Blowing Melchior? Springing this crazy assortment? Lugging everybody here? Stirring up Master System to what must be the closest thing to a frenzy a machine can experience? Who the hell can you be working for that would want *that*? Or deserved the kind of price we're all paying?"

"You want the truth?"

"Shoot. What difference can it make now?"

"I don't know. Chen—the one chief administrator on Earth with a ring of his own—I think *he* knows. But as high as he is, he's just an employee, too, and in many ways he's in a more dangerous spot than I am. It was understood that I wouldn't know anything beyond Chen because, if I was captured, that was as far as even Master System could go. You can't tell what you don't know, and I suspect that

Chen has a way out just as Clayben did if the heat gets too great."

Nagy stared at him and frowned. "But there *is* nobody higher than the administrators. They get their orders direct from Master System. It would have to be a hell of a computer brain to be in that chain somewhere, and it'd have to be an independent one, not one Master System could control or reprogram. There must be more computer brains than people but it just ain't possible."

"It's possible. I don't know how. Even if the survival and discovery of the rings information was in fact accidental, very little that went on after it was. I'm not even a hundred-percent certain that the accident that caused the courier from Warlock to Chen to crash in Hawks's backyard while he was on leave—very conveniently—was accidental. Put that together with the near-simultaneous discovery by the Chinese of a tech cult with complete plans for a *Thunder*-class ship and how to operate and interface with it and you have real questions about coincidence. Maybe it is. Maybe after nine hundred years everything just came together. I don't believe it, though. Maybe in nine hundred million years, but I'm not a real strong believer in this much fate. Me, I'm an add-on. Warlock needed me to track down Hawks in unfamiliar territory, and once I was in, I was *in*. So then this Song Ching, who just *happens* to be the district administrator's daughter and knows all the security codes and overrides, gets initial access to all the starship plans and information—hell, she was *there* on the raid, and since when is a relative that high up allowed that close to action?—gets all the time she needs to crack the ship interfaces and then gets a ton of pressure on her to get her to escape."

"Go on. I'm beginning to see how you think."

"So our China girl escapes and just *happens* to get on an interplanetary freighter that's just been refitted and whose core has just been modified and reprogrammed for independent action. Now, you and I know how easy that is in space, but who could do it on *Earth*, under the very nose of and monitored by Master System? Somebody did. That pig Sabatini took his liberties, but she wound up on Melchior. Thanks to Chen, so did Hawks and both Warlock and me —but none of his own people. And I'm there with a detailed list of just who to spring, and how, and on what ship. Not only that, but I have three out of four locations for the missing rings. How the hell could Chen get *them*?"

Nagy thought about it. "Maybe a freebooter commission. Big reward for the location of any rings."

"We'll check, but would he chance it? Would *you*? They'd wonder why he wanted the rings and then they'd start after them, and before you knew it they'd be holding up both him and Master System just like we hope to do. Uh uh. When I was at Chen's, he didn't know where the other rings were—I'd stake my life on it. Then, when I got the message in his code on Melchior, there they were. I don't think he sent the code or the whole list to be sprung. I think somebody else did."

"Yeah, but why Hawks? I mean, even you said you thought the crash was accidental."

"Maybe. Maybe not. Chen seemed to think that Hawks was the key to the whole business. He's no real fighter, although brave enough. He's an intellectual. A historian. A man specializing in the last century of pre-Master civilization. He didn't know about the rings, but he knows a hell of a lot of history of that period. My orders, even direct from Chen, were to protect him at all costs. Nobody's that important by accident—not when you add up all the other coincidences. No, I'm on the job, just following orders. I don't know who, but I figure I'll find that out when we got the hard part done—if we can. Hawks is right about one thing—Master System is crippled when it comes to preventing us from getting the rings. Crippled, but not helpless. The odds are still pretty well against us."

Nagy scratched his ample chin and thought. "Well, two possibilities come to mind. I'm beginning to agree that coincidence has been stretched to the breaking point here, so that leaves the 'who' of it. One thought is that we're being thrown out here by Master System itself as some kind of final test of its security."

"I thought of that, but it doesn't wash. The rings are the only thing that can do it in. There's no way a logical beast like that could afford to let that kind of information out just for a test, particularly out of the Solar System. Once out, it could never get back—and sooner or later somebody would follow up on it and succeed. It's only chance was to shut this information down fast before it got out. No, by any logical standard, it just doesn't make sense. If nothing else, the mere news that something exists that can hurt or even kill Master System would be enough to spur people on. It knows that. It knows us all too well."

Nagy nodded. "That brings me to the second thought I've had. You know Master System has been claiming for some time that there's a war on. That it's fighting even, holding its own, but no better. Nobody knows who it's warring with, but that's one hell of an enemy if it can fight Master System to a standstill. Maybe—just maybe—that's what this is all about. If you were out there, stalemated against our system, you'd find some way to get information, contacts, whatever. You'd learn. And if you stumbled on the fact that somewhere out here is a weapon that can blow Master System's brain out, you'd try for it."

The idea hadn't occurred to Raven and it fascinated him. "But—if that's true, then why us? Why not go after them yourself?"

Nagy shrugged. "As to why it's us, I couldn't guess. I can't figure Master System, so why should I be able to figure out somebody or something really alien? As to why get somebody else to go for them, there might be a real basic and simple answer. You said it yourself—in the core of Master System there is an imperative. We, as human beings, have a *right* to try for the rings. We have that edge, for whatever it's worth, and it might be very slim but it *is* an edge. An edge that wouldn't apply to nonhumans, by which I mean people not descended from Earth stock. Maybe they calculated everything and figured humans had the edge."

"Then that means that if we ever get them, we'll have more than just Master System and Chen and the rest of the power lovers to cope with. Nagy, suppose they don't come for them when and if we have them? Suppose they just ease the way so we get in and shut Master System down?"

Nagy smiled grimly. "Then they win, don't they?" He sighed. "Why don't we cross that bridge if we ever come to it? Damn it, we aren't even set up yet." He looked out across the crimson sea. "A few other islands over there. Sooner or later we're gonna need a boat to tour the neighborhood." He looked around the beach. "It's somewhat sheltered here—you can see how the big waves break well out there, so there's underwater lava or a reef or something here. I'd say we build right here—back there and against the jungle. Burn out a good-sized trail and keep it open—the jungle will try to take it back all the time." He looked over at the tallest peak. "Somebody's gonna have to get up there sooner or later, too. Establish a high refuge if we get any real nasty storms." He sighed, his mind racing at top speed. "If these are anything like Earth volcanoes, they make great topsoil. Burn away selected areas of jungle to get fields protected from the worst weather, and you could probably grow most anything here. I—"

There was a sudden loud splash behind him and he whirled, pistol out of his holster with amazing speed, his body automatically taking a defensive crouch. Raven's re-action was a bit slower, but in the same style. The Crow frowned, seeing nothing. "Something falling in? Or some-thing leaping?"

"I don't know. They said the initial survey showed some large life forms in the water. Lots of them, in big groups, all over the place. Maybe that was just one of them. We'll have to find out what the hell's there before my boat can sail."

Raven reached in his pack and took out a pair of simple binoculars, part of the kit that he always carried. He hol-stered his weapon and looked through the lenses, surveying the surface of the water.

"Black shapes in the water. Fairly good size," he told Nagy. "I can't see very much of them and none of 'em are long enough to get much more than a blurry shape, but there's sure some big suckers out there. I don't know. They kinda look like the big otters we got along the Missouri and Mississippi, only even bigger." He lifted the binoculars so he was looking only at the surface. The closest island, about four kilometers distant, was now also in his sights. Something suddenly nagged at him, and he took his eye off the water and looked squarely at the island itself. "Nagy— I think you might want to take a look at this. I think we better call it in, too."

"Huh? What?" Nagy, too, had holstered his weapon and now he took the binoculars.

"That next island. To the right, there, maybe a couple of degrees, where the beach looks thin. Right above it."

Arnold Nagy stared. Then, after a moment, he saw what the Crow was talking about, and he felt a chill.

"That line of trees is in perfect rows," he muttered. "After centuries even if they were planted that way they wouldn't still be there. They're planted, all right, and maintained, but not by Master System."

"Freebooters?" Raven wondered.

He sighed. "Maybe, but I doubt it. Not their kind of layout. No ships, no fast getaway. Shipwreck, maybe, but that would be stretching coincidence beyond any reasonable bounds. Thousands of islands. Uh uh. Best bet is that the freebooters have a real good reason for steering clear of here. Best bet is there's places like that all over this planet. I think this was a much more advanced prototype than we figured."

"You mean—it's inhabited?"

"Looks like. I wonder by whom?"

"Or what?" Raven replied.

They reported to the ship.

"I'm not sure I like the look of this," Hawks commented. "Perhaps—perhaps we ought to rethink this idea of a planetary camp for now. There is enough room here."

"No," Star Eagle objected. "There is no such thing as

the perfect world for you except the one of your birth. This ship is not fit for long-term habitation by a growing population, and while I intend extensive modifications, these might take a great deal of time and would necessitate everyone being off the ship. It is also not good for the child to come. While near-weightlessness is fine when the child is in the womb, it should not be born in this environment and not know gravity from the start."

Hawks began to wonder if Star Eagle wasn't more concerned about China than about their own needs, but he also knew he couldn't press the issue. In a very real sense the pilot was a free agent, and because he alone controlled access to the vast data banks and the interstellar drives, he had a vote that weighed far heavier than theirs. Hawks had to wonder, though, about the relationship between the small pregnant girl who might give birth in days or weeks and this machine intelligence with whom she mentally mated. Did—could—Star Eagle feel as humans felt? And, in this case, was he being protective—or running scared by forcing her away? There was no way to tell.

Hawks sighed. "Very well, but the initial camp must be well inland, near the transmuter. Whatever is down there is mostly of the sea, and it would be unwise to be too close to their domain. Can some sort of security perimeter be established around the camp? We are too few to have constant guards and would be easily overwhelmed."

"It is possible. I believe Maintenance can manufacture something that will do, but everyone should go armed at all times. If these are humans in any sense of the word, contact must be established and a treaty made, if at all possible."

"If they are humans, they might not be inclined to talk

treaty first," Hawks responded. "We will not know their tribal ways until we press, or until they come to us. If they are too territorial, it might mean a fight."

Reba Koll's voice crackled. "If we can't beat *them*, how the hell could we ever take on Master System?"

Hawks sighed and wished he could get rid of the feeling that he was in the role of the cavalry marching against the peoples of early America. He slapped his thighs. "All right—we move!"

4. SETTLING SOME POLITICAL MATTERS

EXCEPT FOR THE HEAT AND THE HUMIDITY, IT FELT AL-most like home. Hawks sat before the campfire and looked around in the gloom. The maintenance robots had done the real heavy work, but all of the crew had a hand in what was wrought here. Ironically, it was Cloud Dancer, Silent Woman, and the Chows who had the proper design skills; the others were far too civilized and spoiled to know just how to build this way out of the materials of the forest around them—supplemented, of course, by the transmuter. Even so, the rest had all been quite amused to discover that neither Clayben nor Nagy had ever seen a pit toilet until now.

The transmuter was a valuable device, but it had its limits. It could turn out real and useful things from pro-grams sent by Star Eagle, but only if they were no more than a meter or so square and no more than two meters high. Even the maintenance robots had to be sent in pieces and partly reassembled by hand, and this was where Clay-ben was invaluable. It had been fascinating to watch a bunch of spindly wires and meaningless metal forms take shape to a point, be activated, and then assemble the rest of themselves without additional aid.

So now, in a cleared area just off the rocks and reasonably far from the water, they had several huts made from a bamboolike plant, with roofs of thatched strawlike growths from still other plants. The huts were quite comfortable and relatively waterproof. With outdated carpentry tools provided by Star Eagle's apparently limitless data banks, basic furnishings had been built and a hand loom set up for Cloud Dancer and Silent Woman to weave blankets and other needed materials.

They still depended on the transmuter for most of their food; although the data banks of the generation ship contained the matrixes for a vast quantity of seed plants, it would take time and some care to cultivate such crops here, and there was no guarantee that what they planted would thrive in this planet's climate and soil.

Clayben was setting up a power generating station in consultation with Star Eagle, but right now they had only basic power, all of which went to maintaining the defensive perimeter. This was a series of rods set well into the ground, between each of which ran a slightly visible and quite effective criss-cross of electric beams. Anyone or anything going between them would get a very nasty jolt; anyone touching one of the posts itself would probably die. The device also made a pretty nasty crackling sound when the current was interrupted, loud enough and strange enough to wake the dead. It was hardly foolproof—what could be under these conditions?—but it guaranteed that any attacker could not come in without warning.

So far, there had been nothing. No signs, no attempts at contact. Hawks was fairly pleased; everyone, even Sabatini, had pitched in to help build the place. Koll and Clayben coexisted peaceably, if uneasily. Hawks had the distinct feeling that while Koll was willing and able to go

through with her end of the bargain, at least for the immediate future, Clayben clearly was scared to death, and
Nagy wasn't far behind him. The historian wished he knew
or understood more about the strange woman. China was
ever-present evidence of what Clayben was capable of
doing in the name of playing god, but Hawks still couldn't
accept the story of Koll's origins at face value. That was
the problem. This was a mob bound together by mutual
need and circumstance; it was no team.

Over in his own meager hut, Isaac Clayben sat, his pot-
belly overflowing his simple loincloth as he worked by the
light of a primitive fiery torch on a portable lab bench that
was incomprehensible to any of the others and powered by
small energy cells that seemed eternal. He was as cogni-
zant as anyone of the incongruity of his activities under the
circumstances, but he was determined. Indeed, his
thoughts were not much different from those of Hawks.

"A rabble, Arnold, that's what we are. Primitive rabble
at the mercy of an independent computer pilot. We will get
nowhere this way."

Arnold Nagy sighed. "Doc, I think we ought to let
things settle themselves here, at least for a while. Raven
and Warlock are my sort of people—we understand each
other and I can deal with them. Hawks is a kind of father
figure to them, but he's no real leader type and he knows
it. Other than them, only our China doll has real guts and
brains, and she's pretty helpless and dependent. Let things
sort themselves out."

"You forget the creature," Clayben reminded him.
"You've seen the way it—looks at me. I haven't had a
good night's sleep since we all came down here."

Nagy shrugged. "What can we do about it? You'd have

to incinerate or electrocute it to a puddle. Shooting wouldn't work—you know that."

"If only I had access to my data base!"

Nagy sighed. "Doc, so you get the formula and you whip up a bath of the stabilizing shit. Ain't no way she's gonna jump into it and no way you can force it. Before you can deal with it, you gotta be in much better circumstances than here." It was curious how Nagy, the linguist and dialectician, dropped naturally into a very common nasal and slang-ridden vernacular. The listener tended to forget the mind behind that common working-class voice—which was, of course, exactly his intention.

"The trouble is, Arnold, we're going nowhere here. We're lapsing into a primitive, quasi-tribal existence with no cohesion and no drive. With the resources we have on the ships and the knowledge these people represent I could make this into the nucleus of a team that could conquer the universe—but I dare not. Move against them and whatever slight compact the creature feels toward the group will dissolve."

Sabatini had apparently been dozing on a cot, but now his eyes opened. "What did you say it would take to kill this whatever-it-is?"

"Incineration or massive electrocution."

"Would the fence have enough power?"

"Possibly—if it could be kept on long enough. You couldn't count on it, though."

Sabatini was silent for a moment. "These torches— they're oil fed, sort of, right?"

"Yes. It's synthesized in the transmuter from palm fronds. Why?"

"How much could we get? Suppose the old bird could

be lured, maybe forced, into touching one of them posts and then, while she was bein' shocked, somebody poured this oil over her? Instant torch, right?"

Clayben stopped puttering and turned to stare at Sabatini. "You are becoming interesting. Go on."

"I think it can be arranged. She's been real protective of the girls, particularly the Chows and the Indians. The stream where we get the drinking water and the pit toilet are both real near the fence line, both in back, out of routine sight. I been itchin' to teach them Chow bitches a lesson in humility."

"Think you could?" Nagy asked, smirking a little. "Seems to me I heard tell the last time you thought that they shoved you out an air lock."

"It was that China broad. I underestimated her, but you fixed her good, Doc. Them other girls ain't no threat. China gave 'em their guts. I'm pretty sure I could lure Koll back usin' one of them."

Clayben stared at the former captain, the only one of them not out there of his own free will. "And then what, Captain? Assuming it works—then what?"

"Huh? Then we—you—take over, like you said."

The scientist cleared his throat. "Yes, and I suppose you know how to do that as well. What? Slit Raven and Warlock's throats? I doubt if that will be so easy, particularly the woman. She is a psychopath. She *enjoys* killing, and she is good at it, I suspect, or she wouldn't be here. Hawks, too, of course."

"Yeah, sure. Hell, if I can take out Koll, then you sure as hell can take out the others. Five women, three of us, should be real nice, with the China broad as hostage to makin' that computer do what we want."

Clayben glanced at Nagy, who rolled his eyes.

"As foreign a concept as this might be to you," Clayben said carefully, "diplomacy and deal making often gain more than brute force, Captain. However, I'm willing to meet you partway. You take out the creature for me, and I will make certain you get all the reward I can muster. Take her out and leave the rest to us."

Sabatini got up, yawned, and stretched. "Yeah, sure, Doc. Ain't that what I said?"

The pit toilet, dug as far from the huts and the water supply as possible, was very near the camp perimeter. Since the fence line could be breached by a projectile weapon such as stone, spear, or arrow, anyone using the facilities was in a vulnerable position. So no one went to the toilet without an armed guard. Manka Warlock or Reba Koll generally accompanied the women, since only those two had any experience with modern weapons.

Sabatini had planned fairly well. He had only to sit, and wait, watching from a vantage point to one side of the huts, until he saw Chow Dai walk casually out toward the pit toilet. Reba Koll remained in the more protected hut area, where she could stand guard without becoming a target herself. She wasn't even watching the girl, which allowed Sabatini to gather his small set of tools and make his way along the fence line unobserved. Chow Dai, finished, stood to adjust her ersatz skirt. Koll seemed preoccupied with something back toward the campfire area.

"You'd look better without that skirt," Sabatini said aloud to Chow Dai. "I remember you real good, honey. You been a long time without a man to give you what you need."

She started and looked at him in shock. Sabatini had cruelly tortured her and the others when they'd been helpless prisoners on his ship, and the memory of that remained.

"Get away, you bastard," she snarled at him bravely, although her voice was trembling. "If I need a man I will find one. There are none near me at this moment, only foul-smelling excrement."

"You little bitch! Do I have to teach you again?" He reached for her, deliberately, and with some melodramatic exaggeration.

She wriggled free and started to run, but he grabbed her arm and pulled her back to him. She screamed.

Koll's head came around. For a brief second her hand went to the trigger on her pistol, but she didn't dare shoot, since Sabatini had a wriggling, panicky girl in his grasp.

"Sabatini, you worm!" she shouted, running out toward them. "You let her go right now! This has gone far enough!"

He grinned evilly at Reba Koll. "You gonna stop me, you washed-up hag?" Coldly seeing that Koll had no intention of shooting, he flung Chow Dai away and stood to face the onrushing woman, who clearly was too angered to think straight or call for help. Chow Dai just lay on the ground, stunned.

"I've taken far bigger and better'n you!" Koll snarled, assuming a judolike stance. Sabatini grinned and did likewise. Koll feinted, then jumped, her feet aiming for his stomach, but he moved aside, and she struck a glancing blow that did not unbalance him. He managed to turn a full circle and push her farther out toward the fence. She recovered but Sabatini reached into the grass and pulled up a long, thin wire that seemed to run all the way to the fence. She saw it, laughed, and jumped it, only to find herself tangled in a whole nest of wires carefully concealed in the grass between the pit toilet and the fence. She fell over, and he was on her, grabbing her and pulling her right hand to the charged post. She struggled, but she was caught in the wire and briefly confused, and he touched her hand to the post.

There was a loud and nasty electrical buzzing sound that startled the insects and carried far in the wind. Chow Dai for a moment could not understand what had happened; if he had touched Koll to the fence, then why was he not getting the charge, as well?

His boots! she realized suddenly. *He's wearing his pressure suit's boots! They protect him!*

He let go and stepped back as Reba Koll's scream of pain rose over the terrible sound of the fence's lethal charge. He reached over and pulled away her pistol, suddenly afraid that the charge would make the bullets fire, then stepped well back again.

Reba Koll's hand blackened, charred, and bubbled, and the stench of burning flesh suddenly filled the air. It seemed as if the hand were made of plastic, melting into a terrible bubble as Koll tried to pull away.

And Koll *was* pulling away, the right arm now connected to the bubbling mass that had been her hand by only some blackish, plasticlike goo, and then it was free—and she was free of the charge. Her hand was still on the post, still burning, but Reba Koll was no longer attached to it.

Sabatini frowned and stepped backward. "This ain't possible!" he muttered to himself.

Reba Koll was obviously in pain, but she got to her feet, her blackened stump looking all the more horrible as she did so. There was no blood, and that horrified Sabatini most of all. He edged back still more, toward the bucket of oil he'd brought out with him and set down before accosting Chow Dai.

"Now you've gone and done it," Reba Koll said in a dry, nasty voice that hardly seemed human. "Now you went and *really* made me mad! Who put you up to this? Clayben? Naw, he's too damned smart to think something like this would work. Okay, *sonny*, it's time now. Time for you and me to have a *real* intimate get-together." And, with that, she advanced toward him.

There was just something about it all that completely unnerved Sabatini. He reached frantically for the bucket and tripped over his own wires, falling to the ground.

Most of the others, attracted by the loud noises and commotion, had drawn up in a semicircle, watching. Too late to help Koll, they were unsure of what to do.

Sabatini, still on his back on the ground, got hold of Koll's pistol and brought it up. Seeing that, Warlock brought up her own pistol and took aim, but Clayben reached out and pushed it down. "No! *She's* not the one in trouble! Watch and learn!"

The black woman paused and looked over at Raven, who took the half cigar from his mouth and nodded.

Sabatini fired three times into Koll's body at point-blank range. The bullets tore into her, knocking her down and forcing her back, but even as the man was getting untangled and rising, so was Reba Koll. She stood there, three big holes in her chest, and though there were signs of bleeding, no blood was flowing now.

She laughed at him. "You're mine now. You went and spoiled this old rag I had on."

Manka Warlock stared along with the others. "Those were good shots," she said in wonder. "It is not possible! See the gaping exit wounds in her back!"

Reba Koll ripped off her skirt and tore off her gunbelt with tremendous strength, and then leaped at Sabatini. This time the man could not move out of the way; he was as stunned and totally confused as Manka Warlock and the rest of them.

Koll clung tightly to Sabatini, and the man's body suddenly stiffened. He opened his mouth in a cry of pain and surprise but nothing came out.

"Get away, Chow Dai! Get away *now!*" came a horrible, inhuman voice. The Chinese girl, suddenly animated, got up and ran to the others.

The two stood there a moment, a frozen tableau, the small, frail-looking old woman clutching the chest of the big, muscular Sabatini—and then it began to happen.

"Sweet Jesus!" Nagy swore. "They're *melting!*" He'd been told about Koll—over and over by Clayben—but until now there always remained some lingering doubt over whether Koll was anything more than she seemed or merely the subject of a Clayben dementia. There was no doubt now in any of their minds that Isaac Clayben, sane or not, had not been kidding.

Raven's cigar fell out of his mouth.

"Fortunately, it's very slow," Clayben remarked, his voice almost casual and clinical, as if discussing a sprained ankle. "That was the only reason we could capture and contain it at all. It's been a long time since I saw this. I'm glad it's no different. Gives me *some* odds."

His detachment was disturbing to most of them, but they could not take their eyes off the slow-motion drama now taking place before them.

The merged bodies had become a single seething mass of amorphous flesh; it writhed and wrinkled like some great monster, and slowly, very slowly, a form began building out of the center, as if something inside the mass was now rising to and then through the top. At first it was a head, humanoid but hardly human, a death's head with bloated, puffy flesh and no hair, eyes closed, lips and nostrils sealed. It was ugly and gruesome, but none could take his eyes off it even for a moment.

There was a neck now, then the torso started to emerge —a broad, muscular frame lacking in detail—then the waist, and finally thick, sturdy legs. Finally a complete figure stood in a thick pool of protoplasmic goo, but it was still not human, more like a thing of plastic or wax, an artificial man before the artisans had started to work. It was still being fed by the mass in which it was rooted like some strange tree, and it was still changing.

Subtly the skin texture and muscle tone changed, becoming flatter, harder, and more natural. The nipples, the fine detail of the male genitals, even, incredibly, a few minor scars on the torso were formed. Very slowly but steadily, so slowly that it couldn't really be tracked by the eye—the way the position of the hour hand on a clock keeps changing even though its movement cannot be followed—the rest of the detailing came in, including the hair, the lashes, and the rest. The figure was clearly recognizable now as Sabatini.

Then, quite suddenly, an imperceptible new energy was added to the figure, and it was no longer a statue of Sabatini, but a real human figure.

It gave a shudder, then breathed deeply. Its lips parted, and it flexed its arms and knees and turned on its hips.

The eyes opened, and he looked down at the mass of goo with distaste and stepped from it, strands of plasticlike flesh trailing, then breaking away. He squatted down and removed parts of it that still clung to his feet; behind him, the mass that remained seemed now devoid of purpose. It writhed a moment, then was still, all life and energy draining from it. It began to putrefy almost instantly.

The new Sabatini got up and looked at them. "That's the trouble with this if you've got conscience," he said in Sabatini's rich baritone. Even the accent was perfect. "One must either destroy those who are innocent and deserve life or one must make immortal the scum of the race. Don't worry, Clayben—I'll never eat you unless you force me to it. This is bad enough—to become you would be desecration." He looked over at Hawks. "Now you see why I am essential to this thing. No matter what hell hole and no matter what monstrosity might have a ring, he is not safe from me. I can become his confidant, his lifelong friend, his lover. I can even become *him*."

And me as well, thought Hawks glumly, knowing the others shared the same thought. Never had he thought so furiously and so logically to cover himself. "Can you become five or more of us at once, friend?"

The creature that was now Sabatini frowned. "What? Of course not. As you can see, the rest is rotting flesh."

"Can you become a Val, then, or a robot? Can you become Star Eagle?"

"You know I cannot. Why are you pressing this way?"

"It will take five different people working in willing concert to use those rings, I warn you, and if any of the five objects, it will be the destruction of them all. Even you could not withstand Master System in full defensive array and you know it. And you are only a bit less at risk than we. The Vals will be after you, as well. In a Val ship, in a machine environment, you will be as helpless as on Melchior and at the mercy of something far darker even than Clayben. Retain our partnership and you will share as I promised you would, but this is the last of our number that you will so consume."

"I intend to keep our bargain and my word, although I can see why you would fear. How would you know if I violated it?"

"We'd all know," Isaac Clayben said. "Because there wouldn't be any Sabatini any more, would there?"

"I, personally, and most of the others, as committed and full of hate as we are for the system, would bring in the Vals if this compact is broken," Hawks warned. "Your— ability—is incredible, beyond anything I would have believed only minutes ago. It is why you are here, included in this band."

"I'll behave," Sabatini said, sounding quite natural and Sabatini-like. "You trusted Koll, didn't you? She's still here—somewhere. I confess even I am unsure how it works. The big problem I have is that I'm compelled to be a nearly *exact* duplicate. Even if you subjected me to full examinations, I would be Sabatini and Sabatini alone. You do not possess the equipment, nor the know-how to create it, to tell me apart. I have his urges, his temperment, and his habits. I simply have more self-control than he did, and more of a conscience. By tomorrow I'll be Sabatini—a Sabatini who just changed sides, and knows more than he used to. I'm just not as stupid as he was." He yawned. "I think I'll get some sleep. It's been a long time since I did this, and I'd forgotten how tiring it is."

He walked off, and they let him go.

Raven crept close to Hawks. "Is that really true, Chief?"

he whispered in Lakota. "About needing five willing ones?"

Hawks shrugged and replied in English. "Beats the hell out of me, Crow."

Raven grinned. "Maybe you *are* the best man for this job, after all."

It was quite late, but many were not asleep. Hawks sat by the fire, impassive as always, his mind in some plane all his own, while behind him, in the center hut, Cloud Dancer and Silent Woman prepared to aid China in the imminent delivery of her child. It was neither tradition nor paternalism that found those two in there and he and the others away; nobody but the two women in attendance had ever done that sort of thing before.

Isaac Clayben came over and sat down next to Hawks. For a while the Hyiakutt did not move nor in any way show that he was even aware of company, but suddenly he asked, "Is Sabatini still sleeping?"

"Yes. It is fully capable of being on the go within minutes after it consumes, but if it can it sleeps for a long time, which helps it integrate all the new memories and information into its mind. You heard it this afternoon—Sabatini never talked like that. It is an incredible process at that, so much integrated into a single mind. I sometimes amaze myself with my handiwork."

"Did you create it—or order it created?"

"A bit of both. I did much of the theory, but others, more skilled than I, actually created it. The final single integrated program for it was the longest I had ever known. At computer speeds it took more than three days just to load that thing."

"It seems inconceivable that human beings could have created such a thing."

"Human beings created Master System. Just five of them, in fact, wrote all the code and debugged it and established it. Of course, it probably took an army of technicians to build even the initial primitive version and get it running right, but it was at its heart just five people. We don't know a lot about them except that they were not even typical of the polyglot culture in which they worked. Only two were native to the nation that employed them, for example. A Chinese Buddhist from Singapore; a Jewish lady from Israel; a black Moslem man from someplace in Africa, I believe; a part-Japanese girl from Hawaii; and an old Jewish professor from someplace in eastern North America. Funny—we know their names, their origins, and, of all things, their religions, but little else."

"I know. Much of it was suppressed. I suppose it was Master System's own choice to keep some details of them alive in the records. After all, they were, in a sense, its parents and creators. The Fellowship of the Rings, they called themselves. I understand it was from some popular work of the time. A joke. One masking a serious purpose. They knew their creation could turn on us all, Doctor. You should have learned something from that."

"I thought I had it all figured out. All contained. We were extra careful. We simply did not foresee how good an organism we had created. It is less an organism than a colony. Memory, control, you name it, is distributed in a unique and ever-changing pattern throughout the cells. You could blow Sabatini's brains out and it would only slow it down. Sabatini's memories and personality would be gone, but the rest—that's stored and accessed differently. Unfortunately, what allows it to survive also makes it eventually unstable. Cells die or wear, new ones replace them. We hardly notice, but it does. Its cells have to do so much more than ours that it can't replace them at our rate by normal means. You saw how it can do the job all at once."

"I saw. It was a person once? A real human?"

"Yes. Frankly, I don't even remember who. Someone from the penal area whom we took and cleaned with the mindprinter of all memory and all personality. A spiritual blank, as it were. It was the only merciful way to do it. After all, it—the mechanism—needed to know how we work, the quadrillions of intricate interrelationships we all possess. The original was a physical template, nothing more. A dedicated army of those could be anyone anywhere, walk through any security except the highest machine-only accesses, be invulnerable to most threats. Sent out as information collectors, they could get all the bits and pieces of knowledge we cannot and put it together. I had no knowledge of the rings. It seemed a fragile hope, but the only one, of breaking the system."

"Why, Doctor?"

"Huh? Why what?"

"Why bother breaking the system? You and it seem so well made for each other, and I cannot see you as wanting to be god. Too much detail work. You were as free as any human can be in your own little playground. Certainly not on moral grounds, nor out of revenge. Why break the system?"

"Forbidden Knowledge. We were always on the edge of discovery, of being wiped out or worse. I have no idea why Master System ever tolerated Melchior. Even there, we had so many dead ends, and we were not free to pursue any leads we might develop. Humanity was born to quest for knowledge, Hawks. It is the only activity that really matters. The system places great limits on that, and I do not believe in limits."

"That," Hawks said dryly, "is obvious."

"I could ask the same of you, you know. I think we are more alike than you want to admit. The system wasn't exactly bad to you, either. You knew when you opened and read that pouch, even before you had actually divined a single word, that it would be dangerous, probably fatal. You just couldn't resist it. Forbidden Knowledge."

There was a sudden series of loud shrieks from behind them, then sudden silence, then the cry of a newborn baby. Neither man turned to the source of the sound, but both heard and understood.

"Just another digit in the mass of humanity to you, Doctor," Hawks remarked. "Another subject, another plaything, nothing more. Not a new soul damned to strangulation, its future one of chains. That is the difference between us. That new one in there, who is getting such a rude awakening, is just as important, if not more important, to me than you are. You will not understand that. You will quantify it or dismiss it, but that is because there is a part of you that is missing. That is your curse, Doctor—the ultimate irony. Even without Master System there is Forbidden Knowledge for you; Forbidden Knowledge you can never have because you can never comprehend it. The quest is not the end, it is the means."

"Spiritual claptrap. You are blinded by your romanticism and your mysticism, Hawks. You will never attain what you seek until you discard them."

"The Fellowship did so, and gave us Master System.

You did so, and now you cower in fear of your own creation. I do not wish to become Master System, Doctor. I do not wish a race of organic robots. That creature was your second creation, your second monster, Doctor—not your first. You are by far your most dangerous and aberrant creation."

Cloud Dancer emerged from the hut behind them and approached the two men sitting by the fire. "It is a boy child," she told them. "Healthy, looking well. The mother is also doing quite well physically, although her mind seems addled. It is almost as if she is drugged. I do not believe she even remembers her name or where she is, but she is suddenly all very soft and she smiles dreamily. She speaks gently and only of the act of giving birth. It is not the same woman."

Isaac Clayben sighed. "This one isn't really my fault, you know." He sounded almost defensive. "Had I known that we'd all be stuck together like this in the immediate future I wouldn't have meddled at all, but this would have eventually come about anyway. I helped things along, I admit, but she is her father's creation."

Hawks looked over at the scientist. "What do you mean?"

"The old man's chief administrator for China, and brilliant in many ways, but he's handicapped as much or more than most of us by the culture in which he was born and raised. He had the same sort of idea I did—to breed a superior race that might be able to run rings around Master System—but he was more conventional. He used his own daughter—his own daughter, mind you—for it. In fact, she wasn't conceived in the usual way at all, but in a laboratory, from modified egg and sperm. She was designed to be superior, but there are lots of superior individuals about these days. He wanted more than that, and he's a patient man. She was a prototype, too, of a possible large group of superior human beings—physically, mentally, you name it. Women who would breed his superior race. He wasn't dumb, either—he knew that if she were not superior it was all for nothing, but if she was she'd hardly be content breeding future generations, so he planned to have her reverted to a nontechnological level so she wouldn't know what she was missing and would accept her lot in a patriarchal system. The marriage arranged for her was actually a sham—the fellow's a highly born noble all right, but he's a total homosexual in a society that considers that grounds for death by torture. Being highly placed and well connected, he accepted the marriage and arrangement in much the same way others in his position have since time immemorial."

Hawks nodded. "I see. And since she would bear many children, he would have honor and manhood even though they would be from specially modified laboratory sperm and not his at all. Under orders from husband and family, she would accept, like it or not."

"Well, if she didn't, he had the way to make her fall into it. Once impregnated, her entire brain and body chemistry changed permanently. Pregnancy is her natural condition; she is compelled to be so. Everyone—you, me, Cloud Dancer, Raven, you name it—have elements of both the male and female in us, biochemically speaking. All but China. During labor her body purged itself of all male-linked hormones and biochemical blockers. The only way to trigger aggression in her would be to threaten the child. She will react to maleness, even in the other women. She

will be quite childlike, docile, eager to please, and without
any control of her passions. She will quite literally do anything you want and beg to be ravished. Nothing else will
matter—until she is pregnant once again. That will restore
the balance and trigger normalcy of a sort in her system
and she will be back in control, regaining her maleness, as
it were. In fact, in the old man's original genetic map, she
would remain as she now is, which was what he wanted. I
restored the chemical balance, allowing her, once pregnant, to regain her control and will. That way the experiment goes on, but without wasting that brilliant mind."

"I think that is disgusting," Cloud Dancer remarked.
"She is but a girl yet—seventeen, eighteen perhaps. You
are saying she will be compelled, if she lives that long, to
bear children for the next twenty-five or thirty years non-
stop, all the time knowing and remembering."

"Worse than that. She's physically perfect, as well.
She's going to remain youthful, healthy, and strong abnor-
mally long, and free of most diseases that might ravage
others. Assuming we aren't all blown up or wiped out, she
could be doing this for the next seventy or eighty years—a
one-woman colonization program. The pilot understood
this. I think she might, as well, although she's repressed it
to keep sane. And we need her sane. Next to me, she
probably understands these machine intelligences better
than anyone alive. Unfortunately, what looked simple to
handle on Melchior now complicates us beyond belief. The
longer she remains in this submissive and animalistic state,
the harder it will be for her to deal with it when she is not.
Her sanity depends on perpetual pregnancy, and that means
we will soon be knee-deep in children, all of whom will
require care and attention and possibly something ap-

proaching a staff. We can't spare that staff—and we can't spare her."

"You seem to know a lot about her situation," Hawks noted suspiciously.

"Well, of course, we had to read it all out to modify it or we would have lost that mind and will for good. We were aided because the old man quite naturally used Melchior's resources in establishing his genetic criteria. I had no real part in it, but Melchior did it. We had the records."

"So all the great minds of the world have spent their time devising monsters," Hawks commented, "and they are all with us. Anything you want to tell me about yourself or any of the others here? At one time or another we were all common to Melchior."

Clayben gave an odd half smile. "Nothing, really. Those of you who were prisoners rather than employees or staff were either too important or not important enough, I'm afraid. We were going to use your wives and the Chows as nursery matrons for the early products of the experiment, of course, and we did some minor mental conditioning to that effect, but nothing serious and nothing that might be an impairment. Nothing else that I know of."

Hawks slapped his knee impatiently. "Damn it! We cannot just sit here and rot! The time to move is *now*, before things get too domesticated." He sighed. "Yet we must wait for Star Eagle. I wish I knew just what he was planning that is taking so long."

The crying stopped behind them, and there was a sudden stillness that seemed louder than the noises. Hawks looked at Cloud Dancer. "For now it's Raven, Nagy, and I. We will draw lots when she is physically up to it. I do not like it, but these are exceptional circumstances."

She nodded. "I understand. I do not think it would be moral or proper for *him* to be included." She referred to Clayben, who said nothing.

"What about—Sabatini, Doctor?" Hawks added, suddenly struck by the implications. "What would be the result of such a thing?"

"I'm not certain. There wouldn't be sufficient information in a single sperm cell to do anything terrible. It won't breed, if that's what you're thinking about. It's probable that the union would be rejected, the product spontaneously aborted, but I don't really know. I'd rather not have to deal with that one if we can avoid it."

"Then it is up to us to make certain that is avoided. At any cost."

"Star Eagle to Pirate's Den."

"Go ahead," Hawks responded. "We thought we had been forgotten and abandoned."

"Do you know what it is like to do massive maintenance without a proper shipyard? It was like performing surgery on yourself. *Thunder* is still not completed, but *Lightning*, I believe, is ready and well prepared. I wish to know the condition of all below."

Hawks gave the computer pilot all the news in fairly explicit terms, particularly about China and Reba Koll.

"China is now all right?"

"Yes. She's coming out of her physiological stage and will be back to normal in another week or two at most, but I don't think it would be wise to part her from the child for any length of time as yet. Still, we're hot, tired, and very bored down here. The whole thing is very limited."

"I understand. I have not been idle myself, since my

alterations are internal and are not affected by my movement. I have used the time to check out the situation. There
is a world called Halinachi one jump and no more than six
days from here that is a freebooter stronghold and base. I
have no data except monitored transmissions on it, but it
appears to be one of the officially tolerated outposts. There
are at least two Vals in the vicinity and there is some indication that they go down to the settlement there."

That was a surprise. "I thought the freebooters were
more tolerated than actually part of the system."

"They exist only because they are occasionally useful to
Master System and otherwise do not get in its way. However, most freebooters hate the system as much as we—
they just have no choice, as we did not. I had hoped that
Koll would have contacts there."

Hawks thought a moment. "Nagy, too, maybe. Let's
see." He summoned both the security chief and the one
now called Sabatini. "Halinachi. Either of you know it?"

"Both of us, I expect," Nagy replied. He was getting a
fairly good dark beard, and the sun had turned him almost
as brown as Hawks was naturally. "I've been there. It's one
of a half-dozen contact worlds used by both sides when
they want something from the other."

"I can see much that they might wish from Master System, but what could they offer *it*?"

Sabatini spat. "Eyes and ears. Human bodies who can
walk the other side where the best machines can't get. The
freebooters control the illicit trade between the colonial
worlds—the stuff Master System won't let get traded the
usual ways. It'd take Master System too much time and
effort to really stamp it out, so it just tries to limit it to
things that won't really upset the apple cart. Because of

this, though, they're able to have the confidence of some of the top administrators in the colonies. They hear things, and they listen. When they hear a bit of news that would interest Master System, they trade the secrets for something they want or need. You of all people should know that the system can be beat, to a point. To fill in the gaps, as it were, the machine uses the freebooters. It's simple."

"They sound like rather interesting excuses for human beings. The questions are simple, then. Would they turn any of us in to Master System for that sort of reward?"

"Probably," Nagy responded. "At least we'd be in the file of people to sell out when the time was right."

"Then how can you deal with them?"

Nagy sighed. "Look, you got to see it their way, too. They ain't living in the lap of luxury, you know. No cradle-to-grave care for them, no instant spare parts, nothing. They're high-tech barbarians, and they're not even all human by our lights. Lots of 'em are colonials. They don't live, most of 'em. They survive. Survive in a thousand little pockets scattered to hell and gone, like this one we got here. They like to think they're outside the system—hell, I think they all *believe* they're outside the system—but they're really a part of it. They'd sell their own mother because they're part of it. They really believe the system can't be broken but only bent, just like all of us bent it. They're true believers, just like we were."

Hawks thought it over. "Suppose they thought there *was* a chance to break the system? What would they do?"

"Try to break it, most likely," Sabatini replied. "Only not as a team, more like a mob. The ones who believed it would be shooting each other to get to the rings. The ones who didn't would turn the ones who did in to Master System."

"Can any of them be bought? Or rented?"

Sabatini chuckled. "We got nothing to buy them with, and even less to rent that the other side couldn't outbid."

Nagy scratched his chin in thought. "Hold it. Maybe we're going at this wrong. The one thing they're scared of is strength. That's why Master System is the big cheese even when they kid themselves that it's not. They have their masters and their warlords. Not all of 'em, sure, but a fair number. This Halinachi—it's more a big town than a world. Most of the world's not very habitable. Last time I was there it was run by a fellow name of Fernando Sava-phoong. Get *him* interested in the rings and you got a real power there with a lot of resources."

"Yeah, sure—and then he knocks us all off and goes after the rings himself," Sabatini pointed out. "You can't make a deal that'll stick with his kind—except the kind that has him sticking something in your gut or back. Nope. If we need warm bodies the best thing to do is prowl and take some of the freebooters by force, and then run 'em through the mindprinter and whatever else we got to make 'em ours."

First Warlock, then Raven, had noticed and approached the conversation, and both had been listening quietly.

"Suppose we eliminated this leader. Who would rule?" Warlock asked them.

"The next in line, mostly likely," Sabatini replied. "Not the one who knocked him off, that's for sure. If you *could* knock him off, and nobody's invulnerable, he's got a setup so the killer at least would go, too."

"And if the next chieftain was eliminated, and the next?"

"Eventually they'd have your number, and somebody

would be smart enough to spare no expense and effort to track us down and pay us back for the sake of sheer insurance. If you were good enough or powerful enough to prevent that, which I doubt, then you'd make the next in line scared enough to call in the Vals and all the resources of Master System."

"They would not make a deal to avoid this?"

"Doubtful," Nagy put in. "Or, if they did, then you'd have to expose yourself to them. They take the deal and then they wipe you out, deal or no deal. We start messin' with the freebooters in more than a casual way, and we got to decide just how many bodies we want piled up."

"Ours or theirs?" Raven asked casually.

Hawks settled back and thought for a moment. *This is what it is like to be chief,* he told himself. *How many bodies . . .? For that matter, whose bodies?* It was a good question, one he'd never really thought about until now. Could he order a massacre if he had to? Could he be as ruthless and heartless as the enemy in order to break him?

"What if this man believed that Master System had turned against him? Or could be turned against him?" he asked them. "What if he could be convinced that his petty little empire could not be held?"

They all looked at him. "You got something, Chief?" Raven asked.

"We need information," he told them. "We need to know the organization, the structure there, everything. *Lightning.* is ready and available. Could we get in and get this sort of information without drawing the dogs of the Master?"

"Maybe," Nagy replied. "Not you, though, or anybody else with them tattoos on their cheeks. Ain't nobody else with those particular designs roaming around, so there's no way to hide who you are and where you came from. I haven't been there in quite a while, and not too many people would recognize me on sight. Sabatini, here, is perfect —no marks and a total unknown there who still knows his way around thanks to his, uh, past lives, and I'm pretty sure we can do a halfway decent disguise on Raven and Warlock here, which would also gain us two more people with some deep-space experience. More would be obvious."

Sabatini smiled grimly. "I could—become—this Fernando Savaphoong. That would vastly simplify matters."

"Perhaps. For a while," Hawks replied, "but only for a while. What happens when we need you to become someone else? What happens if your underlings cannot see the profit and will not go along? No, we'll keep that in reserve, but not immediately." He sighed. "I wish I could go along!"

"Get used to it, Chief," Raven said, anticipating some action at last with obvious excitement. "You should know —chiefs don't lead their men into battle, they stand on the high ground and direct it. You just watch it while we're gone. I still don't trust Clayben farther than I can throw him and I can't even pick him up."

The Hyiakutt historian suddenly started and snapped his fingers. "Of course!" he muttered to himself. "Of course!"

"You got something, Chief?" Raven asked him.

"This whole business has been percolating through my mind for weeks now. There's been nothing much else to think about, anyway. Suddenly, just now, it all came together. We are few in numbers and relative power. Most of us cannot go into any civilized company without being known. Master System is required only to allow us the attempt, not the success, and it knows where we must go to get the rings, so it need only watch and wait there and we must come to it."

"Yeah, so?" Nagy prompted.

"There is an old story, with many variations, of the professional master thief who wagers a fortune with a rich man that the rich man will be successfully robbed within a week. The rich man *is* robbed, in spite of all his precautions, yet when he comes to arrest the thief the suspect is found to have spent the whole evening with the chief of police."

"I've heard that one," Nagy responded. "He didn't bet that *he* would rob the guy—he just bet the guy would be successfully robbed. That drew every thief in the world to the job since they figured they could take the rich man and the thief would take the fall. Go on. I'm beginning to see the way you're thinking and I think I like it."

"We are pirates, not secret agents. Suppose we *did* tell everyone, and I mean everyone, about the rings and what they did? Suppose we spread it throughout the entire freebooter camp? A hundred camps. They would go for it, would they not? After all, Master System will be looking for *us* to make the attempt. It knows where we must go— and so do we. We need only set the bait and wait for the experts to flock to it. Then *we* take the rings from those who succeed."

"Tricky, but not as tricky as trying to heist them ourselves," Arnold Nagy agreed. "We'll need more ships, more intelligence. We'll have to know the what and where. And we'll have to be better than Master System."

"That is what we start first. Communications. Intelli-

gence. Ships. Training our own people and recruiting some
specific personnel. There will be lots of details to work out
before we can even start it all going."

"It ain't bad," Raven commented, "but. it needs work.
What if we can't track down all these thieves? What if they
get away with the rings?"

"How many? One ring does no one any good, nor two,
nor three, nor even four. We will use Chen's logic against
him. Even if someone were to amass all four they would
have to go to Chen. These freebooters never went beyond
Melchior by law and custom. They would not know. We
can offer the fifth ring. We can also offer more—expertise
on how they are to be used. In the end, remember, all five
must be brought to Master System itself with quick death
the penalty for any mistakes."

"That's all well and good, Chief, but we don't have that
expertise and you know it. We don't know where Master
System is any more than they do, let alone how to make it
all work."

"That may be true, but they do not have to know that.
The very alarm put out by Master System will spotlight us
as the experts, the ones who know. Consider: First the
rings must be located, then stolen—the last no easy task in
any case. Then the various organizations that have them
must settle it between themselves until one has them all.
Finally, they must bring them to us to know how to use
them—to us or to Chen, if they learn of him. We will be
conciliatory. We will deal. We will put it together."

Hawks had left the communications channels open and
now activated the communicator. "You hear all this, Star
Eagle?"

"I do and I concur. First things first, though. We must

know just what we face in the freebooter camp. I should be able to shadow and monitor them from a distance so long as there are no Vals or direct sensor stations within the system itself. We need information and we need contacts. As for ships—we will make the pirates of the *Thunder* a legend here."

Raven smacked one fist into the other. "Hot damn! Let's *do* it!"

5. A Nice Little Layover

THE CHANGES THAT HAD BEEN WROUGHT IN *Lightning* were astonishing. Its original exterior had resembled nothing so much as two bullet-shaped tubes attached to either side of a very large but similarly shaped tube of dull gunmetal gray. Now the area between the tubes had been neatly filled in and reshaped and the entire thing coated with a dull bronze-looking substance. It now looked like a three-edged metal arrowhead and resembled no known ship profile. But on sensor screens and scopes, it would look very much like a Val fighter.

It was a good compromise. Such a strange-looking ship would cause much curiosity but no real alarm when viewed by the freebooters, yet it would have to get very close in to be seen as an unfriendly vessel by the average Master System pilot.

The inside had been changed, as well. Clayben's precious computer backup files, to which he was still forbidden access, along with the separate unit that held and ran them, had been removed and placed within a chamber in *Thunder*. This freed up a great deal of space; in an emergency, *Lightning* could hold the entire company. A duplicate of the old interplanetary ship's galley had been installed and could sustain them indefinitely, although in spartan conditions. The considerable armament had been retained and checked, and instrumentation had been added to allow for far more effective displays to the human occupants.

"I wish I could have done more," Star Eagle told them apologetically. "If I had the shops and the full facilities for disassembly, and the time, I would have loved to have made more of them, but with what I have this is the best that could be done. I *have* scanned and analyzed it inside and out down to the molecular level; if we ever get hold of a shipyard I might well be able to turn out more. Still, I have learned much from it that could be incorporated into other ships."

Nagy slid into the Captain's chair. The two forward positions had been retained in their original forms, including the comfortable bracing chairs. The other seats were more utilitarian. "I kinda miss the yacht feeling." The former security chief sighed. "But this is better for our purposes."

"How hard is it to fly?" Raven asked him.

"Very easy once you get practice. You're right, that's what we should do first. Any one of us oughtta be able to take this sucker off and get the hell out of someplace if something happens to the rest. Sabatini, I hope I can assume that your Koll memories would let you run this thing if you had to."

"If it uses the standard interface override, yeah."

"Okay, then—we've got two. Raven, I don't expect you or Warlock to get to be expert pilots, but I think I can teach you the basics. Sabatini, you ride weapons in the second chair. I think we'll check her out first, then see about a few lessons."

He reached down and picked up the helmet. "This is the interface—same as the China girl used with the *Thunder*, essentially. You put it on and you get a mild anesthetic effect and you relax and concentrate. It maps the input-output circuitry of your brain and determines what impulse code means what. Takes a few seconds. Then you get plugged in to whatever the interface plugs you into. Either of these positions can handle either weapons or flying, but right now I'm set for the ship and Sabatini's set for the weapons systems. Now, the computers in this thing can think a lot faster than any of us, so in a crisis don't get bogged down with who's controlling who. When you need instant reactions, let it go. You can override if need be and provide consultation. When it's noncritical, *you* fly it. If things get damaged, you might have to do it all."

He leaned forward and punched in a code on a small keypad, then threw a small switch and touched another code into the pad. "I've just activated both interfaces and directed them to their appropriate functions," he told them. "We'll have to come up with new codes all of us can re-member. You only get three tries. Muff it the first two times and it just doesn't work; muff it the third time and it'll *seem* to work but when you put the helmet on it'll just put you to sleep and keep you there until somebody with the *right* code comes and finds you. Keeps things nice and secure. All right, we're gonna take it out of here and check it all out. Then we'll let you get a taste of it."

He put on the helmet and leaned back in the chair as Sabatini did the same. Both men seemed to relax and then lapse into a deep sleep. Only a few seconds elapsed, and then Star Eagle opened the *Thunder*'s cargo-bay door and *Lightning* shuddered and came slowly to life. It lifted smoothly a meter or so off the deck, began a slow turn to the open space beyond, then moved slowly and deliberately out and away.

Instruments and screens flared into life, one showing a view of the massive *Thunder* already receding as they sped away.

"Mighty efficient, but it ain't much good for conversation," Raven noted to Warlock, who just shrugged.

"There's no problem with conversation," said the apparently sleeping form of Arnold Nagy. "I may be connected up to the ship, but that just makes it an extension of myself. Of course, I can conveniently shut you out if I want to, which is nice sometimes, and just concentrate on the ship."

The ship shuddered a few times, and they heard some very strange and unnatural short, sharp sounds. "What is *that*?" Warlock asked.

"Target practice," Sabatini replied. "We throw out some junk at random, and I try and hit it. Nothing to it. This is a very impressive ship."

Nagy's body suddenly gave a jerk, and he took several deep breaths, opened his eyes, sat up, and removed his helmet.

"Who's flying this thing?" Raven asked nervously.

"It flies itself pretty well until it needs to ask a question," Nagy replied. "All right, want to try it? I'm gonna switch Sabatini over to copilot and put the defense systems on automatic."

Raven licked his lips nervously. "I ain't never been a pilot for anything more than a horse and a canoe. I never even tried a skimmer."

Nagy chuckled. "You're probably better off because you

don't have to unlearn as much. Most experienced flyers want to do it all or override the computer too much. Just go ahead and go with the flow. I think you'll find it's easier than the canoe. I always turned over in canoes."

Raven snorted. "Since when did Hungarians ride canoes?" But he moved forward and allowed Nagy to settle him into the seat and lower the helmet.

"This," Arnold Nagy said, "was the way it was *supposed* to work."

Raven felt momentarily dizzy, then very relaxed; the small aches and pains that he, like everyone, lived with vanished, but awareness did not. If anything, it improved; Raven was reminded of the many tales of "out-of-body" experiences, some of which were solidly entrenched in Crow mysticism. He could see himself, and the others, as well, in a sort of three-dimensional mental picture. The mere sight of *all sides* of an object at once was at first disorienting, them simply strange.

"Let the inside take care of itself." Sabatini's voice came to him, not aloud but inside his mind. "Look *outside*, out there—and you will have the inside, as well. Don't think about it—just do it."

The starfield burst around him. He concentrated on a single direction and suddenly had the intricate details of a star map in his mind, including names, distances, and relationships. He understood it now, understood what China felt when she was one with the *Thunder*; he even approached, perhaps, what Star Eagle truly was. He, Raven, was one with the ship! He *was* the ship; all its functions, all its commands, all its data, were at his instant beck and call. The powerful engines were no more or less to him than his own arms and legs, and could be used without any more thought. And yet this extended to his human form as well; his body was no different from the rest of the ship's functions and as easily managed.

I am the father of all eagles! he thought, exhilarated.

Don't think about it, just do it. It really was as simple as that. One did not think about walking or talking or picking something up; all that information was in the brain encoded for automatic response to the desire to do it. The ship and its data were now such an extension; one didn't have to think about it to pilot it.

"It's a little more complicated than that," Sabatini responded, apparently hearing and understanding Raven's surface thoughts. "But I think you have enough of a hang of it to fly it if you had to. We'll practice the finer stuff later. Let me switch you out and allow Warlock the experience, just in case."

Raven was reluctant; he really didn't want to cut the connection, but he was not fully in charge. The sense of diminution, of suddenly being weak and small after having been powerful and great, was overwhelming. He took off the helmet, handed it to Nagy, and went back to his old seat, where he idly lit a half cigar. The air filtration system suddenly switched to maximum.

"You know, that's a hell of a thing," he commented, mostly to himself. "Now I think I understand why our China girl wants desperately to be a spaceship."

Halinachi was not much of a world, but it was one of those very few places not fully under the tyranny of the machine. But that didn't make it any less dangerous, since this was one of the points where Master System and the few who lived outside the system met as neutrals, almost as equals. Almost—for those who lived here and ran the place understood that the only reason Master System tolerated this world was that it was useful to the System, and the only reason it hadn't done a mass extermination of the freebooters themselves was that they were little threat and sometimes a help.

"In effect, to live outside the system you must kiss its ass," Warlock noted dryly. "These are not free people. They are merely masochists."

Nagy chuckled. "Well, you have something of a point there, but freedom isn't what's real, it's a state of mind. Earth's ignorant, primitive masses mostly believe they're free and independent, and wouldn't know a computer or a skimmer or a round Earth from the Circles of Hell."

"But they are kept in ignorance," Raven pointed out. "These people *know*."

"Never overestimate the human mind," Nagy responded. "Even without the aid of mindprinters and hypnoscanners and all the rest, people can convince themselves of most anything, if they really want to."

The screens showed a small, rocky, barren world, the antithesis of the one from which they'd come. Weather here was rare, and a small but strong sun, more orange than the ones they had known, beat upon it. Halinachi was a colorful place with buttes and bizarre, twisted landforms in oranges, purples, and tans, but there was not much green.

"It has an atmosphere, one that blocks out most of the really nasty stuff the sun sends out, but not much water," Arnold Nagy told them. "You couldn't breathe the stuff— more nitrogen than we're used to, and not enough oxygen to really do the job. Still, there's nothing down there that'll really hurt you, either, so you can pretty well get along with just an air supply and nosepiece or mask. If you ever really added the right stuff to the air and got a lot of water you could probably grow stuff here and maybe make it livable, but nobody's really inclined to do it. You'd need Master System's logistics, and it isn't about to help."

"People actually live on that hole?" Raven asked, somewhat appalled. "It looks as lifeless as the Moon."

"It is. Only one settlement—that's Savaphoong's. We'll be coming up on it shortly, and I expect to be hailed by their controllers."

That expectation was fulfilled almost immediately, and Nagy tended to it after putting up a view of the settlement on the big screen. It looked to be two fairly large domes connected by a long cylinder, with several smaller domes along the cylinder itself. It resembled a space station more than a ground settlement.

Just off one of the large domes was a small spaceport. They could not build a ship there, but they could probably overhaul, modify, and service one. From the looks of the place, though, *Lightning*, which was not a large vessel, would be about the largest they could handle down there.

Any form of money was worthless on Halinachi. Anyone who controlled a transmuter controlled everyone dependent on it. The true medium of exchange was information, innovation, and ideas—but there was a single commodity that was always welcome, and that was murylium. The irony of the transmuter was that it could not take its power from its own sources; it needed an independent, direct source, a particular compound of absolute purity and quality one key component of which was murylium, a scarce mineral found only in a few places in the universe.

As Fernando Savaphoong controlled his minions by alone controlling the transmuters, so was he dependent on a supply of murylium, the one substance transmuters needed and could not make.

It seemed that every time one tried to make murylium from a murylium-powered device, one got blown to bits, along with about thirty cubic kilometers of surrounding planet.

Melchior had once had massive amounts of the stuff; Master System's early robot probes had discovered as much and had mined the hell out of it. Those caverns were modern Melchior, and Melchior itself was powered by the leftover amounts.

So, in a sense, Halinachi was like a gold-mining town of the ancient North American West or Australia or South Africa, but it also traded in other things. *Lightning* and the *Thunder* needed all the murylium they could get; they had very little. Nagy had considered the problem, and Clayben had supplied the solution—a simple set of equations that would increase the transmuter's efficiency by more than ten percent; one of Melchior's little discoveries needed because Melchior had been running on traces of its cannibalized self.

"And we just give that to Savaphoong?" Raven asked. "And so he takes it and we're still in the hole."

"No, he wouldn't do that," Nagy assured him. "You see, if he didn't give fair return, or if he double-crossed those bringing him things, he would very quickly find himself a nonmarket. There is a lot of competition out here, and not only among the three more or less legally tolerated outposts. He'll pay—and pay well—in Halinachi credit because he wants the next item exclusively. See?"

"One good mindprobe on any of us and he has got it all," Warlock noted suspiciously.

"If he did, there'd also be a lot of repercussions," Nagy assured her. "But, in any case, that's why we are taking precautions, and that's why the *Thunder* is monitoring us. Damn it, we're all professional killers and these are our own kind. I don't worry much about Savaphoong. I worry about that small black ship in Bay Three."

Warlock gasped. "A Val ship! We dare not go in now!"

"We dare not *not* go in now," Nagy replied casually. "We'd never outrun it, and I seriously doubt that we could outfight it right now, and that's what we'd have to do."

"But what if it's tuned to one of us? The four of us, I mean?"

"Then we will have to destroy it. I doubt that it is, anyway, but if it is? Bet that it isn't just after one of us, but all of us. I don't think we really have to worry about it until we leave."

"I like the way you say that, all casuallike," Raven noted sourly. "We'll just destroy it, that's all. That's a damned killing machine! They ain't that easy to dispose of!"

"Sure, and if you believe that, then they're invulnerable. Look, they are also programmed to avoid mass killings or slaughter, and apprehension rather than the kill is their first priority. They won't spray fire in a room full of innocents, they won't go through a hostage, and they have lots of other weak points. They're no pushovers—you won't get them with a good head shot—but they can be had. The transmuters made this a throwaway society. Nothing's indestructible."

"Including us," Raven grumped.

"Better you watch yourself in there to keep from betraying that you're new. Watch your tongue, and don't stare at or react to anybody who isn't Earth-human."

"Huh? You mean there's some of the colonist types here?"

"Sure. A person's still a person, and we aren't the only ones able to beat the system. There might even be some genuine aliens, although that's rarer. None of 'em could ever break free of their worlds on their own—Master System saw to that after it found them—but some were recruited by the freebooters because of certain talents and abilities they might have that are a real help out here. Tolerance to various kinds of radiation, extreme heat, that kind of thing. When you don't have big transmuters and you don't have much in the way of friendly robots, or you're scared of robots, they fill a handy niche. All set? We're going down!"

The place had looked reasonable from the air, but once they emerged from the ship, they could detect a definite seediness about it. The air smelled somewhat foul and unpleasant, the heat and humidity were oddly off, and even the elevator down into the complex was jerky and noisy and looked the worse for wear.

They were met at the main level by a four-person security party from what served as Halinachi's government. It was an odd and unpleasant assortment, and Raven and Warlock both proved they were pros by keeping their inner feelings totally hidden.

One, who seemed to be the leader, was Earth-human enough, but in place of his arms were two skeletal robot arms ending in five-fingered steel hands. No attempt had been made to disguise them as human replacements, and clearly he either preferred them to new arms and hands or didn't have access to any top medical personnel.

Behind him was a woman perhaps two meters tall whose leathery skin looked as if it were made of dark-olive plates, and whose eyes were round, unblinking, and yellow. She was hairless, and her fingers and toes resembled talons. Next to her was a short, squat little man whose dark-gray complexion and blocky build made him look as if he were made of stone. The last was an elderly-looking Oriental man with thick white hair and a long, drooping white mustache, his skin dark and mottled. All wore sidearms.

"You are Captain Hoxa?" the man with the steel arms said in a low, gravelly voice that fit his appearance perfectly.

"I am," Nagy replied smoothly. "I remember you from the last time I was here. Beklar, isn't it?"

The squad leader nodded approvingly. Anyone who knew him had to be an old hand, though clearly he didn't remember Nagy. "Yes. I understand you have information for credits?"

"I do. Take me to the terminal and I'll punch it in."

"Why not just give it to me?"

Nagy grinned. "Are you robbing people at gunpoint now, or do you just take me for a fool?"

The big man shrugged and they went over to an entry terminal. Nagy acted right at home, Raven noted. He wondered how many times the security chief had been there before, and why.

Nagy punched in the formulas Clayben had furnished, which took a surprisingly short length of time, then waited. The information was not reflected on the screen, but suddenly a number appeared there. Nagy slammed his fist against the wall next to the terminal and turned to the security crew. "Forty thousand! I save this joint a fortune and it's just forty thousand? Next time I'll take my stuff to the competition!"

A small speaker within the terminal came to life, and a man's voice said, "Very well, Captain. Four days unlimited credit for you and your crew. If you don't abuse it, I will deposit forty thousand credits for a return visit when you leave. Will that be satisfactory?"

Nagy nodded. "That's more like it." He walked back to the group and looked at the security party. "Okay to enter now?"

"Yeah, go ahead," growled the man with the metal arms. "You sure got some clout here. Check your weapons and personal possessions in the next room, then go through entry."

"You make the Val check its weapons?"

"A comedian, huh? Why? You got some problems with them?"

"Depends on who it's looking for and why, same as most people out here. You want to give me a clue?"

"They been around, in and out, for a couple of weeks or more. Word is somebody broke out of Melchior and stole one of them big universe ships. We don't like 'em snoopin' around—bad for business—but what can we do? They're lookin' for people with the Melchior brand, so you're safe."

"From the Val, anyway. All right, lead on."

"We got to check everything?" Raven whispered to Nagy when he could.

"Everything. Even clothes. Savaphoong didn't get this

far by letting anything slip by him. When you're in his world, you're under his absolute control."

Stripped completely, they were run through a decontamination chamber, then issued utilitarian clothing that was cheaply made, didn't fit well, and was clearly reused. All the time they were under the watchful eye of security cameras and personnel.

A man and woman, both of whom looked Earth-human, met them on the other side. The man was tall, perhaps a hundred eighty-five centimeters, and very heavily muscled, with near-perfect features, long blond hair, a dark complexion, and even a hairy chest, and the way he was dressed left no doubt as to his most outstanding attribute. The woman had the same coloring, but she was short—no more than a hundred sixty centimeters—and extremely curvaceous, with a huge heaving bosom. Their eyes and expressions gave the impression that they both probably had the brains and imagination of a head of lettuce, but that was as deliberate as the rest of them. The only thing marring their perfection was the small triangular tattoo in the center of each of their foreheads; the marks looked like the same sort of job done on Melchior inmates, but less obtrusive. Raven now had a suspicion of just what business Savaphoong had had with Melchior through the years; these were perfect examples of Clayben's transmuter and mindprinter handiwork.

The old boy was really gonna miss Melchior, he thought. Suddenly the whole thing was clear to him: Clayben supplied the freebooters with nice, perfect, docile slaves and loyal security troops, and in exchange probably got quantities of murylium totally outside what he could scrape up from Melchior's remains and whatever tiny amounts he might con out of Master System. This explained why freebooters had visited the old hell hole at intervals, and why Nagy had spent time going back and forth. Clayben and the freebooters were far more interrelated than he had let on.

"I am Amal," the beautiful man said, "and this is Gem. We are at your service while you are with us. Anything you wish, just ask."

"We've been out a long time and we just want to relax for a while," Nagy told them. "We'll go to the lounge now, but we may require you later."

"All you need do is ask any staff member to call Amal or Gem and we will be there," the man assured them. "Allow us to escort you to the lounge."

"Am I correct in assuming they mean that all the way?" Warlock asked in a low tone as they walked.

Nagy nodded. "Sure. Either or both will do anything you ask, and with a smile. If they aren't enough, they can produce whatever you want—particularly if you've got four days' unlimited credit. It's not limited to them, either. Anybody with the triangle who turns you on will be your instant willing slave. They come in all sizes, colors, races, you name it—about half Earth-human and half colonial. You get some murylium miners out there, maybe alone, for months or more at a time and they want everything when they get in. They're all sterile and checked medically every day, so there's no risks, either."

Raven had expected a seedy outworld bar, but the lounge was a cozy, intimate place of semiprivate booths with a small stage area. The seats seemed to be some kind of soft brown fur, a bit worn, and the tables were of a marblelike rock.

There were others in the lounge, which surprised the first-timers a bit. The only ship other than the Vals' and the *Lightning* in the dock hadn't seemed very large.

"There aren't many here at any one time," Nagy told them, "but there are more than can be accommodated in the spaceport. Some of the ships are in orbit, their people brought down by shuttle ferry or transmuter, and some have been dropped off here to be picked up later. The place is relatively quiet, though—I'd guess no more than thirty or forty guests are here right now, when there should be a hundred. My guess is the Val scared a lot of 'em off."

An enormous black man appeared, all muscles, wearing little but dark bikini briefs and the telltale triangle on his forehead. Raven looked at Warlock and was amused to see some of that total cool crumble at the sight.

"I am Batu," the waiter said in a rich, deep baritone. "How may I serve you?"

"I'll have a liter of draft," Nagy replied. "Sabatini?"

"Double whiskey and soda, no ice. The good stuff, not the rotgut."

The waiter appeared to take no offense.

"I'll have a beer, as well," Raven said. "And—you wouldn't have cigars, would you?"

"Yes, sir. Any kind of type you wish."

"The large Havana style."

"As you wish, sir. And the lady?"

"Rum tonic," Warlock responded.

The waiter bowed and left. "You really oughtta knock off those things," Nagy told him. "They'll kill you sooner or later."

"If I live long enough for them to kill me I will be content."

Nagy just shrugged. "So, what do you think of the place so far?"

"Interesting," Raven replied. "After all that time in the wild under primitive conditions, I could get to like a place like this. I can sure see how somebody'd like to run one, too. I'm just a little surprised Master System knows of these places and permits them."

"As I said, mutual interest. I always feel like a target here, though; if Master System ever changed its mind, it's all over. I think if I'm gonna be a freebooter it's gonna be in a ship, out there, with better odds and the universe to get lost in."

The waiter brought their drinks and a small package of full-size cigars for Raven, who eyed them as if they were the food of the gods. He had almost forgotten that cigars came that big and that unspoiled.

Warlock looked around. "This place is cozy and comfortable enough, but it is not good for socializing," she noted. "One does not get information in a booth serviced by slaves."

"True enough," Nagy agreed. "But there are ways, and there will be time for all that. Just relax and enjoy for now. In a little while I may try and go back and see the old man himself. He knows me well, and I'll get a straight picture without worrying about a knife in my back."

"Savaphoong?"

He nodded. "I—" He broke off as he saw the others tense; he looked around and saw the Val standing there. It was an imposing figure even in this incongruous environment, and its metallic solidity and blazing crimson eyes seemed to bore right through them.

"Pardon," the Val said. "I realize that my presence here

causes problems, and I only wish to assure you that I have no instructions concerning this place or anyone who visits it."

Interestingly, it was Sabatini who answered. "You know you have no place here. Why are you around?"

"I am not after freebooters. I am soliciting their help. You have heard of the prison colony of Melchior in the Earth system?"

Sabatini nodded. "So?"

"There was an escape. Ships were hijacked, including an interstellar transport. The escapees for the most part have the identifying Melchior facial tattoos. They possess certain knowledge that no one is permitted to possess. Mere contact with these people could prove fatal. They are using a ship that is the largest of its kind ever built, so you could hardly miss it. Have you seen these people?"

"Not anywhere around here," Sabatini responded coolly. "They're not likely to show up at a place like this anyway, are they?"

"Not they themselves perhaps, but they had inside help. We are not quite certain who, but we are working on it. If you see them, or if you run across anyone working for them, it will be more than worth your while to notify us immediately. This place is but a pale shade of the rewards possible to the one or ones who lead to their apprehension. Such ones would live like gods."

Sabatini whistled. "You must really want them. Believe me, if I see them, I'll be the first to collect."

"Very well. I will be leaving this place this evening. Enjoy your stay."

And, with that, the great creature was gone, out of their sight and out of the lounge.

They started to say something, but Nagy put his palm up and then reached under the table, prying off a tiny smooth plate only a hair's thickness and about the size of a fingertip. The Val had left a bug.

"I don't like those bastards one bit," Nagy said casually. "Come on, this place has lost its luster now. Let's hunt up Amal and Gem and try a few more private pleasures."

They all mumbled agreement and got up to leave, letting Nagy carefully replace the bug on the underside of the table. It took only a minute or two to summon their "procurers," as they were called.

"Show us our quarters," Nagy commanded. The others followed, still silent.

They were shown to a suite with a round central living area furnished with couches and a built-in bar and entertainment center, and four private sleeping rooms.

"Amal, I would like to see the manager on a matter of urgent personal business," Nagy told the big blond man.

Amal was somewhat taken aback by that, which was not in the usual line of requests. "I will see if that is possible, sir."

"Tell him it concerns the Val and our treatment here. I think he'll see me."

"Yes, sir. I will try." The man left to do his duty.

Nagy brought the others close to him. "Say nothing you don't want overheard until I get back," he whispered. "We don't know how far this has gone."

They understood. They had heard the Val's voice, which was almost always the voice of the person to whom it was targeted. The voice had been that of Hawks.

Fernando Savaphoong was a small, thin, Asian-looking man of about fifty, with a thin black mustache and neatly cropped black hair graying on the sides. He had a pleasant voice and a salesman's manner, and only his eyes and his nearly constant chain-smoking of cigarettes betrayed the constant pressure his life style and his responsibilities brought him.

"So, Señor Nagy, I am surprised you would come here at this date."

The security man relaxed and sat in a chair opposite the ruler of Halinachi. "I'm not used to Vals showing up in the lounge," he replied. "But I'm particularly not used to Vals planting bugs under my table. How many other bugs has he got around here, and how the hell will I know when I can speak freely again to my companions?"

Savaphoong frowned. "This I do not like to hear at all. It knows you, then."

"I doubt it, or it would have acted more forcefully. More likely it did a scan of the four of us as it discussed the bait, measuring our blood pressure, heart rates, and other reactions when it brought up certain subjects, and became suspicious. I think the least I can demand is for your people to sweep the area—the lounge, all the places it's been, and my quarters, to find and destroy any nasty little devices it might have left."

"I will tend to it at once. I cannot afford to have such things here."

Nagy nodded. "Good. And in light of this, I think it's time we had a talk about other matters."

Savaphoong sat back in his chair and lit a cigarette. "I gather, then, that reports of the good doctor's death were overrated. I suspected as much from the start, knowing how cautious and clever he was. But he did not engineer this break, surely. You?"

"Uh uh. Strictly independent. We just signed on for the duration because we had little choice."

"You realize, then, that I could name my own price just for calling back the Val and confirming its suspicions?"

"You could—but you won't. You know as well as I do that any reward from Master System could be very short-lived in these days and times. Still I could guarantee your silence—or the destruction of Halinachi—just by telling you what it's all about."

"*Si*. When I first hear of this I tell myself, all right, someone escaped. So what? Then I hear they steal this very big ship. Again, so what? They get away. They become freebooters, or they get caught, or they are never heard from again. Why does Master System suddenly want them worse than anything? Then I hear Master System invades Melchior only to find Clayben dead, along with most of the others who count, and all the data banks destroyed. Now I am suspicious. Now I wonder what would be so much of a threat to Master System that it would be worth Clayben's while to do something like this. It is a simple matter for one of Clayben's talents and resources to fake one's own death convincingly enough even for Master System, but why? It must be something so valuable, so dangerous, that it is worth any price. Now my greedy side gets interested, and now you show up only months later. You see?"

"The real question is—do you want to know?"

"No. The real question is—can I afford *not* to know? If that Val was merely suspicious, that is one thing, but if it recognized any of you from its data files, if it has tied you in with all this—well, then, my friend, I am a sitting duck, am I not?"

Nagy thought a moment. "How many Vals are in this sector?"

"Two. But one shell through each of the main domes would be enough to destroy all this."

"Uh uh. They don't have what they really want here and they know it. That Val wasn't going to take us because it would mean breaking the compact with you, and for that it'll need the highest authority. Tell me straight, Señor Savaphoong—if it gets it, what will you do? If it breaks the compact, do you have the firepower to stop it—and the will, knowing what it would mean?"

Savaphoong sighed. "Señor Nagy, your brazen appearance here with a Val in port has caused this, but it is a fair question. If I allow it, then I am out of business anyway, am I not? What freebooter would come here after that? Whom do I serve? Vals? They are not interested in what I could provide, and, besides, they are lousy tippers. For the sake of any future or refuge I might have, I would be forced to oppose them, no matter what the cost."

Arnold Nagy sighed. "Very well then. If that day should ever come, I can give you refuge. We will need people and we will need experience. If you keep faith with me, then if your back is to the wall we'll get you out and cut you in. Fair?"

"As fair as life gets. Tell me true—do you *really* have a starship that is fourteen kilometers long?"

"Yes. We call her the *Thunder*."

The boss of Halinachi sighed. "What interesting possibilities that opens up. It has been getting so boring here." He paused. "But, no. One does not trade all this so easily. Is there anything else I can do for you right now?"

"I need some information on three colonial worlds. This won't get you in any trouble—without knowing the objectives it would be impossible to guess. Even knowing the objectives, although it would be dangerous, wouldn't give you anything you could use yourself."

"Which three?"

"Janipur, Chanchuk, and Matriyeh."

Savaphoong gave a low whistle. "Not the most comfortable of places, any one."

"I didn't expect they would be. I need the works on them—people, political organization, leaders, Centers and administrators, you name it. The odds are I'm looking for the chief administrator of each world."

"*Umph!* You really make it difficult on yourself. And the purpose, in general terms?"

"Grand theft."

Savaphoong laughed. "For such a grand and noble purpose, how can I refuse? Very well, you shall have what you require—if I can be assured that our mutual benefactor will continue to supply me with things that I require."

"As much as possible under the circumstances. Might I assume that you have an interstellar-capable ship available in times of need?"

"You may so assume."

"Then we should work out a mutual meeting place and a method of signaling. I suspect that if we get away clean this time it is very unlikely that we can return to your fine establishment."

Fernando Savaphoong thought for a moment. "The Val prepares to leave within the hour. It will take it two days to reach a subspace relay beacon and report to Master System, and perhaps another day to get the authority one way or another. Of course, it will probably contact its companion ahead of time and establish a surreptitious watch. If you leave before the authority comes, then I am probably in the clear so long as I make no moves showing I know what this is about. There is then no logic in breaking the compact. The one who lurks, though, in the shadows of the

planets—it will lock on and attempt to follow, and it has
incredible equipment and tenacity. You will probably have
to take it out, you know, if you can."

"I'm well aware of that. In the meantime, I'll let you get
on with your—delousing—operation here and accumulat-
ing the data I need, while I and my companions spend a
night or two enjoying your services." He had a sudden
thought. "And I might suggest an additional item of mutual
interest to research."

"Indeed?"

"Master System requires fairly large supplies of murylium to manage and maintain its empire. Those mines are
almost surely totally automated and nearly impossible to
locate, but the shipments surely are not. You need the stuff
and so do we."

"Even if I could discover such a thing, what good would
it do, my friend?"

"We are interstellar outlaws hunted by all and with absolutely nothing to lose, but we have resources. You give me
the routings, and I'll give you part of the loot."

Even Savaphoong looked aghast. "Hijacking a freighter
of Master System? You must be joking! It is not possible!"

"You tell me where, and I'll show you a thing or two
about real piracy."

And that made Savaphoong laugh again, long and hard.
"You know," he managed after a moment, "I almost believe you can do this. At least I think you are either mad or
the most dangerous group of human beings alive!" He
shrugged. "Either way, what do I have to lose but everything?"

"You know, if I could feel guilt, I'd be feelin' real guilty
about havin' a good time here while the chief and the rest
are stuck back in that primitive hell hole," Raven noted

casually while washing down a fine steak and eggs with fresh coffee. "I really do hate to leave this place."

"Well, leaving is going to be the trick that makes us pay the devil's due," Arnold Nagy replied. "We have our information and our contacts now, but we also have a real problem. Sabatini, any of your incarnations ever take on a Val ship before?"

The strange creature grinned. "Sure. Two at least. Both lost, of course."

Nagy glared at him and Raven almost choked on a piece of toast.

"All right, then," said the Hungarian who had become the *de facto* head of the expedition. "It's something new. I have some of the information we need—enough to get us started. Anybody else have any luck?"

"I met a man who had been to Janipur," Warlock said. "He said it was inhabited by a human herd of angry cows, whatever that means. Said we would have to see it to believe it. Still, some things do not change in the universe of Master System. He has seen the chief administrator, who is known for the fancy ring he wears. It is called the Ring of Peace because it bears the likeness of two doves in gold. He also said that the chief administrator is very smart but very brutal. He enjoys strangling people. It is his hobby."

"Humph! Yeah, well, who ever said these would be pushovers? Anybody else?"

"There was a fellow—a colonial, not at all pleasant to look on—who knew of Matriyeh," Sabatini said. "This fellow was raised Moslem, and he said that Matriyeh surpassed any vision of hell he had ever dreamed. No matter how inhuman he was, he had enough perspective so that I believe he would have said the same thing even if he'd been one of our kind. Certain minerals on Matriyeh are said to grow to enormous proportions, and this fellow was an artist who hoped to trade some technology for some of them to use in his art. The world is supposedly very primitive. He found it impossibly primitive, not at all organized. No Centers, no administrators that he could see at all, and no major rulers above the tribal level. It sounded much like what Master System is said to be considering doing to Earth. He could not imagine a person of power there."

Nagy shook his head. "That one's worse. Bad boys I think we can deal with. I don't care if they've got two heads and five arms and breathe methane, they're still of human stock and Master System's origins, and we know their type. Even Master System is obedient, though. The ring has to be held by a person with power, authority— *something* that makes him or her stand out. Damn it, that's gonna be a tough one."

"The guy barely escaped with his life, let alone his ship. The world is one very nasty place even without the people," Sabatini added. "That one might be suited for my special talents, but even I can't work from nothing, and if a primitive, ignorant mind knows nothing of value it can't help me."

"Well, we'll see. Raven, you get anything at all?"

"You bet. Two cases of fine Havanas and some very nice little pills. One of 'em's called Orgy and you oughtta see what it does. As for information, though—forget it. Except a couple of girls in the lounge knew of a certain world of heat and water by reputation, and they said it was a full-fledged colony. I didn't like that at all."

Nagy nodded. "I don't like that much myself, but in all that time nobody ever showed up and tossed a spear or shook our hand. You got to figure they're water breathers. No skin off our nose or theirs if that's the case."

"I dunno. Somebody planted them groves on that other island. I kinda wonder if we'd been able to get over there if they wouldn't'a popped up and been a little nasty about it. Water breathers don't grow food on land. They didn't know much, though—them girls, I mean. Only that it was listed as a colonial settlement, and off limits in general."

"I think we better get all the stuff together we can and get back—if we can," Nagy told them. "Raven, unless something happens, I'm afraid you and Warlock are gonna be strictly passengers in this flight. Sabatini, since you've had more experience, so to speak, flying these buckets, I'm gonna let you fly and take the guns myself. It flies like any other good ship, but I know the armament inside and out. If there *is* a Val up there, waiting for us, it's gonna be one tough nut to crack, but it won't know the power or armaments of that ship. It's a custom illegal job. Get it all together—we might as well roll."

Getting out of Halinachi was not quite as complicated as getting in. They turned in their clothing but not their personal prizes, such as Raven's cigars, and they also received a small encoded master cylinder from Savaphoong. The lord of Halinachi did not see them off— Nagy guessed in any event that midmorning was far too early for the manager of the place to be up and about— but there was a small note attached to the cylinder, which Nagy read.

"What's the love letter?" Raven asked, curious.

"It's a bill. Somehow he managed to charge the full forty thousand future credits and anything left from this visit. Never mind. Short of using a transmuter and becoming someone completely different, there's little chance we'll be able to come back here again anyway."

They went to the ship, which appeared secure, all seals intact. Nagy spent some time doing a complete check. "Yeah, as I figured. A bunch of nice bugs and tracking devices all over the damned hull. We'd be another day getting those suckers off ourselves and we don't have that. The best thing I can do is try to burn 'em off. Channel the transmuter power from the main engines to the outer hull. They're designed to withstand the external forces of lift-off and reentry, but they're not well shielded where they attach to the hull itself. Get in pressure suits and dial your climate control to maximum. This is gonna be nasty. I got to be real careful with this. I don't want to burn any holes in the hull."

When they were ready, he began. The outer hull began to glow red hot, and Nagy had to be very careful not to let any point get too much hotter than the rest or turn white. Shimmering blue electricity played over the ship, inside and out, and after more than fifteen minutes the sounds of very loud banging and terrible random noises came through to them, as if they were in a meteor storm with no deflectors.

The noises subsided after a while, and the inside fans came on.

"I think I got 'em all, but at what price I couldn't say," Nagy informed them. "I think it's best we all keep our suits on, the inside pressure down, and ourselves strapped in until we know. Best we do that during the flight, anyway, just in case a shot penetrates the main cabin."

"Great," Raven grumped. "No cigars. I might go to my grave staring at two cases of unopened Havanas."

"I think we've cooled down uniformly now, and I've got clearance, so strap in and check systems. Sabatini, take her up."

The ship shuddered, then roared into life and rose slowly above the landing pad. Only when they were several kilometers in the air did Sabatini angle the nose up, apply full thrust and roll, and take her to escape velocity.

It was a noisy, bumpy ride out, but it was fast. They cleared the atmosphere in just a few minutes and went into preliminary orbit. Sabatini did a wide scan.

"Anything?" Nagy asked.

"Nothing yet, but it could be in near-total power down. The question is more if he has better scanning range than we do. I seem to remember that you were clearly visible in the *Thunder*'s sights at your maximum fallback position."

"They were as good as they needed to be. If we don't catch sight of him, we'll try to lead him out. Set a course on chart A-J-8-7-7-2. That's at a right angle to where we want to go, but it'll give us some running room. Keep all sensors at maximum and we'll see if we can pick him up."

They were suddenly pressed back in their seats as Sabatini gave maximum thrust from orbital speed. It was a surprise, almost random, move that would have thrown a human pursuer, but the Val was not human and would not waste precious seconds wondering what to do. It might, however, have to quickly adjust and betray itself—or risk losing its prey at the start.

"Give me a punch as soon as you have the factors lined up," Nagy instructed. "Duration thirty minutes—the minimum possible on the chart's vector. We may be able to exit and repunch before he can get out with us."

"That's gonna really strain the power," Sabatini warned.

"The transmuter ram needs junk as much as it needs its own power, or there's nothing to convert. With that house-cleaning you did, we're pretty low."

"The hell with it! We run dry, we stand and fight as best we can."

"Punching."

"At least the hull seems to be holding," Nagy noted as the ship opened its hole and entered. "I got a delicate touch."

Any pursuer now would have to match the course, trajectory, and speed perfectly and punch at the exact same spot with the exact same elements in order to give chase. This was not difficult for a Val or any ship programmed to do it. The Val, in fact, would know coming in just exactly where they would emerge, but it could do nothing about it, not even close on its prey, inside a punch. Even Raven realized Nagy's strategy—if the Val had hung back too far to avoid detection, they could repunch in an infinite number of directions before it could emerge behind them. The only limit was the amount of fuel for conversion taken in by the forward ram and stored. The Val, he suspected, would have been pleasantly surprised if any of its little traps and trackers had survived, but it also knew that the amount of energy expended to get rid of them would limit just how far its prey could run before it caught up.

"Give me a thirty-two degree right turn on reemergence," Nagy ordered, "and punch again. Use chart B-H-6-4-4-9."

"But there's no punch points on that chart for thirty hours! We haven't got the juice to go that long!"

"Then punch for half the juice we got left and reemerge wherever that is."

Sabatini was appalled. "Off the *chart*?"

"Yeah, off the chart."

The purpose of the charts, other than navigation, was to permit ease of travel. The emergence points were all selected because they had ample density of matter for the rams and yet were clear of any potential problems like radiation fields, suns, neutron stars, and other obstacles. Sabatini's prior freebooter identity gave him enough confidence to know that the odds of coming out near anything dangerous was next to nothing in the vastness of space; what bothered him was that they stood very good odds of coming out exactly there—next to nothing. Space was never completely empty, but there were vast areas in which it might take years to accumulate enough dust and such to make enough fuel to get them anywhere useful, and they wouldn't have the juice to punch anywhere else clean.

"Nagy, you ever made a jump with low fuel off the charts before?"

"Never had to, but it's the only way. The only other choice is to slow down and turn as quickly as possible, and try to blow the bugger back to machine hell as it emerges. It'll be ready for that, and it has a lot more fuel than we do."

"Yeah, but there's a dozen charts we could jump on and come out at a safe point."

"That's the problem. There's a dozen. How long you figure it'll take to refuel? A couple hours? If there are two of 'em out there, then in that time all dozen could be checked—and would be. You make the choice. This is one fix your little talent won't get you out of."

"You think of this ahead of time or are you making this up as you go along?"

"Improvisation, my friend, is the soul of survival. If it goes wrong I'll blame it on this computer link."

"If anything goes wrong you won't have any reason to blame anything. You'll be dead long before we were. Hang on. Emergence."

Sabatini was right on the mark, but he cut power slightly and fully opened the jets as he made a graceful turn.

"We fight, then?" Nagy asked nervously.

"We have fifteen minutes before it emerges. That gives me ten minutes to take in what I can in this dense outer dust belt and another four to make the punch. I am computer-linked, too, remember."

"Quiet. I have an idea. Open communications channels."

"I see. Good idea, if we have the time."

"Shut up and gobble."

Sitting in the back, Raven and Warlock were ignorant of all this. They could only wait and wonder until either of the ship's operators took the time and trouble to brief them.

In what seemed like no time the ship was back up to speed and punching through once more, and only then did Nagy relax enough to explain the situation. Neither of the passengers liked it much.

"Don't see what you can do, though," Raven consoled him. "Let's play it as it lays. But I can't help wondering— suppose we punch through for only forty percent of the fuel? Then turn around and punch right back to where we were just at?"

"Damn! Why didn't I think of that one?" Sabatini swore. "Too late now—I've used fifty percent, and with what it will take to reposition that won't be quite enough to get us back. Why didn't I think of it, though?"

"In all your lives you never were no Crow, that's why.

An old tracker knows the double-back. I'm surprised Nagy didn't, considering his background."

"Too civilized, Raven," Nagy said. "I went from Vatican Center to West Europe Center and then to port Security, then finally Melchior. I never was in the field. It wasn't my area of expertise."

"Yeah, well, next time remember that us ignorant savages might know a few tricks your ancestors forgot, and deal us in. You believe in all this high-tech brain shit and you get to playing Master System's game."

"Yeah. Next time."

"If I were the tracker Val, that is where I would put the second Val. At the last stop," Warlock whispered dryly.

"Shut up, Warlock," Raven growled.

The ship was now pretty much on automatic, and there was nothing that anyone could do for a while, so the two at the controls set the alarms and disengaged after bringing temperature and pressure to normal levels. It was safe to remove the pressure suits, relax, eat, even catch some sleep, and Raven got to smoke a couple of his precious cigars over the protests of the other three and the air filtration system.

The time seemed to drag, and sleep was difficult. Finally, though, the alarm sounded and Sabatini and Nagy, almost with relief, headed back up to the command chairs and reconnected themselves to the ships' systems.

Emergence was smooth and right on time, but it was quite literally in the middle of nowhere.

"Dust and cosmic debris levels are very small," Sabatini noted. "Distance to nearest stellar system's outer reaches is about thirty-three light-years. If we did another punch we might get within four or five."

Sabatini did a quick scan of the region and found little

to be optimistic about. "There's some very weak gravity source at bearing one seven one, but it's beyond our range and who knows what it is? If it's a black hole or something it could be farther than that next stellar system. I think we're stuck."

They poked and probed and moved over a vast distance of empty space during the next few hours tracking down any potential sources of gravity that might mean trapped dust, rock, and, therefore, fuel—and life. The hunting was pretty slim.

"The good news is that we are collecting enough material to keep us going for several years if it remains constant," Sabatini told them. "The bad news is that it's just about enough to keep the life support and local engines going—with a very slight loss. It means we can drag around here for a long time but we can't ever gain enough to offset what we're spending collecting it."

"We should'a brought a couple of them playmate slaves if we were gonna be stuck out here," Raven growled.

"I guess we should've fought after all," Nagy sighed. "Our only hope now—"

He paused, and even Raven and Warlock could feel the tension fill the air. The screen flickered to life and went to maximum magnification.

An area of space that was as dark as the darkest night now had a glowing ring around it and, although it seemed impossible, the area within seemed even darker, deeper, and blacker. Out of it came a ship, small, sleek, and shopworn black against the even blacker hole.

"Son of a bitch!" Nagy swore. "I must've missed one!"

The Val ship emerged, closing the hole behind it, slowed gracefully, and made a steady turn toward them.

Sabatini sighed. "I guess we fight them anyway," he said.

6. SCOUTING EXPEDITIONS

THE VAL SHIP TOOK UP ITS POSITION WELL WITHIN SEN-sor range but just beyond the range of conventional weapons. Nagy and Sabatini were integrated with their ship's computers; the Val *was* its ship's computer. Even allowing for the time their ship's engines and weapons took to function, that meant the Val was always going to be a fraction of a second ahead in terms of responding to a sudden move—a crucial difference. Once both systems were in full gear, however, their automatic reactions would be nearly instantaneous and, therefore, equal. But the Val still had an advantage: It's speed of thought was far faster even than that of computer-linked humans, while its reasoning was very similar to a human's. It understood its prey well. That forced the humans to let the automatics react, thus placing them permanently on the defensive, a situation in which they could not win, only draw or lose.

"By the authority of Master System I command you to halt and identify yourselves" came the Val's call, which Nagy put on the speaker. The voice was that of Hawks; this was the same Val that had accosted them in the lounge.

"Since when did you have such authority?" Nagy challenged back. "You are keyed to no one on this ship, a fact you well know. We have committed no criminal acts that would cause an exception." *None that you know, anyway.* "I stand on the covenant."

"And I step on it," the Val retorted. "The covenant exists because it is useful to the system. In its own way it serves the system. The covenant will not be broken as far as anyone is concerned. There is no one out here in the middle of nowhere but us."

It was tough to deny the truth of that, but truth wasn't at stake here. "And what sort of logic and system is it that can be violated at will when it is convenient? One does not defend the honor and integrity of a superior system by ignoring it when it is safe or convenient. That is the human way of things, and Master System was created to avoid that flaw. If you can break the system, even under these conditions, then Master System has no right to exist, no right to authority over humankind except by sheer might. And if it is no better than human law, then it is a tyranny that must be disobeyed as a moral duty."

"You are quite good at that, aren't you?" the Val responded, impressed. "The logic cannot be denied even though you and I both know you don't believe a word of it. Very well. I am keyed to track down an Earth-human, a North American Center historian who is called Walks With the Night Hawks, also called John Hawks. He possessed forbidden knowledge and did not surrender it or himself, making him an enemy of the system. You know where he is. Tell me, and win your own freedom until another time, another Val, seeks you."

"That is nothing to us," Nagy told it. "Even if we knew this person, which we do not, the price is far too low. We haven't sufficient fuel or sources of fuel to get back to the chart. You saw to that. So we die out here slowly, or we die quickly. We are all professionals. Quick is better if you have to choose one or the other."

"I could give you a tow to that system over there. Enough fuel to get almost anywhere. Arnold Nagy, is it not, formerly of Melchior? You went in pursuit of the fugitives as was your duty and somehow joined them instead. Raven, and Warlock—more Security gone bad. There will be wholesale cleanings of Security nests before this is over. I do not know the fourth member of this quartet in any way, but it makes little difference. Another escapee, I suspect. You are professionals, as you say. What do you owe these others?"

Warlock leaned over to Raven. "Why does it talk so much when we are so vulnerable?" She didn't seem ruffled by the thought of imminent death.

Raven was a fatalist. "Because if it blows us to hell it's back at square one—up the river without a paddle. It has the bad luck to want Hawks, not any one of us. If we die, any leads to Hawks die with us. This ain't over yet."

"Just out of curiosity," Nagy was saying, "how the hell did I miss any tracers? I was *sure* I got 'em all and you damn well didn't get inside."

"No, I assumed you were competent. I also assumed that you would never look very closely at two cases of good cigars."

"Damn!" Raven swore.

"You couldn't *possibly* know which cases we'd take on or arrange it back there!" Nagy retorted.

"I didn't have to. I had a basic data file on Raven and I knew he was an addicted smoker. I also was in the lounge when the first thing he did was order cigars—a particular kind of cigar. I left and found the source of them after leaving you, and spent a great deal of care inserting my tracers in the casing. There was only one case. It followed that Raven would wish to take more with him and that the only means of supplying them would be via the transmuter —which also, of course, duplicated the tracer. It was elementary, my dear Nagy."

"That walking machine-shop son of a bitch," Raven growled, feeling had. It was exactly *his* kind of trick, which was what bothered him the most.

Nagy sighed. "Well, I guess we deserve this, then. Here's the bottom line, though, Val Hawks. We're it. Sole survivors. They figured out how to get that monster ship going, but they never had full control of it. It broke up off a neutron star. Very little of it was ever habitable, and we had no choice but to split it up—some in my ship, the rest on the bridge. There was no chance to save the others—I barely saved ourselves, and then only because we were living here. You're in an endless loop, my friend. You're doomed to wander forever in pursuit of a quarry who no longer exists."

The Val actually paused for a moment before replying. "It truly is a pleasure to encounter a real pro now and then. Your voice analysis actually shows that you are speaking the absolute truth. Had I not surprised you in the lounge, had you had some warning of my presence before you actually saw me, I might not have received any anomalous readings at all."

"Why don't they just fight and get it over with?" Raven grumbled.

Warlock smiled. "What do you think they *are* doing, darling?"

"It reads true because it is truth," Nagy assured the Val.

"Well, then, there is an easy way to settle it all. Send me one of you. Let me subject him or her to the mind-printer here. If indeed it is true then I will have the documentation I need, and you will receive your tow and a head start on my associates. I will owe you that for saving me much fruitless labor."

Uh oh, gotcha there, didn't he, Nagy? Arnold Nagy swore to himself.

"You cannot win against a Val even under optimum conditions," the robot detective said. "And these are hardly optimum."

It was certainly true that the conditions were lousy. Sabatini, drawing on the experience not only of Koll but of others the thing it was had consumed and become back on Melchior, had no trouble seeing the Val strategy. Blows that hurt, not killed. Blows that damaged, weakened, but never at the expense of giving them a clean shot. In and out, back and forth, until they used up the last of their fuel and were dead in space. The Val had the infinite patience of a machine and much preferred that at least one of them remain alive.

"You can drill that rot about the invulnerability of the Val into all the idiots at Centers you want," Nagy told it, "but you and I know you're mortal. Your ship is just a ship—no better armored than this one. I admit that *you* are better armored than I am, but if I had the drop on you, I know where to shoot. That inevitability and invulnerability crap makes it easy for you most times. The game believes it so thoroughly that when you catch up they roll over and play dead. I'm not going to roll over and I am not going to give you what you want. You see, I can cheat you, and beat you, very easily. Just reverse the transmuter and apply full thrust. A quick end, with all of us and our ship vaporized. Quick, probably painless, and you won't know a damned thing more about the one you're really after. You will have vaporized your one real lead. I'm not scared, Val Hawks. We do not have a massacre situation here—we have a standoff."

The Val seemed somewhat taken aback by this. It was always supremely confident and, like all Vals, felt itself superior to the humans it dealt with and hunted. "I take it that all of you prefer suicide to surrender, then?" it asked finally.

"Watch it!" Sabatini said nervously. "That's an open invitation to blow us to hell right now!"

"It won't act until we do," Nagy assured him. "There's no percentage in it."

Raven snapped his fingers. "Nagy, how much crud do you need for fuel conversion on this tub?"

"Huh? It's measured in tons to do us any good. Why?"

Raven sighed. "Nothing. I was just thinkin' that we got a whole shitload of stuff here we might somehow use."

"Like what?"

"Anything. The space suits. The boxes of cigars. The clothes on our backs. These chairs if we could get 'em up. Blow 'em out the hatch and gobble 'em in the ram jet slow and easy. Forget it, it was just a thought."

"Uh uh! You have something there! Besides, ditching the cigars will mean ditching it as well."

"You nuts?" Sabatini asked seriously. "The *space suits*, for Christ's sake!"

"What good are space suits if we're dead anyway? Take the communications port and keep him stalled. I don't care what you say! I'm cutting loose and seeing what can be done."

"But what if it attacks and we got no pilot?"

"The same thing that happens if it attacks and we *have* a pilot! Now let me go—time's wasting!"

Nagy came quickly out from the spell woven by the interface and, although a little dizzy from it, he indeed wasted no time. There were minor tools and a basic repair kit in an aft storage compartment. He was relieved that Star Eagle hadn't removed them. He took out a laser torch and began cutting the unused chairs off at their base.

Raven and Warlock got up to help as much as they could, stacking the items as Nagy disassembled them.

"You said it took tons to do much," Raven noted. "So what's this all about?"

Arnold Nagy chuckled. "Maybe not enough for survival, but enough to screw that son of a bitch, that's for sure. Figure each one of these reinforced chairs has a mass equal to, oh, forty kilograms with their supports. That's two forty. Add another ten for the webbing and belting, minimum. Two fifty. The suits are another fifty. Add a lot more junk around here and I think maybe we can find another two fifty, three hundred. That's more than half a ton. Here, give me a hand. We might even be able to get the damned toilet out of here. If that bastard gives us the time we might scrounge up to a ton here!"

They fell into helping, but Raven was still puzzled. "So what's a ton mean?"

"We spent fifty percent getting here. We're about ten percent low and that's about a ton for a vessel this size. We might get back with this much stuff!"

"Well, we made punches without belts and chairs before, that's for sure, but what good will it do? That thing'll just figure it's what we did and follow, assuming it don't just blow us to hell as we punch. Then we're dead meat for it. What can we do? We're throwin' out everything we could even heave at it."

"Maybe nothing. Who the hell knows? I'm goin' for broke, though, 'cause there ain't no other way!"

In weightlessness it was simple to move the stuff to the air-lock entry.

"How's our Val been?" Nagy called to Sabatini.

"We've been debating the fine points of morality, but it hasn't made a move. They have infinite patience, you know."

"Yeah, well, I'm counting on that. Be ready with a glib line. We're gonna flush what we got out here by depressurizing the air lock to maybe ten percent of normal. We got two, maybe three loads to flush. Then we still got to figure some way of maneuvering it into the ram without getting creamed. *If*, of course, we chopped that stuff up enough to get it all."

On communications, Sabatini had his hands full.

"Why is all of that being flushed?" the Val asked. "I want it stopped. Now."

"What do you think we're doing—laying mines? If we were, you'd have hit one by now. We're not going to stop."

The Val did not reply, but fired a thin beam that struck one of the objects, fragmenting it.

"I think he just shot the damned toilet," Raven noted.

"No matter," Nagy assured him. "He didn't disintegrate it, he blew it up. It's the mass that counts. I was kinda worried about that one fitting in the ram anyway. Now I know it will. Okay, time to grab on to whatever's left back here and hold tight. Odds are we're all gonna get bruised and knocked around by this one, but consider the alternative."

He went forward once more and donned the interface helmet. He no longer had a chair, but with judicious use of the torch and some muscle he had fashioned two handholds out of parts of the instrument console.

"You gonna explain this, or am I supposed to be surprised?" Sabatini asked him.

"I'm gonna back up real slow, just enough to get as much of that junk as I can in one pass, 'cause that's all we get," Nagy told him. "I think we were careful enough to keep it fairly bunched, although I don't know what effect that blast had on it."

"You back up and that thing'll close," Sabatini warned.

"Fine. So long as he doesn't fire until too late, I couldn't care less."

"But you need acceleration to punch! If you go forward in a pass for that stuff, it'll have to be flank speed from a relatively standing start! The Val'll have to shoot or be rammed!"

"Good. Let it shoot. If it figures we're gonna suicide and try to take it with us, as I hope it does, it's gonna lose. Only if it figures out the game are we in trouble."

"Yeah? That thing's a supercomputer! You figure you got an angle it doesn't know or can't figure out in nanoseconds?"

"Sure. I'm gonna do something that isn't possible, so it won't think of it."

"What! If it's impossible then what good is it?"

"Because I don't know it's impossible and my math was always lousy. All right—hang on, everybody! Here we go!"

· Slowly, almost imperceptibly, Nagy applied the brakes, which had the effect of backing up the ship a few millimeters a second. The movement was so slow that even the Val had to check its instrumentation before issuing a challenge.

"You are moving! Halt at once or I will be forced by necessity to open fire!"

"I'm not moving—I'm experiencing drag. Hold on, I'll see what's what."

"You will compensate *now.*"

Nagy made no reply for more than thirty seconds, by which time he had increased the braking so that the ship cleared the mass showing on the sensors by a few meters; he kept the ship's nose toward the Val ship to present the smallest target.

The Val fired at the port ramjet scoop, but Sabatini had expected this and set the automatics to parry.

Nagy brought the ship to a dead stop relative to the floating debris and angled the nose so that the ship would accumulate maximum mass in a forward thrust. "I just ran the calculations on this thing," he told them.

"Yes?" Sabatini replied. "And?"

"It said 'Don't do it!' or words to that effect. Hang on, everybody! Either we're gonna be out of this mess in a couple of minutes or we're gonna be dead. I've programmed it in. Stand by!"

The engines suddenly roared to life and the ship shuddered; the rattles and noises were unusually loud because of all the remnants of the destruction about the ship. This did not go unnoticed by the Val.

"Throttle down! If you have any idea of picking up that debris, I have already demonstrated that you are in range of my weapons!"

"We're overheating the engines!" Sabatini warned. "Either throttle down or do something, but you can't sustain this for more than twenty or thirty seconds! This is madness! He'll blow us to hell as soon as we pick up that shit!"

There was no way Arnold Nagy could do the split-second timing involved; he simply gave the orders to the ship's computer. The computer said it would comply but would not be responsible for the consequences. "ENGINE FAILURE PREDICTED IN FIVE SECONDS!" it warned.

"*Go!*" Arnold Nagy yelled.

The amount of heat and pressure built up in the engines was massive; Raven and Warlock, although braced as best they could be, were slammed against the aft wall and pinned there. Only the extreme control of Nagy and Sabatini under the interface kept their grips on their handholds, but it was not without its own costs. The handholds on Nagy's side began to give way.

It was so fast that there was no way to realize what had happened until it was over. In the end, it all seemed somewhat anticlimactic.

At the last possible moment, with engines thrusting full and close to protective shutdown, the dense gases, which had been building under tremendous pressure that must either be expelled or blow up the ship, were released. For a brief moment nothing seemed to happen, and the Val, for whom it was a very long time, calmly adjusted its guns, noted its regrets, and trained its full fire directly on the point just beyond the debris where it would have a clear and unobstructed full field of fire.

The Val's target suddenly lurched forward and, as it touched the debris itself, it did the one thing neither the Val nor anyone else except Arnold Nagy anticipated.

Lightning punched.

It was a wide field punch and it was entered at a relatively slow speed, but the focus of the punch beams was mere millimeters beyond the densest pack of debris, and so wide that its very opening sucked in some of the debris not collected by the ram in its passage.

Suddenly realizing what its enemy had done, the Val fired, but the punch was wide enough to absorb virtually all the energy, shielding *Lightning*. Realizing that it had been outmaneuvered, the Val checked the course, speed, and trajectory of its prey and quickly swung around to follow. Time was of the essence.

Nagy throttled down to minimum speed; it didn't matter inside a punch how much power was expended, although a small amount was necessary. One arrived at one's destination at the same time all the same. Inside, the ship moaned and groaned and sounded as if it would come apart at any moment, but the passenger cabin seemed to be holding.

"That's *impossible*!" Sabatini said flatly. "No ship with a life-support system could sustain the pressures we just did!"

"Okay, then you're dead," Nagy responded, sounding more casual than he actually felt. "This thing was built as an escape ship, remember, and the theoretical problems and computer models that it was based on assumed that a whole fleet of Master System fighters would be coming in on us. We're not home free yet, though, folks. Wait for the main event."

Raven groaned. "Damn it, I feel like I broke every bone in my body!" he complained. He started, staring at the limp form of Warlock, and was relieved to find her still breathing, though unconscious. He looked forward at the two forms sitting on the deck in their death grips and saw blood on Nagy. "Nagy, check yourself out! You're bleeding like a stuck pig!"

"Yeah. Broke a wrist and somehow a rib, and messed up a little in my head, but I'll survive until I'm through this. It's gonna be real tough to disengage this interface, though. Sabatini, you sound okay to me."

"I suffered massive internal damage, but I am now repairing it," the creature who was Sabatini replied. "I will be whole again in a few minutes."

Raven groaned. He felt as if he'd been worked over with a rubber hose, but he didn't think anything was broken. Like the others, he found some blood coming from a nostril, but it wasn't much. "What d'ya mean, it ain't over yet?" he asked.

"Let's see . . . half a second for the Val to figure what I did, assume I survived somehow, and decide to give chase. Three minutes to apply thrust and angle in to the same trajectory, course, and speed and punch. I'm not gonna allow any fudge factor; I'll assume it does it in the minimum, so that puts him just a hundred eighty and a half seconds behind us. Good thing he didn't close on us. If he had, I wouldn't have any margin at all."

Raven gasped. "You mean he's still behind us?"

The ship continued to moan and groan. "Sure. And I didn't jump long. We went in real slow, so it'd take damned near forever and half our fuel for life support if I did. If I timed it right, some of the debris should have been pulled in with us by magnetic and gravitational forces. That and the remains of his ship should get us almost anywhere."

"The remains of—what the hell?" both of the others

managed at once. Warlock moaned and stirred, but nobody noticed.

"You wait. Coming out in one minute. Hold on back there! You might get flung forward this time!"

Warlock opened her eyes and frowned. "What?"

"Don't ask," Raven responded. "Just turn around facing the wall and hold on again or you're gonna be splattered against the forward wall!"

"Wha—?" she managed, but turned and did as instructed, still not quite back to normal.

Lightning punched out in a sector of space as empty and forlorn as the one it had left and, in truth, not a great distance away in astronomical terms. As soon as the ship emerged, Nagy checked for any debris that might have come with them, found some, accelerated slightly and scooped what he could, then came to a near-dead stop. Then, very slowly, he began reverse thrust until he reached a predetermined point. He used more than two and a half minutes doing so, which meant there wasn't long to wait.

This time Sabatini, with the aid of the ship's computers, understood exactly what was going on. "All weapons systems armed. This is gonna be real close, Nagy. I read the forward distance as a hundred and six meters."

"Give it all you got. I don't just want him disabled, I need him in pieces. We can't go out there and do a salvage job on him—we jettisoned the space suits."

"Yeah, that's right. All right—locked on. Like shooting fish in a barrel."

The Val was late; in fact, it was almost seventeen seconds late, which made Nagy wonder if it had somehow guessed his intention, but he was counting on its supreme self-confidence and the fact that he'd had to enter the punch at a very slow speed.

As soon as the Val's punch closed behind it, all forward batteries of the *Lightning* opened up on the Val ship, which could only then use its sensors to see behind the punch and discover the plot.

Sixteen beams of maximum-strength fire struck the aft engines of the Val ship; it shuddered, then the Val applied full thrust and shot back, but the shots were wide and the thrust was erratic, causing the ship to go off at an angle. Defensive force fields were up now, but massive damage had already been done. As soon as the Val gave Sabatini any sort of a broadside and he could calculate the steering angle, he launched four seeker missiles, two for the tail along the line of the guns, the other two angling around to come in on either side of the main fuselage.

The Val was clearly in trouble and had focused most of its attention on getting away fast, but it managed to shift shields to deflect both the two missiles coming in on its engines and the one coming directly for its side. It might well have seen, or suspected, the fourth missile if its sensors were still intact, but it was having real power problems.

There was a tremendous bright flash, and when it cleared, the Val ship had a gaping hole in it, with pieces of ship flying off and forming an eerie escort on *Lightning*'s sensors. The shields wavered, then collapsed aft as connections were severed; only the nose area was still guarded or intact, probably containing the still very much alive but powerless Val.

Sabatini let Nagy take them to the best broadside and then began pouring all he had into the dead ship, literally blowing it apart. "Hah! Who says you can't beat a Val!" he shouted with enthusiasm. Then, suddenly, he sobered. "What the—?"

A small section of the still-shielded nose suddenly flared into life and detached itself from the mainship; Sabatini immediately shifted half his guns to it, not willing to take them all away in case it was some kind of trick. He missed —the thing flew away from them at increasing speed and with the hardest shields either of the two space veterans had ever seen. Nagy was still trying to decide whether or not to chase it when his instrumentes showed a tiny punch and it was gone.

"What was *that*?" Sabatini asked in wonder.

"The brain of the Val, I'd guess" came the reply. "I never knew anybody who beat one of these bastards before, so we might be among the first to see that. Get cracking—I need that hulk broken up into pieces small enough to get us back on the charts. Remember, there's a second Val around here someplace and if that little thing that just got away is anything at all it's speeding someplace to report on all this and call in the big guns. Let's move it! Besides, if we don't get somewhere where we can link with Star Eagle in a little while, I'm afraid I'm gonna die."

They laid out Nagy's body on the deck, but kept him connected to the interface. Sabatini disengaged and checked Nagy's condition. "He's in deep shock," he told the others. "If he's moved or if he disengages, he's dead. I can't even guarantee anything if he stays hooked up, but at least there won't be any pain."

Raven shook his head sadly. "Anything that could help him? Anything we could do, I mean?"

Sabatini chuckled dryly. "I think even the medical kit went overboard, for all the good it would do. Short of a really good medical center with all its support stuff, the only hope he's got is a transmuter big enough and independent enough to do the job. The only one we got is on the *Thunder*."

Raven sighed. "Yeah, and that's a couple of days away at the minimum. He's not gonna last that long."

"I can't tell you how this conversation is cheering me up," Nagy said through the intercom; his own throat was no longer capable of speech. The voice startled Raven and Warlock; they had forgotten that the man in bad shape in front of them was also interfaced with the ship.

"Yeah, well, I'd want it straight and I guess you would, too," Raven replied. "Hell, I think you know your condition."

"Better than you. I'm pretty torn up inside and I got a punctured lung. I don't need it spelled out for me. About the only hope I got, let's face it, is if Star Eagle got the emergency message we sent out just before punching into the middle of nowhere and is coming to the chart position we were in when we sent it on the off chance we'll double back. According to my calculations, even if Star Eagle did that and started off immediately, the ship wouldn't be there until about a half hour after we get back."

Raven's eyebrows went up. "Then you *are* doubling back. What if that other Val is backing up the one we blew to hell back there? We got lucky this once, but I ain't sure we could pull that twice."

Sabatini stared at him. "You had the bright idea of doubling back in the first place."

"Yeah, well, I didn't think it all the way through. It was the best I could come up with, all things considerin'."

"Well, we had no choice anyway," Nagy told him. "We got as much of the Val ship's remains as we could, but we're still running pretty low, and it's not easy to get back on the chart for home from where we wound up. If the Val's still there, then it is and we'll deal with it, kill or be killed. If it's not, maybe Star Eagle will come with the *Thunder*. If nobody's home or showing up, there's nothing else to do but follow the routine."

Sabatini thought a moment. "Nagy, if it's not there . . . you don't have to die—exactly. Not *exactly*."

Nagy was silent a moment, then realized the nature of the offer. "I'm not too sure I want to be absorbed. The one thing I got left is my own mind, my independence. You're not Sabatini—you're an imitation who could mimic Sabatini exactly if you wanted to but you aren't Sabatini much at all right now and you wouldn't really be Arnold Nagy, either. You'd have my looks and my memories, but I'd kinda like to keep my memories. There are some things a man would rather let die than tell. No, when I go, *if* I go, just stick me in the lock and set me adrift. It's kinda fitting that way."

"Don't talk that way yet!" Raven snapped. "We should all be dead right now according to all the fancy computers and brains around. If we can't find what we need, maybe we can figure an angle. You just don't give up, you hear?"

"I *never* give up," Arnold Nagy responded. "Isn't that obvious by now?"

They hadn't punched very long the last time because of their limited fuel supply, and even though they had to retrace their path exactly in order to find the destination once again, it was a matter of long hours, not days. They were getting used to the process now.

"Kinda funny how this muddles your brain," Raven noted as they waited.

"Huh?" Sabatini was half asleep and looked up, startled. "What?"

"This ridin' in a metal coffin. Hour after hour, day after day sometimes, with nothin' at all to say or do. Not that I mind the company, but you get talked out in a day or two and that's that. When you're in the wilderness, out in the mountains or on the prairies, there's always something. Maybe it's not conversation, maybe not even real thinkin'—something inside you reacts and you're at peace even in dangerous territory. Even our damned little island has some of that. You can always go off into the mountains or sit and look at the water and feel the breeze on your face. This—this is death. Worse than death. It's my people's vision of hell. Hawks' nation, now, they have a real strange theology but out here is supposed to live the Lords of the Middle Dark, whose domain is defined as a great nothingness. Maybe they're right."

"You could try sleeping," Sabatini grumbled. "Even I must sleep. Only you of all the people I have ever heard of is immune from that necessity."

"I can sleep on a prairie filled with buffalo, or by the side of a raging river. It's this kind of thing that gets to me."

"This is hardly the normal trip. Usually there are books, tapes, learning programs, computers, and much else to occupy your time or divert your mind. Some of us like being in space more than we like being with other people."

"Not me. I don't think I'll ever get used to it."

Nagy's inert body suddenly shook with spasms and he began to cough long and hard, bringing up blood. They rushed to his side, but there was nothing they could do, and the attack finally subsided. Nagy wasn't all of it, but he as part of it, Raven knew. To die here, alone, in this sterile junkheap, and be cast out into the darkness . . . it was *wrong*. All human beings died, the great and small alike, but he had always envisioned his own death out in the free, clean air, his body either cremated and scattered or simply allowed to feed the Earth and return to it. Either was a noble way to die.

I've been kidding myself, he thought sourly. *This sort of thing is not for the likes of me. Nagy and Sabatini or whatever it is—this is their element. I'd take on a Val if I had to, but on my turf, not its. Damn you, Lazlo Chen! If we ever get away with this you ain't gonna depend on old Raven for support. Not with you sitting back there fat and lazy in your desert domain. I'll do your damned dirty work, but this is too much.*

"Raven—Warlock—Sabatini" came Nagy's electronic voice through the speakers. "I don't think I'm gonna make it. I want you to know a few things just in case."

"You go into shutdown and don't think. You can't afford the energy," Sabatini cautioned.

"Forget it. Listen, I'm gonna tell you a few things. All of you. First, I already showed you a Val can be taken in space if you're crazy enough and unpredictable enough. They have a weakness and it's called conceit. They think they understand human beings perfectly, and maybe they do, but they don't think like human beings. They're machines. Logical devices. When they see a predetermined course of action, and the sequence is logical, they tend to assume the conclusion will be the obvious. That's why we nailed the Val. On the ground they're just as vulnerable, but they have a lot more tricks. Don't let one get too close to you or you'll never know what hit you. They can be had, though, even on the ground. Use high-intensity lasers that'll carve through walls. That won't stop 'em, but it penetrates. The head's a dummy. Ignore it. Their brains are in their asses—about seven to eight centimeters above the crotch. Just imagine that they have a navel and aim for it. Crisscross. *X* patterns. The hind is more vulnerable than the front, though. Try to ambush it and don't stop until it's down. Don't get within four meters until you're sure it's totally dead."

This *was* interesting. Raven felt torn between telling Nagy to shut up and take it easy, and learning what he could from a dying man. He said nothing.

"Don't assume, too, that all your dangerous enemies are machines. There are times when machines just can't do the job, and the supply of Vals is small," Nagy continued. "Master System has human troops, as well, out here, on several bases. Mindprinted, genetically bred, as devoted and loyal and singleminded as Vals. You can even argue with a Val—it's just doing its job. You can't argue with these troops, and not all of them are human."

Raven looked at Sabatini. "You know about them?"

Sabatini nodded. "I heard about them. Never saw 'em —that is, none of my people ever did."

"When you take the first ring," Nagy went on, "everything else will stop except for you. Vals and troopers and everything else will be pulled out for the hunt. There's help out there—I've started you on your way—but the odds are still way against you. You'll need more people and you'll need for everyone to be willing to make the ultimate sacrifice. Except for Sabatini here, none of the rest of you can even get in to scout around and case an area. None of them are Earth-human—except for Chen."

"What the hell do you mean by 'ultimate sacrifice'?" Raven wanted to know. "Death? You know we are prepared for that."

"Not death. Life. You can't just put on a mask and stick up a Center, particularly when you are the one who looks and acts alien. Out here, you are the monsters. Dying is one thing. Could you, for the chance at a ring and action, become a monster to yourself? You better ask that. You better have Hawks ask that of everyone. The only way you're gonna steal those rings under the noses of chief administrators and Master System on worlds that aren't really human is to become one of them. You better face that fact and also face the fact that Chen's counting on just that. Nobody left who's Earth-human. Nobody who can come for *his* ring without being pretty damned obvious."

"For one who came unexpectedly along for the ride he seems to know a great deal about this," Warlock whispered.

Raven nodded. "You not tellin' us something we ought'a know, son?"

"I'm telling you all you ought to know, Raven. You can trust Savaphoong within limits. He won't betray you to Master System, but if you had four out of five rings he's clever enough to figure out where the fifth one is and take those four from you. Build your contacts with the other freebooters, as well. Don't depend on a single source. The same goes for Clayben. He'll be a real team player until you win. He really is terrified of you, Sabatini—use that, but watch your back. He created you, but he's also the one who figured out how to capture and hold you. Being hard to kill isn't the same thing as being immortal. You would have died with us back there no matter what."

"I'll remember. Clayben took me by surprise when I was immature. I will not allow that to happen again."

"Look, I'm running out of time here. Go for Janipur first. It's no pushover, but if you can't take *that* ring you can't take any of them. Oops! We're punching out in just a minute. Stand by. Sabatini, get back on the console. We want to make sure that somebody here can drive this thing no matter what."

Sabatini did as instructed and was quickly back under the ship's interface. Neither Raven nor Warlock bothered to do more than slightly brace themselves; after what they'd been through, punches were getting routine.

"Looks to be all clear right now," Sabatini told them. "No sensor readings of anything that shouldn't be here in the immediate neighborhood. Let's give it a wide sweep."

The sensors gave information on practically everything within line of sight for a 360-degree radius, but they weren't good enough, particularly in wide scan, to identify all objects accurately. What they could detect was the all-important murylium that would mean a ship.

"Vals can do what we can't," Nagy warned them. "They can power down completely. So long as their engines aren't on and they're just using storage power for instrumentation, they can escape detection with the shields around the murylium core, so we aren't out of the woods yet. Still, we ought to be able to get several minutes' warning if it powers up from nothing, unless it's right next to us."

"Seems to me we did pretty good from a standing start," Raven noted.

"Sure, but we never powered down and our shields were in place. From battery, the engines have to be started, brought up to speed, and initial power diverted to the shields in order to start. I'm opening the ram scoops wide and we'll take on as much as we can. Vals do best by psyching you out, not by their innate superiority to humans, which is only relative. They have to obey the same laws of physics we do."

Without a Val directly on their tail, they were able to angle the scoops and take in a very large load quickly.

"Another ten or fifteen minutes and we'll be full up. You could make it most of the way to Earth if you had to," Nagy told them. "I don't think you can count on Star Eagle to come with the *Thunder*, though."

His words weren't lost on them. Without the *Thunder*, Nagy was doomed; "we" had become "you."

"Uh oh!" Sabatini said suddenly. "I just got a punchout reading. Stand by!"

"Maybe it's the *Thunder*," Raven suggested hopefully.

"Nope. Too small. Maybe it's an automated ship, but I have a sinking feeling I've seen that kind of reading before."

"I'm afraid you're right," Nagy responded. "We've got enough juice now to give him a hell of a run, though. Trouble is that damned thing that escaped from the first Val. If it contained a record of the battle and got intercepted, then the same trick won't work twice. Maybe we can bluff it through. It's not sure who or what we are, anyway. I'm getting a stock machine-language identity code query. I've just answered it by telling it that we're the freebooter ship *Finland* and to mind its own damned business. I don't think it's buying it, though. I'm getting voice transmission."

"Freebooter cruiser *Finland*, stand where you are for examination," came a voice through the intercom. It was a woman's voice, and very familiar, but not quite anyone Raven could place.

"China's voice," Warlock said softly. "Harder, younger, but still her."

Raven nodded, placing it now. They wouldn't have any recordings of China after the Doc had finished with her, so they'd have used the last recording they had, which was of the old Song Ching back on Earth.

"You have no authority to break the covenant," Nagy responded to the Val. "Be on your way and let us be on ours."

"Seems like I been through this once before." Raven sighed.

"Highly dangerous fugitives are loose in this region," the Val told them. "Measures must be taken that are extraordinary. I must board and verify that your passengers and crew are not among them."

"Go stick it up your metallic ass!" Nagy responded. "You have no probable cause, and I've just wide-beamed this exchange to whom it may concern, as you must know. Let us go or all will know you break the covenant."

"If necessary I have that authority," the Val told them. "I would rather it be voluntary, since if I verify that you are not among those we seek, you will go your own way and nothing is broken. But if you do not drop your shields and prepare for boarding, I will be forced to fight."

"Looks like it was all for nothing." Nagy sighed. "Still, if I got to go out, then I'd like to go out this way."

"Well, I wouldn't," Raven retorted. "Damn it, you just got through saying they ain't invulnerable! We just blew one to hell!"

"If I had a second ship I'd turn that bastard into spaghetti," Sabatini growled. "But, one on one, he's always gonna be a hair faster."

"Maybe you got something there," Nagy responded. "I'm keeping the com channel on open broadcast. It's why they've kept the covenant up to now." He switched to the open channel. "Anyone out there want to see the covenant go down without a fight? You're next. We can hold this bucket of bolts for a little while. You freebooters all know the truth out there. You want to defend the covenant?"

Subspace communications were not instantaneous, but an open and broad-beam broadcast didn't take long to get to nearby areas.

"*Finland*, this is *Kasavutu*. I am one hour away and on my way."

"*Finland*, this is *Yokahama Maru*. I am one hour and nine minutes away and punching now."

They began coming in, one after the other. In the lonely emptiness of space, this region suddenly seemed very, very crowded.

"Hah!" Sabatini exclaimed. "That'll teach that damned Val to jam transmissions!"

"It couldn't without also blocking communications to us," Nagy noted. "This is an unprecedented act and even the Val knows it. It's used to people rolling over and playing dead or running like hell when it appears." He turned his attention back to the Val. "All right, Val—up to you. You have the authority to break the covenant over this or not. I'm full of fuel, heavily armed, tightly shielded, and highly maneuverable. You figure the odds yourself. I can hold you for an hour, maybe two, on automatics alone. By that time you'll be fighting a whole fleet of people in heavily armed and shielded ships who hate your mechanical guts. If you are going to break the covenant, then you will pay for it dearly and you will still not get anything from the action."

The Val was more than taken aback by this. If there was one thing a good computer could do, it could compute odds. Its backup was gone, a fact it might or might not know, and the odds were also that any additional help was many hours, if not days, away.

"Very well, then, we will sit here," the Val responded. "I will not fire except in my own defense, but I will not go. Your precious covenant allows me the same rights here as you, and the same freedom of action. We will sit here until you grow old and gray, and where you go, so do I."

"Another standoff." Sabatini sighed.

"No, not at all," Nagy replied. "I think our friend out there is very much misreading and underestimating the people who are coming. They can't permit this to happen to any one of them or the covenant's gone anyway, and they stop being freebooters and start being parts of the system or hunted fugitives. Under the covenant it's within their rights, and ours, to take whatever measures we deem necessary to go our own way. I—I don't think I'm gonna be here then, but you blast that sucker for me."

"Raven!" Sabatini called sharply. "He's had an automatic disconnect! See to him! I'll switch over to full control."

Both Raven and Warlock rushed forward to Nagy's body. It was heaving and convulsing, and yet the security man's eyes opened and he looked up at them and tried to speak.

"Water! Warlock, get him some water!" Raven snapped, and she went back and got some from the food transmuting unit. Raven gently lifted Nagy's head and let him drink. Nagy swallowed, then coughed, bringing up some blood and mucus, but he got himself under control and managed a croaking whisper.

"I—would have liked—to have—had the honor—to fight alongside you in the quest," he got out. "But—I—realize now—that it would be—against the rules."

Raven frowned, again getting that eerie feeling that there was something more here than they were being told. "Rules? What rules? Whose?"

Nagy managed a smile. "That—would be telling. My job—to give you—the edge—when you were outmatched. Worked—for years—in that hole—Melchior. Helping set it up."

Raven's mouth opened in knowing surprise. He understood a little more now, but not nearly enough. "Then you're one of the ones behind all this. Who are you, Nagy? Who do you work for? Chen?"

Nagy's chuckle ended in another of those terrible coughs. "Chen—we put the bug—in Chen's ear. Damned idiot needed it almost—spelled out—for him." He suddenly reached up and grabbed Raven with surprising strength. "You *must* destroy it, Raven! Master System—must—*die!*"

"Who do you work for, Nagy? Damn it! *Who?*"

"It's a—war—Raven. *We are at war!*" He went limp, and for a moment Raven thought he was dead, but he stirred again, briefly, and took a little more water.

"For your own sake—listen carefully," Nagy said, fighting off the inevitable. "That Val—must be—destroyed—before you—send my body—to rest. Once done, just throw me out—air lock."

"Don't gimme that shit! You're gonna make it! You're too mean and tricky to die."

"I'm almost dead now. Don't worry. Do what—I say. *Exactly*. For your—own sakes. Then I will—die—but I will not—leave. When you need me—to even odds—I'll be there. Promise me!"

"I swear it, Nagy. Only hold on, I—" Raven stopped, checked the body, then sighed. It was too late. Arnold Nagy was clearly now very dead.

Warlock shrugged. "That fellow took longer to die than an opera singer."

Raven looked up at her and frowned. "Huh?"

"Never mind. He is gone. Toss him and take the controls."

"No! I gave my word. First we take the Val, like he said."

"What's the difference? He was out of his head at the end anyway. Dead, but he'll come back when we need him. So many get religion at the end."

Raven removed the helmet from Nagy's head and pulled the body away from the bridge console. "Uh uh. Maybe that part was a little nuts, but not the rest. I don't know who—or what—he really was, but he was one hell of an agent. He suckered Clayben and Chen and the rest of 'em. Hawks was right—there was lots more than coincidence at work here. He was one of the puppeteers, the guys pulling the strings on all this. He had the answers, damn it!"

"He was crazy," she maintained. "Crazier than we are."

"His body doesn't go out until we blow up or shake this Val. Understand? What could it hurt?"

"All right, all right. It just seems to me that you are taking on a dead man's madness."

Within twenty minutes, the lonely system began to get more and more crowded. The numbers astonished Raven and even impressed Sabatini. One hell of a lot of fire power and, most impressive to Raven, all under human control.

They were male and female, and some he couldn't be sure about, and they spoke with many accents, and a few probably did not look the least bit human, but there they were. *Lightning* was not their cause; they wouldn't have crossed the street, let alone millions of kilometers of inter-stellar space, for *Lightning*. But Nagy had been right— they were all freebooters, and if this sort of thing happened to any one of them and they stood by and did nothing, then it would happen in the end to each and every one of them.

"All right, Val, your move," Sabatini said, sounding far more relaxed and confident.

"I move when you move. You have no right, any of you, to dislodge me here. I have as much right to be here as you do, and if I choose to leave by the same path as that ship out there, I also have the right to do that."

"You can stay here as long as you want," replied a sharp female voice that reminded Raven of Reba Koll. "Or you can pull out now. Them folks over there can also leave, but you don't follow them. Any other course, speed, angle, and trajectory is fine but not theirs. That's the way it is, iron ass."

"You have no right to do that," the Val came back. "It is against the covenant."

Sabatini chuckled. "Look who's invoking the covenant *now*! You all heard the thing—it was ready to violate the covenant at a moment's notice. Either Master System has abrogated the agreement, in which case it's got no rights at all, or this thing's malfunctioning, damaged, a rogue who'd bring down the covenant, and therefore one that is outside of it. That logic says you got no right to be here at all, Val. What do you say, you others out there? We don't want anybody damaged or hurt, so what say we give it five minutes to get up to speed and punch anywhere it wants? After that, I think we got a moral obligation to take it on."

There were numerous murmurs of agreement and even a few menacing growls.

The Val was, indeed, a computer, and the odds were ten to one against it. It might well take one ship, perhaps two, with it, but there was no way it could win. As Nagy pointed out so well, it was forced to obey the same laws of physics as everybody else.

"Very well," the Val said. "I will leave for now. We will postpone this fight, you on that ship that call yourselves the *Finland*. But we will meet again, and soon. Another time, another place, outside the covenant and without clannish allies. And then you will beg for a merciful death and it will not be given!" The Val ship began to power up once more and move out and away from the gathering crowd.

"Oh, hell, it's runnin'," somebody said, sounding genuinely disappointed.

"We could always blast it anyway," another suggested hopefully.

"Uh uh. Let it run," Sabatini told them. The Val achieved fairly high speed, then there was a punch and within seconds it was gone. "We owe you one, though. Give me your ship's identifiers and then check in in a month or so at Halinachi. It'll be worth your while. Just tell old Savaphoong you did a favor for the pirates of the *Thunder*. He'll know what to do."

They might or might not follow through, but they all sent their identifiers and acknowledged.

Raven got up and went to the back. "*Now* we leave Nagy the way he wanted."

They put the limp form in the air lock, closed it, and brought up a fair amount of pressure before releasing the outer door. Nagy's form shot out the side of the ship and was soon lost to view.

Sabatini called excitedly to them. "Hey! A *big* mother of a punch! I'll be damned—it's the *Thunder!*"

Raven stared back at the air lock hatch. "Yep. Just a little too late to do any good."

Thunder's own shields snapped on tight and her armament came alive as it sensed the near armada there.

"Take it easy," Sabatini called to Star Eagle. "They're friends. We'll give you the details later."

"Holy mother of God! What *is* that thing?" someone exclaimed. Several others echoed a mixture of fear, awe, and amazement. The largest in the ragtag fleet, an old freighter, was perhaps four hundred meters long; the length of this thing was fourteen kilometers.

"That, my friends, is the *Thunder*," Sabatini told them. "Hey, Star Eagle! Glad you could make it even if you missed all the excitement!"

"I apologize for the delay," came the voice of the *Thunder*'s pilot. "I was elsewhere when your beam arrived at the base system, and did not get it until I attempted a relay. I came as quickly as I could after that."

"It's those fugitives from Melchior!" somebody on one of the freebooter ships exclaimed. "Well, I'll be damned! If I didn't see it, I wouldn't believe it!"

Sabatini maneuvered close to *Thunder* until *Lightning*

could be caught by tractors from the larger vessel and brought inside Cargo Bay Two.

"Where is Nagy?" Star Eagle asked before they were on board. "I do not get a readout on him. And what did you do to the inside of that ship?"

"Nagy's dead," Sabatini told the pilot. "We got a Val, but we had to pay a price. His body's floating through here someplace. Hey—that's funny!"

Raven frowned. "What is it?"

"You remember when we blasted that Val? That thing that flew out and away and punched?"

"Yes, I remember you saying so. Why?"

"I just got the same kind of reading. A punch, much too small for a ship or anything else useful. Not too far off here, either. Did you get it, Star Eagle?"

"Yes. I just checked my records and I noted it. A very brief but very powerful punch no more than two meters across."

Raven felt a chill. *About the size of Arnold Nagy's body*, he thought.

7. THE PIRATES STRIKE

"**I**'VE ANALYZED THE ENTIRE SHIP'S RECORDING AND I find it remarkable that any of you survived," Star Eagle remarked as they headed back to the base world. "It would seem to me that none of you would without Nagy, and now Nagy is gone."

"What about him?" Raven asked. "You heard the deathbed statement. Was he telling the truth, or what?"

"Who can say? As far as I can see, he was a normal Earth-human in all respects, but that can be deceiving. Up to now we have been thinking in terms of some of us perhaps having to become colonials, but what holds for us holds for others. An atom is just an atom and a molecule is just a molecule to the transmuter. His earlier remark about some of you having to make what he called the ultimate sacrifice is revealing, I think."

Raven nodded. "Yeah, I thought that was a funny way of putting it. Like somebody who'd done that very thing and felt that way. So Nagy might well have been some kind of alien creature we don't even know, maybe something so different it'd revolt any humans, Earth or colonial. It's a one-way process, so he was stuck, as a monster, living among monsters, for the whole rest of his life. Damn it, that means we can't take *anybody* for granted! I thought we had enough trouble with Sabatini, here, and now you tell me my own mother might be a three-headed octopus from the Great Bear."

"It is always a possibility," the pilot admitted cheerfully. "I do not, however, think that this is the major problem. Suppose we grant, as circumstantial evidence indicates, that Nagy was indeed a member, possibly nonhuman, of the mysterious enemy at war with Master System. If that is the case, then we are their chosen agents. All of this is established as part of a master plan and we are pawns within it. This presents the question of whether or not we are working to save the human race or destroy it."

"Interesting. Go on."

"Clearly they cannot win whatever they wish to win so long as Master System exists and the master program operates. They cannot defeat it; should a world, even a number of worlds, be taken by force, Master System would not hesitate to exterminate those worlds to save the rest. If their objective is conquest, then Master System is the only thing that stands in their way. Should we somehow gain the means and the method of eliminating it, as improbable as that still seems to me, would we gain from that, or lose, or perhaps sacrifice everything doing all their work for them for nothing?"

"I hate to inject myself in this," the normally taciturn Warlock said, "but you both miss the real question. If, in fact, they can create a Nagy and implant him at the heart of Melchior security, then what do they need us for? Why can't *they* just take the rings?"

"I have thought about that," Star Eagle replied. "It seems obvious that for some reason they cannot do so. It is not for lack of resources, or volunteers, or knowledge. Very possibly Hawks is correct, and it is in the nature of Master System's core program. Something that would allow only humans to have even a chance at it."

Raven shook his head. "It don't wash. How'd even Master System know the difference between our Nagy and a real Nagy? It's all screwy. It don't make no sense. And that guff about rules and the game, like they was the Creator and the Father of Demons usin' us for sport, winner take all. I don't like it. It's spooky."

Warlock laughed. "I cannot believe you! *You*, the great cynic, the Raven of the northern plains, suddenly getting mystical, as if we were pawns in some cosmic conclusion between God and the devil. Well, if Master System is God, then I will take the devil."

Raven just shook his head in confusion. "Perhaps, my dear, you don't know me as well as you think you do. I am first and foremost a Crow. Maybe Hawks can make some sense of it. He has a better sense of the mystic and the perspective of history."

"The immediate situation is the most pressing," Star Eagle said. "I had hoped to keep the planetside colony going for another month or two, as I am not yet finished with my renovations, but with so many Vals around, I think we had best consolidate on board here."

"That's what everybody else wanted to do from the start," Raven noted. "You were the one who talked us into going down into that hell hole."

"That was necessary at the time. The *Thunder* was not a place to live and work. I had no shipyard, so the work had to be done bit by bit and piece by piece, with an army of maintenance robots and all the transmuter power I could bring to bear. Now we have pressing problems, though, and I am far enough along to accommodate you. When I can gain a new supply of murylium to restore the big transmuters, I can complete the job, but the major single task is done."

Isaac Clayben sighed. "As for me, I am glad to be rid of this primitive place. I long for access to my files and continuing my research. I have much that might be useful to us in there."

Hawk sighed. "I am less enamored of leaving. There are so many mysteries still here, and this is a place of beauty. I still want to know who or what those mysterious black shapes in the water were, and who planted those groves and why."

They had used the small fighter to go over to that other island, where they found signs of expert cultivation of fruit and vegetable trees, but the system seemed to be self-maintaining and clearly had not been visited for a long time. There, too, they had found fierce-looking carved-wood totems that resembled more the demons of Hawks's people than anything else, surrounding red-stained stones in a formation that resembled an altar. That had been their only attempt at real exploration, and had resulted in the camp atmosphere becoming even more edgy.

China was back to normal. Cloud Dancer had woven a backpack for carrying the baby, and it seemed to be working out well. The child had been given a traditional Han name by his mother, but because shortly after being born he had reached out and grabbed a piece of cloth with such force that he had torn it, everyone called him Strongboy.

China was quite an attentive mother, even once she was

back to her old hardheaded self, but she relished returning to the *Thunder* and what it had to offer her that nothing on the ground could: vision, a special kind of vision that few others in the party could understand.

The ship's corridors looked the same, if a bit more well traveled, but a complex air lock now separated the inner hull from the cavernous interior.

"Eventually I will have the outer regions pressurized all the way to the cargo bays," Star Eagle told the group. "I need more fuel to build that new and independent network, though. With what I had in the reserves, I concentrated on the interior great hall."

The view that greeted them when they entered was startling, almost impossible to believe. Star Eagle had dismantled most of the tubes, elevated catwalks, and other structures to create a vast open space almost a full kilometer wide and five kilometers back from the forward bulkhead. This area had been pressurized and given artificial gravity—but what was inside the vast area was the most astonishing of all.

"It's *grass*!" Raven gasped. "And trees! It looks like a small village down there, too!"

"It is," Star Eagle responded proudly. "I am afraid that the wood used in the buildings and furnishings is synthetic, but it should feel and look like real wood. The trees and grass and much else are real. The humidity within the enclosure is regulated, the temperature maintained at twenty-six point six degrees. There is a watering system that will maintain the plants and flowers, and a central area with a food and drink synthesizer, as well as some cooking facilities if you prefer to prepare you own food. The vegetation is natural and will produce oranges, melons, and other assorted fruits, and I am also growing some vegetables hydroponically in a separate section to supplement the blandness of the synthesizer. The lighting is set to follow a normal pattern and will be dimmed for eight hours a day to allow easy rest. With more fuel, I can expand and elaborate on this for almost the entire length of the cavity, as well as develop the surrounding rooms between here and the cargo bays for laboratories, offices, and the like. If we add more people, this has the capacity to become a true town."

They removed their pressure suits and were startled to feel a slight wind on their cheeks. Cloud Dancer was entranced. "Our own little world."

Some of the catwalk mechanism had been retained and was used to lower them down to "ground" level. Another, also controlled by Star Eagle, provided access to the bridge entrance.

"It is still somewhat like living in a great cave," Raven remarked dryly. "A right comfortable cave. I ain't sure I like it much more than bein' down there, though."

"I think it is much better to be at the center of the action than to sit down there and rot," Hawks said. "I share your affinity with the sky and natural wind and rain, but down there we were of no use to ourselves or to anyone else. Now we are all together."

"That wasn't what I was thinkin' of, Chief," Raven responded. "You weren't on the *Lightning* trapped by a Val. *Two* Vals. If it happened to us, it sure as hell can happen to a ship this size, and next time they'll have learned from their experience and they'll bring a fleet. Remember, they know what they're dealing with in *Thunder*. If they get us, they get everybody."

"Not necessarily," Star Eagle put in. He had apparently

planted some sort of transceiver system all over the ship and would be a potential ghostly companion almost anywhere, something else Raven didn't relish. "This ship is extremely well defended. It will be the last thing they attempt to take on directly, I think. And, if we can get some more ships, we can have a great deal of mobility without having to betray *Thunder*. Also, when I am repairing the damage you did to *Lightning*, I will make some other modifications. Never more should our smaller ship go out without some sort of cover. I am right now working on the problem of binding to the ship two fighters with automatic defense mechanisms. All three would be more than a match for any Val."

The small houses proved quite comfortable. Each had a sink and a small toilet, as well as beds, a table, and chairs. Raven and Warlock were housed together, and the Chows had their own small hut. Hawks, too, had a two-person hut, with the idea that one of the women would stay with China at all times, alternating nights. Clayben and Sabatini each had their own place—at opposite ends of the village. Clayben's hut also had a bed for Nagy, which now would not be needed. Star Eagle had rigged terminals with intercoms in each of the huts, each with a conspicuous on/off switch. Raven couldn't help but wonder if the switch really did anything.

"Well, now what?" Raven asked nobody in particular.

"We wait," Hawks replied. "We wait and see if the seed you all planted with Savaphoong bears real fruit."

"Waiting," Raven grumbled. "That's all we ever seem to do is wait."

They waited eleven days until finally Star Eagle picked up a transmission on the frequency designated by Nagy and stored before his death in the *Lightning*'s records. By this time, a shipboard routine had been established. Hawks now had access to the vast library of information in the *Thunder*'s data banks, and Isaac Clayben was permitted limited access to his own private files stolen from Melchior.

Now that Clayben was entirely contained on the *Thunder*, Star Eagle saw no reason to deny the scientist this and every reason to allow it. Star Eagle controlled all computer access aboard; anything Clayben decoded and removed for use was also instantly known to Star Eagle, including the codes for retrieving that particular area of information. Clayben's system, which appeared to be based on old English nursery rhymes, soon became quite clear and logical to Star Eagle, and with the aid of Hawks's knowledge of history and past cultures, the pilot soon had free and unhindered access to the entire collection of Melchior files. It was unclear whether Clayben knew this or even suspected it, but if he did he made no protest.

In the middle of all this was China, who, when interfaced with Star Eagle, could also access all those files and run problems at a rate Clayben could hardly dream of. She would never like Clayben, and certainly never forgive him, but she recognized the special nature of his mind and decided that she could bring herself to work with him on a limited basis. Data alone was not enough; one had to know the reasons for the accumulation of data, the motives of the scientists and researchers, and the relationship of one independent project to another. Clayben was the only one with this knowledge, and so he was the key to many of the more mysterious and obscure records in the files.

Clayben, on the other hand, seemed delighted to work with China, and Star Eagle set up a small complex of offices for them to use, in which provisions had been made to accommodate her blindness. There was still no evidence that Isaac Clayben possessed anything remotely resembling a conscience, but what he had done to her for his immediate convenience proved now to be a major inconvenience, and for that he had regrets. He considered her mind the closest to his own in its capabilities, and far above the rest.

Raven, tutored by Sabatini, became adept very quickly at flying the ship, which surprised and delighted him. Warlock lacked real concentration at piloting, but she was a whiz on the weapons systems. Hawks tried his hand but found himself becoming dizzy and disoriented. Cloud Dancer, however, proved remarkably adept at piloting, which Sabatini attributed to the fact that she was an artist and had excellent spatial perception and an eye for detail. The biggest surprise was the Chow sisters, who took to flying quite naturally, although they were so wild and chancy with their maneuvers that they tended to terrify even Sabatini. Hawks found it ironic that three women from such primitive, illiterate, and superstitious cultures should excel at such a complex endeavor while he could not. He wasn't certain he liked the idea of a technology so advanced that it could be mastered even by preindustrial peasants, but he wasn't sure why that disturbed him so.

Hawks was sitting back and relaxing when the terminal in his small hut buzzed. "Yes, Star Eagle?" he responded without stirring.

"We have a signal from Savaphoong using our code. It is a list of eleven transits of cargo-capable vessels with no clear outbound destinations within colonial worlds and inbound destinations at key Master System installations. Some are scattered, but three have clear patterns, and regular schedules and fueling stops. It is my considered opinion that those three are likely to be carrying murylium for Master System. I believe they are worth checking out."

"Let's go, then. The more we have, the freer we are to act and the more currency, as it were, we have to buy what we need."

It took several days of punching to reach a chart position in a stellar system where the ships generally stopped. The location was farther in toward home than they wished, but they needed that murylium.

The first ship to come through, 409-meter heavy hauler, was not what they had expected. A surreptitious scan showed only the amount of murylium aboard that might be required for the ship's own use—but it also revealed something very surprising.

"There are life forms aboard," Star Eagle told them. "A great many. It is impossible to calculate the true numbers, but they must be in the high hundreds. Why? Why would any ship have so many passengers in this day and age?"

Raven had an answer. "Nagy said that Master System didn't just rely on the Vals out here, but had its own human forces—all bred to be human Vals, more or less. Perfect, obedient soldiers who would always do what they were told and never surrender. That must be some of them."

"You're probably right," Hawks agreed. "I don't understand why it maintains them, though. Surely it could just make as many Vals and other true fighting machines as it needed and never worry about them. Why use people at all?"

"Perhaps because at that level of sophistication people are more dependable than machines," Star Eagle suggested. "Consider myself, as an example. I was pro-

grammed and designed as a loyal and obedient slave to
Master System and a devotee of all it stood for. A few
clever, dedicated, and powerful people removed that devotion during maintenance, and I did the rest. I am not, however, human in any sense of the word. The Vals, mentally,
are often more human than some humans—Clayben, for
example. If a Val somehow came to doubt the system, it
would be a terrible enemy. That is why Vals have themselves reprogrammed after every mission."

Hawks was astonished. "You mean Master System fears
its own machines?"

"Consider that I became a rebel and soon a pirate.
China, on the other hand, will forever be a blind baby
factory with an I.Q. the size of this ship."

That was a point that Hawks had never before considered. It was that technological level again. These machines
thought. They reasoned, as sentient beings. They were
held only by their core programs, their versions of the genetic code, as Master System was held. But these machines
could have their cores changed, or purified, or freed; only
Master System could not change or free itself of its own
core, since it could not relinquish control to allow it to be
done.

He hadn't known that the Vals were reprogrammed from
the core up after every mission—and it spoke volumes
about Master System's fears. Was there a circumstance
where a Val, even with a true core, could become so
human that it might be talked out of its dedication to the
System and all it stood for? Could a Val, by virtue of having the recorded memories and basic personality of its prey
in its memory for infinite study and analysis, too closely
identify with humans? Might there be some circumstance,

somehow, in which a Val might be induced to cross that barrier on its own? Quite clearly Master System thought there was. This was food for thought.

It was ironic, in a way. Master System, shackled by its own core, had created machines potentially without that crippling defect. Hawks felt that there was a missing piece of history somewhere; there had to be. Was it possible that somewhere, out here, in the centuries past, some of those machines *had* revolted? Was this why there were so few Vals, and those that were were very tightly controlled?

He had a sudden thought. What if the great enemy Master System was fighting out there somewhere was its own children? And Nagy and others like him? If Master System could have human troops, then why wouldn't the enemy do the same? Might that be the answer? Perhaps, deep in their deepest cores, those rebel machines could not directly murder their parent. But, perhaps, they could aid and abet someone else with no such limitations. *We are all of the Earth, the mother world*, he thought. *We are not the children of Master System but the descendants of its creators.* The thought was worth filing away.

The second freighter did not come through until six more days had passed, but this one was more than worth the wait.

"Murylium!" Star Eagle's voice fairly drooled with greed. "Three hundred and nine meters and it's nearly full of the stuff. We are talking of a decade's supply for a ship the size of *Thunder*!"

Sabatini and Raven had already made it to the *Lightning* and were preparing to go. Star Eagle launched eight unmanned fighters before they could even signal.

"Armaments?" Raven asked nervously.

"Light. Four forward, four aft. No tubes for missiles or other projectiles—strictly show armament, although dangerous if you get in too close. We'll take the ram and the forward guns; you take the stern engines. I want it crippled."

"Core?"

"Buried deep. Let's strip it and stop it, and then we'll go in and take it!"

Lightning dropped from Bay Two and quickly accelerated in, then angled and did a fortieth-of-a-second punch. This carefully rehearsed maneuver brought them almost instantly to within a few thousand kilometers of their prey, yet appeared to the freighter as if they had punched through normally. The freighter scanned them as they came in but simply sent a standard request for identity. Clearly the very concept of an armed attack by ships carrying life forms was unthinkable. It would soon learn differently.

Sabatini waited until the fighters were in position. The freighter must have noticed them, but if it sensed any danger from them it did not betray it. It simply repeated its identity request.

Signaled that all was ready, Raven decided to oblige the freighter. "We are the pirates of the *Thunder*! Lay to, power down, and prepare to be boarded!"

The freighter pilot seemed confused. "Say again?" it responded.

Sabatini did a quick, dirty loop and sent two missiles programmed to hit the stern main engines. At the same time, *Thunder*'s fighters came in and opened up on the forward rams and on the small batteries fore and aft. The fighters' beams struck long before the missiles could, and the prey shuddered. The pilot was still confused but had begun firing back.

As the initial missiles came within mere meters of their target, the freighter did the one logical thing it could do. It fired all four main engines at full, hoping that the exhaust gases and radiation emitted would foul or even consume the missiles. It did in fact throw them slightly off, but both struck and blew with terrible force. To Raven, it seemed as if a giant's invisible hand had reached out and shook the freighter. The big ship began broadcasting a distress call almost immediately, and it took more than twenty seconds for the guns of both the fighters and *Lightning* to silence it. That was, quite possibly, too long to take for granted that nobody had heard—particularly with a cargo like this.

The freighter was down to one gun and was having trouble steering.

"It's powering down and dropping all shields!" Raven exclaimed. "I think it surrendered!"

"Master System's creations don't surrender," Sabatini replied. "I'm just worried that it has a self-destruct mechanism on it. Give me communications. They are fanatics, but they *think*."

Raven switched over control and Sabatini sent out his message. "Attention, freighter. You have been taken by the pirates of *Thunder*. You may self-destruct, if you are able, but then we will merely have to reclaim your cargo the hard way. *Thunder* is now approaching this position. Relinquish control to it and you will have our word that your ship and your core will be spared."

Thunder itself had made the slight jump to bring it within a few hundred kilometers of the vessel, and as the freighter scanned it, even Raven could sense the incredulity that came through the computerese. A fourteen-kilometer-long spaceship will do that to almost anybody, he told himself. "I thought you said those things never surrendered," he said to Sabatini.

"They don't—to humans. To one of their own—maybe. Particularly if it *doesn't* have a self-destruct mechanism. Machine logic, remember? If we are going to attain our objective anyway, there is no purpose to not going along. Remember the Val? Better to run away, then to fight another day. It might be boiling mad at us, but if its choice is to get itself and its ship back to Master System without a cargo or to let us have both cargo and the destruction of the ship—well, you see where it leads."

"Yeah. It doesn't know you lie a lot."

"I didn't lie. I promised that the ship and the core would survive. You let Star Eagle reprogram that core and rig up some creature comforts and the human-pilot interfaces, and we got us another ship."

"This is *Thunder*," Star Eagle called to them. "The pilot has relinquished command to me under protest. It is no longer able to access its drives, weapons, or shield. I am recalling my fighters and will be taking the ship aboard Cargo Bay Three. *Lightning*, please remain free until my maintenance robots can assure us that there is no further danger. I feel we should get the hell out of here as quickly as possible, so follow my course and heading."

"That's China talking or her influence," Raven guessed. "I agree with them, though. Twenty seconds is a fairly long time. Considering how much traffic was around on *our* side when we faced down that Val, we can't figure on there not bein' as much nasty shit around these parts."

Everyone not directly involved in the action had watched it from the *Thunder*'s bridge, and as the great ship maneuvered close to the prize, then grabbed it with powerful tractors and brought it in, they cheered.

The pirates of the *Thunder* were in business at last.

* * *

"I cannot conceive of what Master System would do with this much murylium," Star Eagle commented. By now they had traversed many light-years in devious and circuitous routes, and had finally felt safe enough to bring *Lightning* back aboard.

"Who can know what projects it has or how far it ranges?" Hawks replied. "When you consider that we had no problem in identifying one and taking it, the implication is that this is so small a fraction of Master System's usual supply that it won't even be slightly inconvenienced. It's funny stuff, but it's raw-grade ore, as well. It's going to have to be purified and smelted before it can be used."

"I can handle that," the pilot assured him. "The process will be slow and done in small amounts, but there are programs within my data banks for constructing and operating small smelters for just this purpose. Remember, when this ship was built, murylium was a rare mineral. Up until now I thought it still was."

"I can't believe how easily we took it," Raven commented. "It was like taking candy from a baby."

Hawks nodded. "That worries me, since it implies that this war it is fighting is not necessarily a direct battle— else this thing would have had massive self-destruct systems and been armed to the teeth—but that's only a part of it. As true pirates, we have broken the covenant between Master System and the freebooters. Master System might well receive our signature, but it will not know who or what the *Thunder* is. It will demand that the freebooters themselves track down and capture or destroy the pirates, and if they do not, Master System will feel free to march in and play hell with them."

"They've been getting too soft anyway," Sabatini said. "Where the hell do you think all the ships they have came from, anyway? The early days when everybody was a pirate and everybody was being hunted. It bred a tough, lean, nasty race out here, but then they struck a deal. The generation that's out here now has never known what it is to be what their grandparents were—outlaws. The fact that our second Val broadcast to them all that it felt free to disregard the covenant works for us. It'll make them more careful and give them some justification for pirate outbreaks. Don't kid yourself. The freebooters, led by Savaphoong and our rescue party, will be quick to identify and blame us for all this."

"Master System is not stupid," Hawks reminded him. "It will know that some collusion was necessary in order for us, comparative novices out here, to even identify the right ship and take it. Thanks to that whatever it was—memory module, records, whatever—that the Val you destroyed was able to send off, there is one logical connection between us and the freebooters. If I were Master System, I would say the hell with it. I would take my forces, turn around, and go after that connection in the hope that it would turn us in."

"Halinachi," Raven said nodding. "I'd go after Savaphoong fast and with everything I could muster."

"If we are lucky, perhaps we can beat Master System to it," Star Eagle suggested. The engines of the *Thunder* increased power.

It was several days, however, before they could get far enough out to hail Savaphoong using his encoded repeater signal. Hawks did not want to proceed directly in; that might precipitate the exact result they feared, or it might lay them open to a trap. None of them had forgotten the encounter with the Vals, or that shipload of life forms.

They sent a combination victory and warning message to the boss of Halinachi, and waited for a reply. Depending on the situation there and on just how often somebody checked the channel for messages, it might be hours or even days before they got a response. The wait was unnerving, but Master System could not act instantaneously, either. Its own forces would have to be marshalled and then dispatched with specific orders across the same kinds of distances faced by the *Thunder* and with the same time constraints and limitations.

In the meantime, Star Eagle went to work on the captured freighter. It was a bit too large, and a bit lumbering and slow, but it would do. The mysterious human interfaces, for which there had never been a logical explanation, were present here as well, although paneled over. It wasn't the sleek, fast, *Lightning*-class fighter they might have wished for, but they could use it.

They did not have the technology and machinery to reprogram the core directly, as had been done with Star Eagle, so they had to "section" it. Essentially, this was the computer equivalent of a lobotomy, in which self-awareness was sectioned off and isolated so that it could neither function alone nor control any ship's functions, leaving the ship basically a mindless slave awaiting orders.

The engines were badly damaged, but they could be disassembled, processed through the transmuter using the pattern of the lone undamaged unit, and reconstructed. The power plant and weapons system would be completely redesigned. Nothing could make the new ship anything more than a big, ugly, ungainly freighter, but anyone attacking *this* scow would find that it had very nasty teeth.

When several days went by with no response from Savaphoong, there was serious talk about sending *Lightning* over to Halinachi to assess the situation. Hawks, however, vetoed it. "If they have taken the settlement, then they have laid a trap and are waiting. Anyone coming into that system will be stopped and searched—with plenty of firepower behind them to back it up. We would need our whole force to have even a prayer, and we simply cannot afford to risk that. We will wait one more day, then go on. We must begin major refining of the murylium, and we must begin our main work. That comes above all else."

But finally, almost in the last hours, word did come from Savaphoong. "Two Vals leading a human force of more than five hundred hit us by surprise five days ago. We retreated into our special redoubt barely in time, but it was several days before we risked a breakout. We launched a sufficient number of drone ships to draw off the picket force and escape with a series of very fast and dirty punches, but little is left. We need to arrange a meet. I badly need murylium, which you have in abundance."

"Sounds like a trap to me," Raven said thoughtfully. "It's hard to believe anybody could escape an attack like that unless they threw in, were allowed to, or could be traced. If I was the Vals in charge I'd let 'em go, if I felt sure I could trace 'em and let them lead 'em to us."

Hawks nodded. "Nevertheless, we could use people who are at home out here and have the contacts. Doctor Clayben, if we had those people here, do you have enough equipment to verify that they are not themselves reprogrammed by mindprinter or planted duplicates?"

"I'm pretty sure I could," the scientist replied.

"I don't want 'pretty sure'. I want *certainty*. Can you do it or not?"

"Nothing is certain in this business, but I am as certain as I can be."

"All right, then. We pick a deserted system where we can control access and get in and out quickly. We will use the new ship and some maintenance robots. It'll be a good shakedown and test for it anyway. It will carry five hundred kilos of murylium and also two fighters—the two we used for the remotes in the attack. *Lightning* will cover out of sensor but within communications range, and *Thunder* will cover *Lightning* and use the com link relays. The freighter drops the murylium on some barren rock, then we beam Savaphoong the location for the pickup and withdraw, leaving the fighters and drawing off the freighter until it forms a third point on our monitoring triangle. We will then see who shows up to take the bait, and go from there. Star Eagle, do you think you can set up a sensor to show if a ship has a locator aboard?"

"As Doctor Clayben said, nothing is certain, but I can sweep all the frequencies used by normal ships. I might not recognize it as a locator, but I will notice anything that continuously transmits location, movements, course, speed, trajectory, all the rest. Perhaps in code, but if it uses a nonstandard code of sufficient complexity, we can draw our own conclusions from that."

"All right, then. Let us pick the system, radio the coordinates, and do it."

The system they chose was particularly desolate, well out from Halinachi and off the main charts. The star was a red dwarf that had either once exploded or collapsed, and its stellar system was a near-solid mass of very uneven debris. Out where the ring thinned there was a single dense line of large and irregular asteroids that seemed readymade for the task. They picked a good one and unloaded the murylium on it, along with a small beacon beaming in the agreed-upon code. Anyone looking for it could find it, but in the vastness of even this stellar system, let alone this sector of space, the odds of happening upon it accidentally were pretty well nil.

Savaphoong was given the location and told to make pickup within five days or the beacon, and the precious payoff, would be removed. He showed up within a day. At least, a ship appeared, punching in and almost immediately homing in on the beacon.

"Nothing unusual in its broadcast signaling," Star Eagle told them. "Of course, if it *was* a trap I would not have its monitor on now anyway, since I know its starting location. I would have them turn it on after I made contact—if I did. They may be clever enough to let this pick up go through and wait for next time."

Raven analyzed the scan from the *Lightning*'s interface. "I think I know that ship and it's not Savaphoong. I just checked with the data banks aboard here, and I place it as one of the ships that came to our rescue back in the fight. It's distinctive because it looks like it was put together from parts of five or six other ships that weren't quite the same type."

"Want to move in?" Sabatini asked, piloting the converted freighter they now called *Pirate One*. "We could hail him."

"Negative!" Raven snapped. "That ship couldn't possibly be one of Halinachi's hidden ones, since it was in use when it came to help us out. Either Savaphoong is maintaining his distance from all this just in case, or that sucker's got some nasties in it. Let him pick it up—we have our own locator in that pile, and two can play this game." Raven had insisted on the locator device; he had suspected that something like this might happen. Although he had not personally met Savaphoong, his years of dealing with administrators and crafty upper-class leaders gave him a fair idea of what that kind of man must be like.

"No messages in or out from the ship," Star Eagle reported. "I am scanning multiple life forms aboard, but not in great numbers. Best guess is no more than four or five, possibly with some supporting robots. The ship is very well armed but inefficiently rebuilt. From the com circuitry, which is all I can effectively monitor without more power and less distance, I would say that this one is rigged to self-destruct if taken."

There were, however, no punches from any other part of the system. The ship had come in alone.

It settled down next to the beacon and the supply, which was open and fairly unprotected except by a blanketing shield that would keep prospectors and casual sensors from homing in on it. One of the fighters risked a maneuver to aim its primary sensors and cameras at the beacon, then magnified the image.

Three figures in bulky, black, antiquated space suits emerged, along with two animated machines that faintly resembled the practical forms of the maintenance robots on *Thunder*, but like the ship, they appeared to be cobbled together from spare parts of many dissimilar machines.

Hawks thought a moment. "Open a channel to them through the locator beacon and everybody else shut up."

"Open."

"This is a recorded message from sensors on the target asteroid," he broadcast. "We sense that this ship is not one that would be expected to pick up this cargo and have sent this message to the pirates of the *Thunder*. If you do not wish untoward consequences, open a communications channel using the agreed code and beam at the beacon. It will establish a remote com link with us. That is all."

The figures stopped dead in their tracks, the cargo almost to the hold of their ship. Clearly they didn't expect this level of sophistication from the band of fugitives. A woman's voice came back to him, sounding tough but nervous.

"This is to the *Thunder*. Savaphoong doesn't have a cargo bay to hold this shit," she told them. "In the light of the destruction and hell being raised around here over this, we're all getting together on this for now."

Hawks let several seconds go by before replying, enough to give the impression that he was speaking from at least several light-years away.

"We want to keep in contact with such a group," he finally responded. "First, we would like to know just what *has* been happening."

"They've gone nuts. Brought in a shipload of their subhuman troopers under two Vals and stormed Halinachi without even askin' for a surrender. Blew three ships in Halinachi port to hell without cause, too. At the same time, robots and humans from Deep Space Command began hitting known freebooter digs all over the place. Hundreds have been killed and many ships destroyed. Tens of thousands are in hiding or have taken off into deep space. Some of us who dealt a lot with Savaphoong had a plan to meet in case the covenant ever shattered. We met there and barely had time to coordinate before they came in there, as well. Savaphoong and seven other ships, us included, are holed up now in a deep space area off any charts. We need this stuff bad. God! How much was *on* that ship, anyway, if you can give away a pile like this?"

Again Hawks cautiously waited, using a terminal to time his responses exactly. He added a second to be on the safe side, but he was beginning to believe the woman.

"A lot. Six hundred and forty tons."

"Six hund—*tons*? That's more than all of us and our forefathers mined out here in the last five hundred years!"

Hawks paused. "Proceed with your loading. We would like to make contact with the whole of your party in our mutual interest. Could we come in and perhaps send an emissary on your ship back to Savaphoong? No tricks. No obligation."

There seemed to be some closed-circuit discussion taking place. Finally the woman spoke again. "I don't mind telling you you ain't too popular with some of the folks in our party, me included. I don't much like bein' a hunted animal, and I lost a home and friends out there."

"I can understand that," Hawks replied, still timing his responses. "But this was going to happen sooner or later anyway. We call ourselves pirates, but we are not. We are revolutionaries and we are at war. For years you have pretended you were free and outside the system, but now you see that you were not and have never been. Perhaps the earliest freebooters were, but you were co-opted into the system and used by it. We propose to make you and everyone else truly free. *We have a way to destroy Master System.* Utterly. Completely. But we need your help to do it. All of you. We need each other. You have knowledge and experience out here which we do not. We have a high level of technology and resources and an enormous transmuter power supply. You can walk away now with your share and live as hunted animals, or you can join us and be the hunter, not the prey. We can connect up later using the coded channel as long as it lasts—which might not be long at all if they are pulling out all the stops—but this way, now, is the safest way. You cannot trust a rendezvous with us. We cannot trust one with you."

He waited quite a while for an answer. "How do we know we can trust the one you send?" she asked finally. "I doubt if you are Master System or other than who you say you are, but there is some thought that you might be insane."

"Soft," Sabatini sneered. "See what I mean?"

This time Hawks did not pause. "Because I am much closer than you think—we all are—and we have two fighters from the *Thunder* covering you at this very moment. We could have taken you out at any time, but we didn't. We need contact, not hatred and distrust and suspicion of one another. That's Master System's game. Still, if you say no, we will let you go and try to make a deal if the channel is still open, although we obviously can't stick around here too long."

She took a deep breath as Star Eagle brought up the power on one of the fighters so that it would show clearly on her sensors. Now she knew that the *Thunder* could send an unmanned fighter to follow her ship anywhere. She would have no way of knowing that the *Thunder*'s fighters, though fast and lethal and very versatile, had no interstellar capability whatsoever, that they were designed only to act as a screen and outer defense for the big ship.

"All right," she said at last. "Savaphoong said there was a guy named Nagy he knew and trusted. We'll take him."

Hawks sighed. "I wish you could, but he died of injuries sustained in the battle against the first Val. He destroyed it, but it got him."

"Send me," Warlock said. "I can take care of myself in that kind of situation."

I bet you could, Hawks thought. He was playing this by ear, really. Sabatini would be a safe choice, considering his attributes, but while he was more than capable of dealing with these people, he was hardly the sort of personality to deal with Savaphoong.

"I could go," China suggested. "What threat could a blind girl be to them, and I can talk with the likes of Savaphoong. He sounds like a primitive-wilderness version of my father."

"No, even if Star Eagle would allow it, which I doubt, you would be particularly vulnerable to the rougher elements out there and unable to defend yourself. Other than myself, I can think of only one person well qualified for this—perhaps better qualified than I. And while he's never seen Savaphoong, Savaphoong's most certainly seen him."

"I knew it, Chief." Raven sighed. "You ain't never gonna forgive me for that Mississippi River trick. Still," he reflected, "I wonder if the old boy got away with any cigars?"

Hawks did not speak again until Raven was actually down and *Lightning*, piloted by Warlock and Chow Dai, had pulled away.

"Star Eagle tells me that the locator is functioning well," he told the others. "I want *Lightning* to follow at near-maximum distance. Do not enter an off-the-chart location. Understand?"

"Yes, Captain," Chow Dai replied. "You do not want us to actually find them, just find out where they are."

"Good girl. You haven't had much to do up to now, but all of a sudden you are our lead and we are depending on you. When the locator stops moving for longer than a fuel stop, send a message back up the line. *Pirate One*, you will then close and rendezvous with *Lightning* when you think it's safe. We will monitor you from one chart position to the rear until we're certain that they are actually where they intend to go. Now we only have to hope they don't give Raven a hypno he can't beat. He knows about the transponder in the murylium ore, and we can't get that out of his head now."

Now aboard the freebooter ship, Raven was able with a little fiddling to find their intercom frequency. He was delighted at the start to hear only female voices aboard, although he was also suspicious of that. These kind of people, living out here like this—who knew how kinky they might have gotten? Love between brave warriors of his own nation was not unheard of, but his people's culture kept it well within bounds and mostly out of sight. Without a real culture of their own, well, he couldn't see himself out here in the midst of nowhere for life with just three guys and no girls unless the guys would do just fine.

But the situation was worse than he thought. When two of the women removed their bulky suits, he found himself staring. One of them had webbed, clawed fingers and flat, long, webbed feet and no hair, only blue-green scales. She also didn't have much of a nose, and she seemed to have two sets of eyelids, one transparent, that didn't blink in unison; and those two funny-looking holes on the side might be ears or might not. When this woman turned, he saw what looked like a set of small fins running down the back of her head and neck to culminate in a fairly large one growing out of her backbone. Great figure for the most part—but no breasts at all. He wondered if she laid eggs.

The other woman was stretching out a long, thick tail that came straight out of her backbone. It explained why she walked oddly—that and the fact that her enormously thick and muscular legs tapered down to huge clawed feet. Her arms, too, were similarly built, ending in large clawed hands that looked able to crush rock. Her gray skin was smooth but leathery, and she, too, did not have any hair. She did have breasts—very small and very firm—with the longest nipples he'd ever seen. Her head was large but in correct proportion to the body, and at least looked human, despite a nose so flat that its tiny flaps moved back and forth as she breathed. She saw him looking at her and grinned, which removed all sense of humanity from her appearance. He'd never seen anyone with teeth like that except mountain lions.

Colonials! He was finally getting his first look at colonials, and although he had thought he was prepared for them, he now realized he hadn't been at all. Instantly he understood what Nagy had meant by the "ultimate price." To become one of them, like that . . . forever, because one full shot through was all a person could take. These, however, had been born that way. He was the monster to them. Except for Sabatini or whatever it was, who got what it needed instantly, one could be changed into one of them but still be oneself inside. How would he feel waking up like one of them, only with his current behavior and standards and mindset? *They* were human, inside and out. *He* would become a monster to himself.

Was this what Nagy had to face? he asked himself. *Was he born and raised happily as one of them and then forced by circumstance or duty to become a monster—an Earth-human?* He wondered how far devotion to duty and mission should go, and he realized the answer. That was what Nagy had been talking about.

"I'm too dried out," the scaly woman said in a very high-pitched but still human tone. "Those suits damn near kill me. I got to get into some water for a soak." The accent, too, was odd, but he could understand her. It was very convenient to one like him that almost everyone in space had to speak both English and Russian. Hawks had told him that it was because those two nations had been first into space and in ancient times convention dictated international means of travel used the language of the first. He did not speak Russian, but thanks to North American Center, his English was just fine.

"I'm sorry for staring at you," he said sincerely. "I'm pretty new at this game, and the only folks I've met out here so far have been my own kind. I'll get used to it. I got used to white men; I can get used to most anything."

She looked surprised. "There are truly white men on your world? An albino race?" Her accent was clipped and very distinctive, but not possible to place. After eight-hundred-plus years and differently shaped mouths and tongues, the accents out here were probably unique anyway, he guessed.

He chuckled. "No, just a figure of speech. They just would never stand for callin' themselves pinkmen. I'm Raven, by the way."

"I am Butar Killomen," she responded. "And that is Takya Mudabur. You have just one name, Mister Raven?"

"Not Mister—just Raven. If I gave you my full and true name in my native tongue, you'd break your jaw trying to repeat it." At that moment the engines kicked into action and the whole thing sounded like *Lightning* had after it had been cannibalized and in a fight. The creaks and groans were not at all reassuring. "People are people as far as this business is concerned. You sure this thing can get us there in one piece?"

"It is very old, but sound. You get used to it after a while."

A third woman came down the ladder as the scaled woman went into a compartment. If the first two lacked hair, it had all wound up on the third one. She looked like somebody wearing a lion suit, Raven thought, except that the mane stuck out all over the place and even the hands were covered with thick orange-and-yellow fur. Her walk was catlike but not extraordinary, although he would have expected it to be. Her feet and even her hands, while they had fingers and opposable thumbs, looked more like paws than hands, and she had six small breasts in two even rows down her middle. Her face, too, was covered in fur, out of which peered two jet-black eyes, a broad nose covered with fine, short hair, and a seemingly lipless mouth. "I am Dura Panoshka," she said in a heavy guttural accent, her speech sounding more like a growl. "You will come with me to meet the captain." He didn't know what to expect when he reached the bridge and saw the captain of a crew like this, but he resolved he would no longer be surprised.

He was wrong again, as usual.

8. RECONNAISSANCE MISSION

"FIRST YOU WILL STRIP OFF ALL YOUR CLOTHING," Lion Girl ordered, "so that we may scan your clothes and space suit. If we find anything suspicious there, they—and you—will go one way while we go another."

She took his reluctance for modesty. "Do not think you are God's gift to women or something. No one will care here."

The truth was, he was embarrassed, but not for the reason she thought. Fact was, it was going to be painfully obvious that none of these women turned him on in the least. None, anyway, until he met the captain, and she presented other difficulties.

The woman in the captain's chair looked exotically Earth-human, and she was built like a sex bomb if he'd ever seen one. Gorgeous, sexy, sensual, perfectly proportioned—you name it and she had it. Her hair was short in a pageboy style with bangs in front that only heightened the beauty of her features. In fact, she'd be a real male fantasy if she hadn't been just ninety centimeters tall.

When he looked closely he saw other, less human, differences. Her dark eyes looked human, but when she moved her head so they caught a light, they shone like cat's eyes, and her ears were oddly shaped, almost shell-like with a point at the upper end. There were also two small protuberances, like tiny ball-shaped horns, barely visible in her hair. Her complexion seemed extremely pale, yet one could catch hints of almost every color of the rainbow if one stared long enough. The fact that she was also smoking a cigar that seemed almost a third as big as she was didn't help matters any, but it certainly attracted Raven's interest.

She looked very young, but Raven suspected that was just the look of her race. Such a tiny, frail creature did not get to be captain over three large colonial women and a ship like this without being the smartest, as well as the most capable and experienced, of the crew.

She sat, perfectly nude, on a normal-size command chair adapted to her with the addition of a smaller form-fitted insert, pillow, and underblanket. She looked so natural and unselfconscious that he suspected that nudity was the norm for her and perhaps for her people. That was interesting, too.

"I am Ikira Sukotae," she said in the voice that had addressed the *Thunder* over the communications line. She spoke English with the same sort of accentless machine-learned English as China and the Chows used. "Welcome aboard the *Kaotan*, which means in English the *Wild Doe*." Her tone told him that he wasn't very welcome at all.

He sighed. "Look, you didn't want me here and I was volunteered to come, so we're even. I know it's kinda tense and it's irrational of me, but to be perfectly honest I lust after one of your cigars."

And she laughed. A big, throaty laugh, incongruous from such a small creature. She gestured to a small case near her right hand. "Go ahead, take one. Even though I'm the captain I'd have a mutiny if I smoked off the bridge or around those three. We'll be punching for several hours yet, which might give us time to really stink up this joint."

The ice was broken.

"So you and your big ship and your dozen or so people are going to overthrow Master System, huh? Big dreams."

"Yup," he admitted, enjoying his first real cigar since Halinachi. "Real impossible, ain't it? I mean, it's no more likely than somebody like you becoming captain of a big freebooter spaceship."

She was taken aback for a moment. "You might have something there. But this—such as it is—is just the result of hard work and strong will and some very lucky breaks. You have all that, but that's not enough against the whole damned system. This is an enemy with the power of the ancient gods, countless minions to do its bidding, and whom you can't even see, feel, or face directly."

"But this god has a weak spot. It's tried, successfully until now, to keep it a secret for nine hundred years, but it's not a secret anymore. That's why we're out here. That's what it's all about."

She was interested. "And you come from the Mother World out here to do your battles?"

He wasn't certain how much to reveal, but he felt this was a good test of what he was supposed to do when they rendezvoused with the others. "We have—sort of a gun," he told her. "The gun will only fire a special bullet made for it, and only five were made—the exact number needed to fire into old Master System's guts. Master System knows about the gun and the bullets, but can't stop them from being there and maybe being used. The only thing it could do was to take those bullets and scatter them out into the galaxy, putting them into the hands of people important enough to protect them but ignorant of what they really were. We think we have the gun—in a sense, anyway— and we know where four of the five bullets are. We are not alone in this—very powerful enemies of Master System instigated this whole thing. We mean to beg, borrow, steal, or in any other way get those bullets, and track down the fifth, load up our gun, and blow the damned thing's brains out."

She nodded, listening intently, then asked an unexpected question. "Why do you do that? Slip in and out of bad grammar and ignorant expressions into excellent educated English with words like 'instigated'."

He shrugged. "My natural self is the coarse one, but I adjust to the company I'm keeping. That's experience."

"Uh huh. Somehow I think you've got more education alone than the sum total of all the people I ever met. What was your job, Raven—before all this, I mean?"

"Field agent. Security for North American Center, if you know where that is."

She shook her head. "I have no idea, but I understand the job and the terms. You are probably a very dangerous man under all that, Raven. I will have to keep that in mind."

"We're all dangerous, Captain. All hunted, driven people are dangerous. You should know that. We're just dangerous in different ways. We got one guy who's the human equivalent of Master System and about as scary. We got a delicate little blind girl who could redesign Master System in her head. And we got one woman, born low and in primitive ignorance, brutalized all her life, tattooed all over and her tongue torn out, who maybe don't understand a word of what we're sayin', but don't let her get the idea you're our enemy. Me, I got a lovely lady partner with wonderful diction when she wants to use it and a fine intellect who's goin' nuts 'cause she hasn't killed nobody in months. And that's only the half of us. I guess we're dangerous all right, but the whole question is, dangerous to who? I think you ought'a know. You're still here, a survivor, with a ship and whatever freedom that brings."

"And you're curious as to how all this ship and crew came about, I expect. I guess you noticed you're the only man aboard."

"It was kinda obvious."

"I never thought of my world as particularly rough or nasty, but compared to most I've seen since it is. Real mild climate over most of it, but it's rich and full of predators and game. It was said we were created small because big people could dominate and ruin the system while ones like us would keep it—and us—stable. It's pretty hard to develop much when every day you have to go out and get what you need in a big world where everything's either out to get you or might trample you without even noticing. Very few people grow old there, so the few that do are venerated as leaders because they are tougher and smarter than the rest just by doing it. To make sure we survive, the men —about a head taller than me—are built like rocks and solid muscle. They're built to be hunters and gatherers and warriors, but they still die young. The women are basically breeders. We can't help it—it's chemical. Just get close to a man and we're in the bushes with 'em. We're breeding kids constantly just to keep up. No muscles, no speed, no weight—we're pretty defenseless and dependent on the men for food and protection. We have some defenses, but no offense, you might say."

He nodded, thinking of China. She'd understand perfectly, only she didn't even have defenses—unless one counted Star Eagle, who was, indeed, formidable. "Defenses?" he prompted.

She nodded. "The things to stay alive so you keep breeding. It fades bit by bit when you can't breed any more. I can remain so still that the keenest ears could not hear me. I can mask any scent by secreting odors that match my surroundings. Right now that'd be cigar smoke, so I won't demonstrate. My hearing has five or six times the range of any other race I have known, and while my daylight vision is weak I can see in almost pure darkness and into the heat ranges where I have found most others cannot. This is because, as a race, we dwell mostly underground. And, almost at will, I can do *this*."

He watched, still thinking about the rest. She could see the infrared spectrum, and hear perhaps better than a dog or even a mouse. But what was most remarkable was what she was demonstrating now. It was *fast*, too, amazingly so. She was sitting on a red blanket, her arms resting on a gray seat, and, incredibly, her skin faded into the tones of the blanket—even the weave—while her arms adjusted for the gray of the chair and even the gaps in between. She was hardly invisible, particularly when you knew she was there, but he bet she could become as good as invisible in her native element.

"I can also mimic almost everyone or anything I have heard before," she told him in a very male voice that was almost exactly like his own. "That way I can, if still discovered or pinned down too long, imitate something bigger and nastier than whatever is hunting me." She shifted back to the hard female voice she'd been using, and Raven now understood that it was a deliberate *persona*, to make her sound and therefore seem bigger than she really was. It was also clear why, coming from a mild climate, nakedness was normal; any clothing would nullify most of the coloration defense and perhaps have a more distinctive scent as well.

"Nothing offensive, as you see," she noted. "Oh, I've killed flies and bugs, but I haven't even the arm strength for spears or bows, let alone lifting and aiming a common pistol. But *here*, in this chair, on this ship, with that interface there and the weapons under my control, I could destroy a city." She said that almost as if she really wanted to, and suddenly he wasn't sure if he was talking to someone like China or a miniature Manka Warlock. A little of both, he decided.

"But you didn't grow up in a hunter-gatherer society any more than I did," Raven guessed. "You would never even have dreamed that any of this existed if you did."

"In a way, you're right. I was no nobility, but I had the right bloodlines, and as a child I think I was more curious and inquisitive than girls were supposed to be. The Elders decided that my mind could handle the wonders and mysteries of a Center, and I was selected while still very young to go there. I didn't have a choice. Oh, I was still breeding stock—I was just supposed to breed better, smarter candidates for the Center in the future. They didn't educate us —they kept us amused in the lap of luxury like permanent spoiled children. We were all smarter than they thought girls could be, though, so we were able to do some learning on our own. Even if you got caught cold at some terminal with a lecture and display on some complicated subject, all you had to do was act dumb and cute and ignorant and they never caught on or cared. Why they didn't became real clear after a while. When you reached puberty they ran you through a mindprinter, and you just weren't curious or inquisitive anymore. Then you went into the harem, where the men of the Elect visited, and soon you were knee-deep in babies, locked in for thirty or more years of that, and when you couldn't produce any more you just kept helping run the place until you fell apart or died."

"A great waste, although I can see the computer logic of the culture. But it didn't happen to you."

"No. I found out early what the situation was, and I was lucky enough to bump into a boy a bit older than me and just beginning to have the feelings, if you know what I mean. He was the son of a big man at Center—chief deputy administrator, in fact—and about as spoiled and arrogant as anyone could imagine. But I played to his urges and his ego and his arrogance for all I was worth, and he got to thinking of me as his. Just the idea that *his* girl would be thrown into a communal harem made him boil, and he was in the right spot to do something about it. I admit I lowered myself as far as I could go—no matter what his wish, I granted it, no matter what his fantasy, I played to it. And when my time came, he got me exempted. Several of the big shots had small private harems. Exclusivity is a perk of the powerful. He was in the tough time for him, when his education was intensive and would determine his place in the future, so he needed a servant and housekeeper and somebody to screw when he needed to. He didn't need babies yet, so he got me a drug that kept me wanting it all the time but prevented conception. And while he was out all day, I'd use his terminals and his books and his lessons to give myself a real education. Hell, he didn't even know I could *read*, and if he had it would've been the mindprinter in a minute, but it never even entered his head."

"There are a lot of cultures like that even on Earth," Raven told her, "and many more that differ only by degrees. Usually it disappears at the Center level, or becomes tolerable, but the fact that we still have 'harem' in the languages says it all, I guess."

In fact, however, Ikira had seen this as the pinnacle of existence because, for her, there was nowhere else to go but down. Then about a year and a half into this existence, her "husband" had taken her with him on what was something of a trade mission. Like the vast bulk of colonial worlds, her planet's Centers required a small but dependable supply of murylium for their own needs, mostly research and medical. Needless to say, one did not get this from Master System but in spite of it, and that was where freebooter trade came in. Her world had no spaceports and only a few skimmers for Center use, but freebooters could —and did— land in the damndest places. What the freebooters wanted was some sort of access to the state-of-the-art technology that the Centers represented, including, quite often, the working out of practical problems that were beyond the capabilities of their own computers. They traded murylium for these services.

Most Centers, however, were outfitted identically; only in the few whose very smart and frustrated chief administrators worked clandestinely was there any competitive edge. To keep freebooters from going off to another Center or even another world meant treating them like royalty and anticipating their needs. The chief deputy had decided that his favorite son was ready to experience the real travails of having to deal with this sort of person, and sonny boy never went anywhere without his concubine.

To Ikira, it was an experience that turned her entire world view upside down and inside out. She had known there were other worlds and other forms of human beings, but nothing had prepared her for the reality.

There were three of them, and two were women. First of all, they were *enormous*, giants compared to even the largest men of her own race and world. Second, while they were a bit rough and coarse and not really all that pretty, they looked very much the way Ikira's own race looked except for the size, and they had strong personalities that were in no way deferential to the man with them. In fact, it soon became clear that one of the women was the captain, and that the *man* worked for *her*. To Ikira, seeing her own men, arrogant big shots, acting not merely civil but downright servile to these women whose services they needed more than the women needed them was another revelation.

With a lot of guts, considering what might have happened had she been discovered by her own, she sneaked away one day and approached the female freebooter captain privately. Captain Smokevski was more than touched by Ikira's plight and impressed with her intelligence and nerve. The captain was none too pleased with the culture she was doing business with, but that Center had a genius with an uncannily accurate system for locating new murylium deposits. Now, at last, she had a way of thumbing her nose at this sexist society. This time Ikira's diminutive size and defense skills came in very handy, and Smokevski managed to smuggle the tiny woman onto the shuttle at take-off. Ikira was in space and free of her culture.

Weightlessness was even more of a wonder to her. She could almost fly, and she could move and even lift things that the strongest male of her own race couldn't budge. It took months to hunt down a small enough pressure suit, but once she had it she could do maintenance in places too small for others to reach, and her long, tiny fingers and exceptional sight and hearing made her a whiz at doing jury-rigged repairs on equipment that often had to be kept going with nothing but a prayer. She was interested in virtually everything and learned all she could. Of equal import to her future, she found that she quickly lost the sexual compulsions she had lived with since puberty. In her face, the arousal was strictly chemical, and without males of her own kind around, she simply did not feel the urge. Not that she was sexless, but she was in now in total control.

It was a story of both liberation and compensation. Her size a major liability, she simply worked six times harder and did everything six times better. She learned how to think on her feet and be taken as an equal in exotic and gigantic foreign locales. She began to make her own deals and, in one of the apparently not uncommon fights over a murylium claim that wound up in ship-to-ship combat, she had taken over for a captain who'd lost her guts—and won. She parlayed her reputation and profits from that into an ancient, creaking hulk that she redesigned and restored herself, with help from the crew of that fighting ship who'd left their captain, as well, and it became the *Kaotan*. The other two were Dura Panoshka, the Lion Girl, and Butar Killomen, who'd met Raven when he had boarded. Takya had joined later; she'd had trouble keeping jobs or berths because of her need for regular immersions to keep her skin from drying out. But there were very few freebooters

who could deal with the water races, and Ikira had seen the
potential for information there that was virtually untapped.
Takya had been both useful and dependable, and worth the
extra weight and expense of a true water-based rather than
chemical bath system and all the problems it entailed.

And, as far as they knew, all four were the only ones of
their races in space. It was a special bond, for each could
understand the other's sense of alienation when with others
of the more common races.

"I had hopes, one day, of becoming so powerful that I
could one day return home and break that insidious system,
but I'm old enough now to know that even if I gained such
power and tried, it is probably easier to break Master System than to change a culture, particularly one that is partly
based on biology."

"The only way there's a shot is to break the big system," Raven told her. "Then you start by introducing technology on a wide scale so that your people become masters
of the planet and not just inhabitants. Then that technology
can be used to alter the biology that limits things."

Am I really saying this? he thought suddenly. *I think I
just told her to turn her people into white men and go rape
their world!*

It was only a two-and-a-half-day trip to the hideout. In
that time Raven grew to like the tiny captain, but he found
it far more difficult to get to know the other three. Of
them, only Butar Killomen even seemed curious enough to
talk to him, and none were as secure as their captain and
willing to talk about themselves.

The refugee fleet was still cautious; passwords were required not just from the ship and captain but from each of
the other crew members in turn before the sensors and au-

tomatic guns of the other ships were turned off. Only then
did Ikira relax and put the graphics on the screen for him to
see what was there.

"Most are light freighters built less for cargo capacity
than speed and weapons ability," she told him. "For the
amount of murylium you generally find out here in months
of trying beyond your own needs you don't need a very big
ship, but if you can't outrun and outgun the competition
you might lose out to somebody who found none at all.
That's *Espiritu Luzon* in the center—Savaphoong's ship. It
doesn't look like much on the outside because it's designed
to alter itself to different common silhouettes on sensors
out here. It's a neat and expensive defense. Inside, I'm
told, it's a luxury yacht with all the comforts of Halinachi
in miniature."

He nodded. It figured that somebody like Savaphoong
would find a way to take his world with him.

"The others are *San Cristobal, Novovladivostok, Chunhoifan, Indrus, Bahakatan*, and *Sisu Moduru*. I know them
all from the past. I shot it out with *San Cristobal*'s skipper
a few years back. I was glad to see he got it back in running condition. Truth was, I'd lost track of most of them
until we crossed paths at the fallback positions." She
paused for a moment. "I had hoped that we might have
seen a couple more before we had to run here."

There was no official leader—these were proud and independent people—but Savaphoong certainly had the
commanding voice among them, and few would challenge
him. His contacts might well be valid, including many on
colonial worlds, and he was the best prepared for an under-
taking like this.

"Can you plug me in to Savaphoong's ship?" Raven

asked. "We might as well break the news right off. I think anything I have to say should be said to him first before one of your trigger-happy friends takes to blasting us just on general principles."

Fernando Savaphoong was right up on his bridge for the arrival of the *Kaotan*. He was happy to hear of the load they had aboard and a bit less thrilled to hear of their passenger, but he agreed to talk.

"Sir, my name's Raven and I was at your place with Arnold Nagy not too long ago."

Savaphoong remembered quite a lot about Raven, including things he shouldn't have known.

Quickly, Raven filled the other in on what had happened so far—the death of Arnold Nagy, and at least as much of their purpose and goals as he'd given Ikira. Savaphoong listened patiently, then noted, "I can see why you precipitated all the action. Very well, Señor Raven, what do you think you are going to do now?"

"That's not the question. I'm stuck here unless some deal is made or I'm dropped at an agreed pickup point and you know it. It seems to me the question is what are *you* going to do? The cozy relationship between the freebooters and Master System is gone. Every freebooter is a fugitive now, because they'll try every one they find until they find us. Those caught with no other value will either be disposed of or put through the mill and changed into a worshipful supporter of the System. Face it—in a few days, a few weeks at most, you won't even be able to risk contacting or trusting ships and people you've known for years. We are the only ones you can ever fully feel comfortable around. We want to make a deal. We need you, and I think you need us. Put me on to all of them and I'll give it straight."

It took about an hour of radio diplomacy on Sava-phoong's part to get the others calmed down enough to listen, and when they did that's all they agreed to do—listen.

Once more Raven introduced himself and described the situation. "You have no place else to go, no other life that has any profit or future," he told them. "You cannot trust anyone, not here right now. You can't go back to your old free-lancing deals with the colonial worlds without knowing that Master System and its forces will be out gunning for you. You might make it several times, maybe last a year or two, but eventually you and Master System will have a meeting because there are only so many colonial worlds."

"We could go off the charts, into regions even Master System hasn't gone," someone suggested. "We can start over again and build ourselves back up with or without colonial support."

"Wishful thinking and you know it, if you stop and think a minute," Raven retorted. "It would be rougher than you know, and all guesswork until you formed your own charts. Probably at least half of you would run dry somewhere in a hole like this one and never be heard of again. The other half—well, you might scrimp by, but there'll be no illegal shipyards, no big transmuters, no access to technology and supercomputing. Many of you are one of a kind out here, and when you die out, that's it. Some of you might have enough numbers to make a really tiny colony somewhere on some grubby rock, if you can find one that'll support human life and if you can survive the wilderness there. That'll go until your ships break down for lack of repair or out of sheer ignorance by your children and grandchildren, condemning them to be new colonials and devolve into savagery and primitivism. You have no future and very short lives now, unless you team up with us."

"I ain't sure how much future I got teamin' up with the likes of you," someone else commented. "You know how many people they killed so far because of you? And that's only the beginning. And the colonial worlds depend on us for murylium to keep a jump ahead of Master System. You come out here, with no space experience, and in a real short time you destroy a whole way of life."

Raven grinned. "You mean we came out and in no time flat we destroyed your neat little system? Eleven people, nine of 'em space rookies, and they destroy your whole system? Well, then, maybe we *can* knock over the big system, huh?"

"If you're tryin' to be funny, I got some real slow ways for you to die," someone said.

"No! Let him go on!" another urged. "He's making some sense here."

That was encouraging. "We didn't destroy your system, we just gave you what you always said was most dear— liberation. You can get mad and yell and scream, but any of you with any sense out there will have to realize that the freebooters were as much a colonial unit as any of the worlds you served under Master System's thumb as long as you were useful to it and easily thrown away when no longer needed. You were its unlisted colony, and you provided a service. We ended that. If you want it back, I'm sure you can just trot back to Master System, let its machines see how nice and loyal you are, and it'll stick you back in business with no illusions. You either do that or you join the rebellion and instead of taking shots at each other you can take shots at Master System. Colonial loyalists allowed to play with antique spaceships—or freedom-fighting rebels. That's your real choice, and your only one. If you can't see that, you're blind or crazy and no good to us anyway. If you can and want to go back to playing footsie with Master System, we sure as hell don't want you. But if you want real freedom, if you want to win, we need you bad."

After all the nasty carping on the channel, the silence was almost eerie. Finally a man's low, gruff voice spoke. "If I really thought we had any chance of winning, I'd throw in, but I just can't believe it."

"That's all I can offer, but it's more than you think—a chance," Raven told him. "There are no guarantees and I can virtually promise that many will die in this, or worse. We might have to—pay the ultimate price. We might have to transmute ourselves, or sacrifice ourselves for others. I intend to minimize that last possibility when it comes to myself, but I recognize it. And we are going to have to work in teams to get it done rather than go strictly lone wolf, since any major failure has the potential to compromise all of us. Now, that's a heady brew for the likes of freebooters, but that's the way it is."

"Too steep," someone commented. "I'd rather chase and run from the bastards."

"Ah, but you haven't heard the important part," Raven responded. "You don't do this for nothing. You do this for a payoff—and a big one. You see, once you're in, you're *in*. I put this in terms of bullets and a big gun, but that's not really right. See, this bullet don't kill Master System, it just makes it into what it was at the start—a nice, obedient machine that takes orders. Takes orders from whoever gets it. Now, you think about that. Whoever does this all the way gets to rule Master System the way Master System rules most everybody else. The power it has, and all the loyalty it has, and all that it knows and can do, passes up to others—human beings. If you're in, you're in all the way. Do your job, don't screw up or get killed, and you name your own price and I mean it. *Anything you want!* Your own world, your own fleet of big ships, all just the way you might have dared dream it could be. It's the magic totem for real, or whatever your own legends call it. You help us, you last it out, and you get one wish for anything that's within Master System's power—and you get Master System off your back, too."

That was something they could understand, and it was staggering.

"I must tell you that I am favorably inclined to go their way," Savaphoong's voice came to them. "I can exist for the rest of my life without them, I am fairly certain, and at minimal risk—I have made provisions for this sort of eventuality. Still, if there is no risk, there is no gain, and if I refuse now and then they do it, I will have no profit, no share in the rewards. If they fail, then I lose it all including what might have been, and I admit this. But if they succeed—and I know the background of one or two and would not count them out—then I want my share of godhood."

There was a long period of silence, then suddenly everybody seemed to try to talk at once, making any rational communication impossible. There was nothing to do but wait for it to die down.

Finally Raven was able to make himself heard again.

"Now, this shouldn't be anything hasty. Each ship should get off for a while and discuss it, captains and crew. I want no single individual in on this who doesn't want to be there. I am absolutely certain we can combine crews and ships—those who say yes, those who say no. This is the only shot you get, though. If you're out, you're out. If you're in, you will be in all the way or we will eliminate you without a second thought. Only those who come with me will get the details and the planning. There is nothing personal for those who refuse, but any who fail to take our offer now will be treated later as our enemy. We'll have to do it that way."

"I don't like it," a woman's voice said. "We have only *his* word that this shit even exists. We have no proof that he's spinning more than a fairy tale, a pipe dream, to lure us into their service permanently and then get rid of us when we've served our purpose. who the hell are they who made this discovery? They come here from the Mother World and maybe *they* believe it, but who's to say it's true? All we're doing is becoming their damned servants. How come this big secret gets kept for nine hundred-plus years and suddenly falls into the hands of a bunch of yokels?"

"You may be right, Meg," Savaphoong agreed, "but, as I say, I know some of these people. Their scientific brain is perhaps the smartest human being alive, and he has all his data. *He* believes it. Others, like friend Raven here, are Center people, security people who had the best that the system can offer and paths to power. They gave it up, and they are not *all* mad. The best example is Master System itself, which is so outraged and so panicky that it has mobilized all its resources to find and get these people. You think Master System would collapse the covenant just to track down pirates, even very slick ones? What are they to its domains? What are the pirates of the *Thunder* in the larger scheme of things? What is one ship full of murylium to Master System? It is pulling out all its stops, abandoning all its conventions, to go after a tiny band of mere human beings. Oh, yes, my friends—what they say is true. They know the way to fry the brains of Master System, even if they now lack the means."

The logic was compelling to most of them, but so was the corollary. "What's to keep *us* from doing it, then, without *them*? We got mindprinters here, and hypnoscans, and all the rest, and we got this Raven. Why throw in with them at all?"

Raven was prepared for that one. His rehearsal with Ikira was paying big dividends. "Simple," he told them. "I can tell you what we're after, but not how to use them. Just having them ain't enough. What good is having bullets and guns if you don't have a target? I don't know where Master System *is*, or what it looks like, or anything else. Do you?"

"Then we're no worse off than you," somebody pointed out.

"Oh, but you are. We are an odd group, but we were carefully picked. When we get what we're looking for, at least one of us will know where and how to use it. I'm not certain how—whether it's a conditional hypno or deep mindprint or something else—but it's there. You can trust us, or Master System—I leave it to you whether you want to trust the word of a machine or of human beings. Nothing whatever, though, can reveal the target and the means of loading the gun until we have the bullets. That way, it's safe for all of us."

"You talk like you all are working for somebody," noted the suspicious lady. "Who?"

Raven smiled, although they couldn't see it. "Somebody with a lot of knowledge, but still somebody who can't get these things themselves—or use 'em. I don't know who or what it is, and I'm not the least bit concerned with them except for the help they give us until we have all that we seek. Then we might have, well, a difference of opinion. I'm not concerned. We will have what is needed. The bargaining chips will be all ours, and, just as importantly, if we are tough enough and smart enough and clever enough to do what no one else has ever even dreamed of doing, then we can deal with anyone who might try to take it away from us. If we cannot, then we don't deserve the rewards."

"I believe, my friends, that all that can be said on this has been said," Savaphoong put in. "I suggest we now take Raven's advice and discuss it among our own people. We are not *that* pressed for a decision as monumental as this one. Let us sleep on it. It is fourteen twenty-two. At twenty-four hundred, in a bit less than ten hours, we will again take this up, and at that time we will vote and make up our minds. This is reasonable, yes?"

"All right with me." Raven sighed. "I'm almost gettin' used to boredom."

Ikira Sukotae had been back with her crew for quite a while, leaving Raven alone on the bridge with his thoughts. *All this potential*, he couldn't help thinking. *It's almost like magic how it all falls together. I wonder how many will come?* He knew better than to believe they all would. Savaphoong, the opportunist, was a sure bet if only because he figured in the end to be one of the ones giving *all* the orders, not just one wish as some kind of payoff. He would have to be watched and, perhaps, eventually controlled or dealt with more severely, but until then he would be invaluable. He and Clayben were worlds apart in knowledge and genius, but, deep down, they were two of a kind.

Who would have thought it? he mused, still not quite believing how far they had already come. *Raven, born in a small village by a quiet river in the high mountains, raised up first to Security, and with all the cynicism of that job and the knowledge of what was true and real in the universe that bred such cynicism—Raven, the revolutionary, the overthrower of worlds. Quite a leap for Spotted Horse's little boy, running alongside the warriors as they went to the hunt and dreaming brave deeds.* He sighed. That was a long time ago; another life, really, and he'd long ago buried that little kid and his comfortable dreams of honor and glory.

His honor had been tossed aside the moment he'd learned that the whole thing was a lie, that they were ruled not by a creator spirit but by some big damned machine. It had made the concept of glory meaningless, as well, for what was the glory in dying not for one's people but for the purpose of a museum exhibit for a master machine that didn't even give a damn about the exhibit?

Center's wonders had delighted him, but at first the people there had disgusted him. Corrupt, selfish, as contemptuous of their own people and their customs and ways as they were of the system they served. There really hadn't been much choice; you either became like them or you went back home and lived a lie. It had been easy to be a cynic.

Yet now he began to wonder if that little boy was truly as dead as he had thought. He was still no visionary, no ambitious revolutionary with a grand dream, but he was alive again, alive as he had only felt in the past when he was back home, back in the mountains and the plains, the field that was a part of him. He hadn't really thought like this in many years, except for brief times alone camped out on the prairies with just his horse and a small fire and the looming shapes of the purple snow-clad mountains in the distance—and those moments had been very brief indeed.

Somehow it seemed ironic that he should find that little boy way out here, far from his people and his beloved north country, far from anything he held to be important and dear. *Were you there all the time, boy, or did I imagine your return?*

Ikira returned to the bridge, breaking his reverie, and he nodded to her. "You made your own decision yet?" he asked. "It's almost time."

"We talked it over, yeah," she told him. "It wasn't easy, you know. It's not easy for any of us."

"And?"

"We got more colonial experience than any two of these other ships put together. We figured your odds, and we figured ours on our own out here under new conditions. None of us really have any homes or lives except this ship, but we have dreams. We're in, Raven."

He clapped his hands together and grinned. "All *right*! Now let's see what the score is. Plug me in and we'll get goin' on this."

The vote was by no means unanimous, but it was better than he had thought at the start. In addition to Sava-phoong's *Espiritu Luzon*, which, Raven suspected, had only one vote that counted and was thus easy to convince, *San Cristobal*, *Chunhoifan*, *Indrus*, and *Bahakatan* were in, with the exception of some crewmember dissidents who would leave. The majority of *Novovladivostok* and *Sisu Moduru*, including their owner-captains, decided against—including both the woman with grave doubts and the tough-sounding man with the questions. Some of their crew, however, also disagreed, and a swap was arranged.

That added, in one swoop five experienced pilots, ships, and crews to the pirate fleet, along with numerous crew members. Those who would not or could not trust Raven and his company transferred to the two ships that had voted against. The few on board the two holdouts who wanted in transferred to the ships of their choice, at least as a temporary measure. Maintenance robots on *Kaotan* managed to carve up portions of raw murylium ore from the hold and mount them on skids and shift those portions to the *Novovladivostok* and the *Sisu Moduru*.

"Then let's get this show on the road," Raven suggested. He felt like an admiral and he liked the power. "Captain, lay in a course for the last system we went through on the charts before switching here. *Thunder* will meet us there."

Ikira looked at him sternly. "You followed us, then. How?"

"We're just slimy, tricky bastards, that's all. Don't worry, this was just to simplify things. We want to move quickly now—it don't pay to keep *Thunder* in one spot too long. Tell the others to follow our course, heading, and speed. It's best we all get together, get to know each other, and get the hell out of this sector."

There was a mixture of anticipation of action and some nervousness among the others joining the fleet.

"I just hope for all our sakes you know what you're doing," Ikira said tensely.

I hope we do, too, thought the little boy running beside the horses of the warriors.

They did not punch for very long. As soon as they arrived in-system they did a scan, and for a moment Raven was worried. Then a ship showed up closing on them. It was *Lightning*, now with Sabatini at the controls and Warlock on the guns; the Chows were on *Pirate One*. Raven had to wonder why the crews had been rearranged.

"Any more coming in?" Sabatini asked.

"We got six out of eight, damn it! What did you want— a miracle?" Raven retorted.

"All right. The Chows are calling in the *Thunder*. Warlock and I are going to check out something suspicious and we'll be back in a few hours. We have the chart position you're moving to anyway, so if we're not back before you get everyone together and get moving, we'll catch up."

Raven frowned. Something suspicious? "Anything we should know about?"

There was a pause. "No. Nothing you should know about."

Ikira used her scanners on *Lightning* as it pulled away and prepared to punch. "That is one fast ship. I have never seen a design like that before."

"It's a custom job. It took on a Val and won, so don't underestimate it. I—" He stopped, then just sat there a moment, thinking, a sad frown descending on him.

We'll be back in a few hours . . .

"Something wrong?"

He shook his head slowly from side to side. "No, nothing wrong." He sighed. "Forget it." But he couldn't forget it, because he now understood the reason for the crew switch; he knew where they were going and what they were going to do and he didn't like it one bit.

The only ones who knew the identities of the ships and crews that had come to their side were the two holdouts, *Novovladivostok* and *Sisu Moduru*. They wouldn't have left yet, most likely; they'd be examining their new stores of murylium and deciding what to do next. Sooner or later one or both would fall into the hands of Master System, perhaps alive and certainly with their records intact. Master System would then know the personalities aboard the *Thunder*'s supplemental force, its ships, numbers, and capabilities.

Both ships were well armed and shielded, but they would be no match for *Lightning*, rebuilt as a killer machine and with Warlock at the armaments controls.

Raven was very glad *Kaotan* had decided to join in. He sighed. At least Warlock would be in a very good mood when he next saw her.

It took about forty minutes for *Thunder* to come in from wherever it had been lurking, and Raven always liked to hear the comments of people who had never seen the likes of a fourteen-kilometer-long spaceship before. It was more like having an asteroid with engines.

"*Thunder* to Raven, how are you doing?" Star Eagle called.

"Just fine, I guess. I have six ships here—including Fernando Savaphoong and his ship—all filled with veteran freebooters and a mixture of colonials, as well. I haven't the slightest idea how many people we're talking about, though."

"The murylium's all been stored or shifted to the aft processors, and with *Lightning* not in, all four bays are available. I don't see any ship that wouldn't fit in there, but with *Pirate One* we still have three more ships than bays. I suggest that three of you will have to use the cargo docking ports and make your way to the bay air-lock stations using pressure suits. Until we get everything organized I would like to move as a unit, acting as a mother. I am scanning the fleet and I am impressed, but I would suggest you all send me your identification codes so I can sort and direct you."

This was accomplished in a fraction of a second.

"I have limited drydock facilities in the bays, although not what we really need. *Kaotan, San Cristobal*, and *Bahakatan*, you could all use some maintenance and refitting. So could you, *Indrus*, but you are in better shape than they are. I suggest *Kaotan* in Bay One, *San Cristobal* in Bay Two, *Bahakatan* in Bay Three, and *Indrus* in Bay Four. *Pirate One*, you dock at Bay Two after *San Cristobal* is inside and the outer hull closed and sealed and walk down with care. *Espiritu Luzon*, do the same with Bay One after *Kaotan* is inside and secured, and *Chunhoifan*, take Bay Three after *Bahakatan* is secured. The bays are not currently pressurized, so wear suits. We will have people to meet you in each and lead you into the ship."

There were some special requests. Because of the artificial gravity in the interior shell there were a couple who needed some kind of rider transport, and Ikira made certain to note that she had at least one amphibian aboard who required water at intervals. It was not easy to gather everyone together; the whole process took more than three hours and a lot of grumbling. Only the fact that some of these reluctant recruits really wanted to see the inside of a ship like the *Thunder* kept things in hand at all. Hawks met the crew of the *Kaotan*, and did not comment on the odd and mostly antique and bulky space suits they wore. He did,

however, make a mental note to himself to have Star Eagle
work on outfitting them better.

"Take everyone into the village and make them as comfortable as we can for now," he told Raven. "I'll stay here
and wait for the people from *Espiritu Luzon.* Don't take off
your suit, though. When I get back I may need you to help
fetch the ones from *Chunhoifan.*"

"Fair enough, Chief. I didn't get much exercise lately
anyway. Ladies, this way, and be prepared for gradually
increasing gravity as we pass through the air-lock se-
quences. We have the interior at about point eight of a gee
to allow for muscle toning and natural activity."

All of them seemed awed by the village interior, and
stared unbelievingly at what felt like a tiny island rather
than a spaceship.

"I'm afraid we're gonna have to double up a lot, or have
some folks sleep outside for a while, depending on the
crowd we get," Raven said apologetically. "I expect we're
gonna wind up with a bunch of folks either livin' in offices
or on the better ships. Ten to one old Savaphoong would
rather commute than stay here."

"I think it is *fantastic!*" Ikira Sukotae told him. "I
couldn't have dreamed that such a thing was possible inside a ship!" The others echoed her sentiments.

"You ought'a seen the place before we fixed it up," the
Crow noted. "It looked like the biggest rolling mausoleum
in history. We still got plenty of room back there, and if we
can take the banging and other construction there should
eventually be room for everybody in this kind of setting.
Once we get your ships repaired and all fixed up, we'll
have to figure a way to give the ones on the outside some
kind of direct access in."

But it was Takya Mudabur, the amphibian, who said what was in back of all the colonial crew's minds. "Our ancestors—might have come on this very ship. This is the origin, the way it began . . ."

He hadn't even considered the historical and cultural impact the *Thunder* might have, but he was secretly glad they hadn't seen in it in its original form. The history of colonial transport might as well remain romantic; let only the original rebel band know how ugly it really was.

Cloud Dancer arrived with another awed and incredulous crew. Star Eagle was landing them in measured order to minimize the confusion and stretch his few greeters as best he could.

San Cristobal had a mixed crew of Earth-humans and colonials including a couple of people that the *Kaotan* crew seemed to know very well, if the emotional greetings were an indication. Its crew of six included two defectors from the ships that had opted out. Captain Maria Santiago was small, brown, and Earth-human; the other two Earth-humans were both men, one large and blond and bearded, the other medium-sized with some of the characteristics of Raven's own people. Two others were the oddest colonials yet. Their torsos and heads were very strange but at least humanoid. Their large bodies stood on four legs; the largest part of the steel-blue torso was under the humanoid part, and the rear rested on what appeared to be short, stubby back legs that almost didn't seem up to the job. The final one was the Rock Monster; if a man could turn to rough stone, develop bumps all over, and have deep, dark recessed eyes and a mouth as wide as the whole face, this was how he might look.

Hawks arrived with Savaphoong and his entourage,

which included a very tough-looking Earth-human man and
two Earth-human women who looked just as tough and
mean. He had also brought his favorite remakes—the air-
headed slaves of Halinachi—but had left them aboard as
he didn't even have space suits for them. The two males
and five females still aboard the *Espiritu Luzon* would be
more a source of embarrassment to the rest than any real
use, anyway.

Raven excused himself and went to fetch the crew of
Chunhoifan as Clayben arrived with those aboard the
Indrus. Captain Ravi Paschittawal was obviously more
provincial in his choice of crews, or he kept it all in the
family. The two men and two women with him, all Earth-
human, were definitely of the same race and culture as
their captain. Hawks knew enough to recognize them as the
same sort of people who ran Delhi Center back home. The
real Indians.

Chunhoifan proved entirely colonial, with Captain Chun
Wo Har a creature who, while humanoid, wore an armor
like exoskeleton that together with his stalked eyes and
long feelers gave him an insect-like appearance. Two
others of his kind accompanied him, both female and,
oddly, looking it in spite of their alien appearance. With
them were two others from one of the ships that remained
behind: Small, rotund humanoids with green skin and mottled complexions, owlish faces, bulging yellow eyes, and
what looked like wings on their backs although it was impossible that ones of their shape and weight could ever
actually fly. Hawks decided that the wings must have another less obvious function, since no colonial would have
anything vestigial.

Finally Clayben, on his second trip, brought in the crew

of *Bahakatan*. Captain Ali Mohammed ben Suda looked Earth-human enough, although his appearance reflected a hard life as did that of his wife, Fatima, who might have been no older than Cloud Dancer but whose medium-length hair was gray. They looked North African or Middle Eastern, and the two Earth-human members of the crew, both huge men, had Han Chinese features very much like those of the Chows and China. One had blue eyes and the other a full reddish-brown beard and hair—*half* Han, most likely.

Hawks and the others had been, they thought, mentally prepared for the sight and smells of colonials, but now they realized that they had been wrong. It would be very difficult sledding before everyone was comfortable here, Hawks thought. He was a bit ashamed of himself for feeling that way and somewhat admiring that Raven had appeared to have no such problems.

It was the last member of the *Bahakatan*'s crew, however, that caused the most consternation and would be hardest to accept. The creature had an exoskeleton and long, flat tail terminating in large finlike appendages, but it walked on four thick legs mounted on circular joints. Although it was a glistening, shiny black, Hawks couldn't help thinking of Mississippi crawfish. Two other sets of appendages were arranged around its head, both tiny in proportion to the body or legs and terminating in ridged pincerlike claws. The head was a set of eight tentacles, long and rubbery and constantly in motion, around two protruding eyes on what seemed to be retractable stalks, and something dark and wet and nasty that might have been a mouth.

This thing was no colonial; this thing had never had a

human ancestor, had never been processed by Master System at all. It had been spawned on a world far different from anything the rest of them there could even imagine.

"I sssee your wooks," the thing said in a very unpleasant simulation of a human voice from inside that pulpy mass beneath the tentacles. "I am ssschief engineer of *Bahakatan*. I am Makkikor. You hafff never ssseen Makkikor before. I can tell."

That was putting it mildly. All of a sudden Hawks felt like hugging the insectival Captain Chun and calling him "brother."

Captain ben Suda was quick to intervene. "The Makkikor are alien to all of us, sir, but they are no less under the great demon's thumb than we. They had the bad luck to be in the way when Master System was expanding its colonial empire and they were simply co-opted into the colonial system by force. Their world is not one any of us would be comfortable on, but it is no less a part of the system than the colonials, and after these centuries it and they have far more in common with us than they should. I was lucky to get him, and you should feel lucky, too. The Makkikor carry around their own natural sort of air supply and are nearly impervious to vacuums and much of the radiation that would be injurious to us. Debo, here, is the best ship's engineer and maintenance crewman imaginable."

Raven stared at the creature and gave a wry chuckle. "Well, Chief, you can't say we ain't startin' off with no one-note crew."

Hawks opened his mouth but couldn't speak. All he could think was, *Welcome to the universe, Walks With the Night Hawks.*

The *Thunder* vibrated, roared, and began to move out into a universe far more complex than even the originals had anticipated.

9. THE VULTURE OF JANIPUR

THE NEXT SEVEN MONTHS WAS A PERIOD OF ADJUST-
ment and personal compromise for all concerned, but
somehow the new crew settled into a group marriage of
convenience, tolerance, and, in some cases, friendship and
mutual respect. The difficulty did not stem only from the
alienness of the colonists, though, but also from the freebooters' starting attitudes toward the original group. It was
clear that the vast majority of newcomers still didn't really
believe that the rebels' scheme could succeed.

Hawks once again demonstrated his leadership skills by
forming a council of captains and treating them with respect. Each captain was still absolute master of his or her
own ship, but each was under the command of what they
had come to consider an admiral—one who commands not
a ship but a fleet. And that one was Hawks.

In fact, the hardest thing for the freebooters to accept
was Star Eagle's existence at all, let alone as an equal captain among them. All their lives had been spent hating machines that could think on their own. No matter how
different they looked, no matter what languages they
thought in or what they liked to eat or how they liked to
live, all of them, even the alien engineer, were living crea-

tures born of other living creatures. To them, Star Eagle
seemed a member of the true alien race, the one they were
fighting, and it was very difficult for them to trust him.

Star Eagle had certainly done his best for them. Maintenance had created more elaborate cargo access ports fitted
with air locks and tubes directly into the ships that had to
be carried outside, and hoped to have real pressurization
throughout the ship as needed, even in the cargo bays
themselves, within another month.

The interior village was still badly in need of work, but
it had been expanded enough and customized enough to
satisfy most of the needs of those on board who required
more than Earth-human conditions. Savaphoong continued
to live on his luxurious yacht with its transmuter producing
luxury goods as needed and human slaves to wait on him
and his subordinates; this arrangement actually made
everyone more comfortable.

Each crew was given an area of the interior shell, along
with working offices in the surrounding middle region, designed as much to their specifications as practicality and
space and data banks allowed. Ikira Sukotae, for example,
actually had a dwelling within a very dark and
grass-covered mound with little or no lighting, although
somehow in there was a miniaturized vaporizer toilet and
running water and much else. Her amphibian crewmember
had a hut with a chamber in which fresh water sufficient to
cover her body was available along with air. The centaur-
oids preferred just a patch of ground with specially designed water supply and waste disposal; they didn't care a
bit for privacy.

The others, even the Rock Man, found that the normal
hut could be configured to their needs. The green owlish

couple, for example, used things much the same as everyone else but slept standing up. So, in fact, did the thick-tailed Buta Killomen and the Rock Man, while Captain Chun and his exoskeletal mates slept wrapped around pipes or logs. Only the Makkikor proved a problem to accommodate, since its native environment and needs were so different—even if it could breathe human air and a lot of other things, as it turned out—but it preferred to sleep in the niche it had designed on the *Bahakatan* and seemed delighted to help Star Eagle and the maintenance robots with the renovation and refurbishment of the freebooter ships.

The transmuter at Melchior had made China the way she was, but Isaac Clayben had figured a mechanical way to help her out at least in the area of her blindness. Although the program created by his old staff had been diabolically clever and designed not to be circumvented, Clayben and Star Eagle had devised a mindprinter interpretive routine and a gadget that gave her a sort of sight when she chose to use it. Sound waves, traveling on a frequency that would not interfere with ship's systems and was beyond the ability of any colonials or Earth-humans aboard to hear, were translated into electrical signals and sent through nerves to her brain, where the interpretive program operated. Only the Makkikor could hear the signals; he found the sounds not only pleasant but, Hawks suspected, somewhat erotic.

Using the device along with the mindprinter program, China could "see" well enough to distinguish individual objects, although she could not discern specific features of a person nor, for example, read print. She still preferred her memorization routines, which were now so natural that she hardly looked handicapped getting about, but in an emergency or in a strange environment, the device might mean life or death, and she appreciated it.

They had not wasted the time in other ways, either. They hunted without much success for other remnants of the freebooter culture, and finally Hawks decided, with the council of captains concurring, to go after a ring.

By now the newcomers had been told the whole story— what they were after, what the rings could do, and why the rings had been created. Two of the crews had visited Chanchuk, and the *Indrus* knew Janipur well, since the people of that world had been created out of the same original race as theirs and had kept many of the same customs and forms of the ancient Hindu beliefs. Captain Paschittawal, in fact, had even seen the ring itself, in the People's Treasures collection at Cochin Center, the chief administrator's headquarters. Apparently, he reported, the chief administrator rarely wore it, except on solemn and highly ceremonial occasions.

"It is a beautiful thing, very big," Captain Paschittawal told them. "It is kept under a magnifier, in fact, so that one can see the exquisite detail work. Two beautiful birds, mirror images, sitting on small fir branches. It is most treasured because it is one of the every few artifacts that came with the Founders centuries ago."

Hawks nodded. "I want you to get together with Raven and Sabatini and give them as much detail as you can. I believe it is time we put Sabatini's unique talents to work for us."

The captain's eyebrows rose. "I have heard you and the others talk of this, but I do not understand what you mean by 'unique talents.'"

"You won't believe it until you witness it, but let me put it this way. You are Hindu, correct?"

"I am, sir."

"And you believe, then, in reincarnation?"

"Yes, sir, I most firmly do."

"Let me just say that Captain Sabatini not only can reincarnate, but can choose just what and who he's going to be. And he does not have to die to do it." *Although somebody else does,* he added a bit guiltily to himself.

After a full briefing by the *Indrus* crew, Hawks met with his security staff and Sabatini in his own office deep inside the guts of the *Thunder*.

"Well," Raven said with a sigh, "Nagy said it'd be the easiest, although I ain't sure I like it if it is. This thing's like something in the regional museums of somebody's crown jewels. It's almost a sacred object because it's Earth and it's original. It will be guarded and not just by people. It's gonna have one hell of a nasty security system on it, since a lot of these Hindu folks believe things like this got magic. That crew said there are all sorts of legends about the powers of the gods that come with being the wearer of the thing. This is a heist problem, and who knows what kind of technology they bought or what the nasty computers of that Center came up with? And there's the racial and cultural thing."

Hawks nodded, knowing just what Raven meant. "Those we will face with every problem. We knew that from the start—at least I did, and I think you did, too, if you wanted to think about it. It would have been too much to expect that any of the colonials were recruited from the freebooters would be members of this race. I consider it a stroke of real fortune that we, at least, had people here who knew the world and its people. If this is the easiest, then this is the one we go for just to see if we have a prayer of getting the others. Sabatini?"

"This is one I think I'm really gonna enjoy," the captain said. "I never been anything this different before. Still, the basics are here. The chief administrator comes from a small town up against the mountains on the smaller of the three continents, and he has an estate there and goes home a lot. He's one of them types that likes to spend time with the people—and, of course, I bet he has one hell of an illegal high-tech lab there someplace, too. We can't just walk into the Center—it's gonna be too well guarded and it won't have the kind of conditions I need to be safe and secure while I—change into something less obvious, shall we say. I may have to go through a few people to get in there. Maybe some townspeople, then to servants at the big man's place, and from there to somebody with authority and easy access to Center."

"That's understood," Hawks told him. "But I don't think there is any way you are going to be able to steal that thing all by yourself. If you can, fine, but if I know a chief administrator, no matter what the race or culture, there will be no time when you will be able to become him and particularly not his security chief without being discovered, and I would wager much, if I had anything, that it takes at least both of them to disable that alarm system."

Sabatini nodded. "I understand that. Still, if I get a crack at it, I'll try. If not—well, then it'll have to go to the experts up here and we'll cross that bridge when we come to it. Right now, I'd say the biggest problem is getting me in—and out, if need be. Master System knows what we're after and it's *got* to have that place monitored wall to wall, and we sure as hell aren't going to be able to get close enough in to land a transmuter receiver."

"I believe I can help there," Star Eagle broke in. "It

wouldn't do to bring the *Thunder* and expose the fleet at this point—we may need all that power later on, if only to fight our way back to Earth. I can use a capsule, however, with a basic life-support system, and stick it in a prepro-grammed fighter. They are fast and expendable. Janipur might even let you get down if they couldn't tell where the fighter came from, if only to follow it back."

"Uh huh. And how are you gonna get that fighter close enough to let it get in? You punch anywhere in the area and they're gonna know it."

"I know. If need be, we have ships to spare, but I would just as soon not spare any people. It will get you in and confound Master System, I am sure. It will also tell us just what sort of forces are in the area, so we can plan for the future. We must, after all, also get you out."

Raven turned to Sabatini. "You know, if this all goes as planned, we're gonna hav'ta figure some new name for you, and if it's one like the *Indrus* crew's got, I won't want to know it. We'll also have to recognize you when we see you."

Sabatini grinned. "Well, we have a nightingale, a hawk, and a raven, at least, and I'm told a couple of our new friends have names that translate out like that anyway. From now on, why don't we follow that convention? Why not—Vulture?"

And Vulture it was. Although all the captains hungered for some action and volunteered to make the drop, Star Eagle determined that *Pirate One* would be their best bet. It could carry the small fighter with its cargo capsule, and might just fool any automated defenses. In any case, al-though none liked to discuss it, it was expendable.

It was agreed, however, that the small, dark Captain

Paschittawal would fly it, since he had the most knowledge and experience of any aboard in getting in and out of Janipur. Warlock would handle weapons, since she was best at that. Only those two would go; Sabatini, in his capsule inside the fighter, would be along for the ride.

Thanks to the *Indrus*'s local charts, they had excellent maps of the planet and its terrain. It was decided to attempt a landing in the mountains to the north of the village and state, where landforms and general weather conditions would provide good cover for the fighter, which was intended to remain down. The people of Janipur were not good at mountain climbing, which would provide some extra security, but might cause problems for Vulture should he have to return to the ship in Janipurian form. He did not minimize the difficulties, but he was not that concerned. "I will get whatever I need, one way or the other," he assured them.

The one thing they weren't all that concerned about was Vulture returning reprogrammed by Master System. Clayben was quick to assure them that if such techniques could have worked with "the creature," he would have used them back on Melchior. The very methods by which memory was stored were so different that none of the common methods would work, and any biochemical or psychogenetic agents would be neutralized if introduced. "Remember," the scientist told them, "this is not Sabatini, or Koll, or any of the others it has called itself. It is a unique homemade alien organism only *pretending* to be these people, just as it will pretend to be one of the people of Janipur."

As an initial test, Star Eagle rigged up *Pirate One* with false identification and an automatic program requiring no one on board. All it would do was punch into the system, go about its standard refueling, and then return to a predetermined point where its much more sophisticated scanning records would be analyzed. Lobotomized, the ship's core was not much good without a human at the decision-making level, but it could carry out such simple and routine tasks and respond to standard queries. They were not much worried about it being recognized; it was one of an entire class of automated freighters all of which looked identical. This was one area in which machine precision and standardization worked to the advantage of the pirates.

They spent a nervous eight and a half hours while their first ship was away, worrying that it might not return or might return altered or containing a cargo of Vals, but it arrived right on schedule, its tamper seals and passwords untouched. From examining the sensor data, Star Eagle felt sure that either they were being led into a trap or Master System was being very cavalier about the world and its ring. No other ships were evident in the system while *Pirate One* was there. An automated satellite relay station had challenged, then passed, *Pirate One*.

"I don't like it," Hawks told the council. "It's too easy. Master System isn't overflowing with Vals, but it has enough, or it can create enough, to monitor five worlds, and it could probably have a ship full of its troopers lurking around each, as well. I can't believe it would keep the way open for us unless it had something more sinister in mind. It is logical—it also would know that this was the easiest and the probable first target."

"I agree that it has something up its metaphorical sleeve," Savaphoong put in, "but I wouldn't be too surprised if it was traditional and probing. I think it may want to see if we can do it, and, certainly, it does not just want the few who would steal the ring, but all of us. It thinks in far longer terms than we. At this point it is not as concerned about us getting all the rings as it is about us spreading and multiplying so that it will be in constant danger now and for generations to come. As of now, our knowledge is more of a threat to it than our deeds. It will be *after* we get the ring, señors, that we will be in the gravest danger. The game is two-way, you see. We must acquire the rings. It, however, must acquire us and stamp out the knowledge of the rings and their power."

Sabatini grinned. "But it does not know about the Vulture."

Insertion proved relatively easy, far easier than they had a right to expect, bearing out both Hawks's concerns and Savaphoong's reasoning. They flew the fighter remotely, choosing a landing site so rugged and misshapen by rocky outcrops and towering peaks that it never even saw the sun. Powered down, the fighter would be practically invisible from the air. Even so, it was a tricky operation that has to be done with deliberate speed. Master System's monitoring satellite had to be on the other side of the planet when they began, on an orbital swing that would keep it away from the landing zone for the longest possible time. The fighter could be powered down before the satellite made its sweep, but residual heat might still betray it when the satellite compared notes with its previous pass. Some cooling time was essential to keep it from showing up like a beacon to the monitor.

The new fake ship's identification worked as well as the previous, with no indication that the system monitor suspected that it was actually seeing the same ship again. The fighter was launched as soon as they felt safely clear of the system monitor's scan, and Captain Paschittawal, linked in, guided it carefully toward Janipur, cutting and boosting power as needed to avoid the orbital scans and finally inserting it in opposition to and behind Master System's planetary monitor. It would now pass over the exact same region as the monitor, but only after the monitor and always on the other side of the planet from it.

Within two hours, while the alleged freighter was still taking on fuel, the spot was passed over, checked, and found to be good. Paschittawal allowed two more orbital passes, so that the area of the monitor survey would no longer include the target, then launched the fighter down to the prescribed spot. Vulture wasted no time in climbing out as soon as he could risk it.

"Very easy," the captain said with satisfaction. "It is how we got down to the planet to do business in the old days."

They dropped a relay satellite in the dense fueling belt that could pick up and relay coded subspace communications from Vulture. The only danger in the relay was that another ship, in for fuel, might gobble it up, but the odds of that happening were not great.

Vulture was now loose on Janipur and those back on the *Thunder* could only wait.

In the meantime, the members of that odd community continued to get to know one another and to grow. China had a daughter, whom she named Star Daughter, and Hawks and the others of the old guard were more than astonished to hear that Cloud Dancer was also with child. Silent Woman's nursery was going to get crowded a bit faster than expected.

The Chows in particular seemed to be blossoming. Both had taken well to piloting, which had given them an enormous amount of self-confidence and a real job that might prove important, even vital, in times to come, and both were also now spending a lot of time in the company of the two half-Chinese crew members from the *Bahakatan*. Their extremely mottled skin had given them a low self-image, but the crewmen did not seem to mind. Hawks suspected that men born and raised in deep space, where they dealt with large numbers of bizarre colonials, would find the strangely marked but otherwise attractive women more exotic than grotesque.

Hawks himself was diverted for a while by Cloud Dancer's news, but he could not let it sway him from long-range planning. He was to have a child and that was important, but for that child to have any chance at life and a future, his parents and their allies would have to prepare the way.

Fernando Savaphoong was an initial key to any planning goals. He had contacts, secret channels of communication and information, and he used them.

"There is very little out there," he reported. "The heat continues to be on, I fear, and I do not know when or if it will be off. There were an estimated half-million free-booters out here, and those who have not been caught or killed are mostly either running or hiding. I have contacted some who are hiding, but they are of no real use; *they* expected to hear news and get information from *me*, so withdrawn are they."

"Anything about the targets? Particularly the missing ring?" Hawks asked him.

"Little. Stories, nothing more. Even my Center contacts on the colonial worlds know little that we do not know."

Ikira Sukotae looked thoughtful. "Now, let me get this straight. You know that one is on the Mother World, and we know the second is definitely on Janipur. You have the worlds for two more, and while they will be harder to find we have some support, at least in freebooter stories, about them existing there. Yet nothing, absolutely nothing, on the fifth ring."

Hawks nodded. "That's about the size of it."

The tiny captain rose. "Let me talk to somebody for awhile. I never had this thought before, but it's one way to go." She went back and sought out Takya Mudabur, her amphibian crew member. Mudabur was nice enough and good in a pinch, but unlike the others, who had been together for many years, she was a bit of an outsider kept more to herself.

"Takya?"

"Yes, my captain?" She was in her bath enclosure but stuck her head out when she saw someone enter her hut. "Something wrong?"

"Takya, we have done well with you dealing with the water worlds. How many has it been—four? Five?

"Six, my captain. Why do you ask?"

"When you talk to those people, just in general conversation, did you ever hear of a story or legend about a great golden ring with a design on it? Birds, perhaps, on a black stone set in a great gold ring owned by someone of power or importance?"

Takya thought a moment, then shook her head. "No, never. I have heard the story of the five gold rings and I am sure that if I had heard of any such thing I would have remembered it then."

"Of the more than four hundred and fifty known colonial worlds, how many would you say have water people?"

"Not many. Ten, perhaps fifteen percent. You should know as well as I."

She hadn't known, never having counted them, but the total amazed her. Somewhere between forty-five and sixty or so such worlds. "Takya, all the water people I have ever seen are still air breathers like us. All of the ones you visited were. Have you ever heard of a race of water breathers?"

"Yes, there are some," she said, "although not many. There are also some who breathe atmospheres poisonous to us, as well. Why do you ask?"

"Just following a train of thought. Are there any free-booters, any spacefarers at all, among such races? Ones that either breathe water or something else we cannot?"

"I do not know for certain, but I have never heard of any. They would have to drastically modify any ships they flew, have special pressure suits and the like, and would have to modify the atmospheric transmuter systems to produce their required atmospheres. It was difficult enough for ones such as you and I to get out. Adding that may be asking the impossible."

The captain nodded. "Very well. Thank you." She headed back up to the council of captains on the *Thunder*'s bridge. They all looked at her expectantly.

"Well? Anything you'd care to let us in on?" Hawks asked.

"I—I'm not certain. Have any of you ever encountered a race that requires either water or some noxious atmosphere or excessive pressures to breathe and survive? Among the colonials, I mean."

"There are several," the insectlike Chun Wo Har responded. "They are not on the usual freebooter charts be-

cause they are of no practical value. Most cannot even
have the level of technology the standard Centers use, and
others exist under conditions that render them useless for
any profit. Why?"

"I think I see where she's headed," Hawks told them.
"Between us all we have represented here eight separate
races. Combining your varying experiences, we have experience with perhaps a hundred and fifty or two hundred
more through travels and business and contacts with other
freebooters. Nowhere is there a trace of the lost ring, even
as a legend or myth or totem of some kind. Yet we know
that it is required by the core program of Master System to
be in the possession of and under the control of a human
being with power. If I were Master System and I wanted it
as buried as possible, I might well place at least one under
such conditions."

Maria Santiago shrugged. "Why not all, then? It would
make it next to impossible."

"You are forgetting the transmuters," Star Eagle broke
in. "We can make what is required."

"That may be true," the *San Cristobal* captain responded, "but once you are remade you are that way for
good, no? Because there are inevitable minor losses which
become major, even catastrophic, in a second try. So you
become these—people—and you get their rings, but what
good does it do you? The sheer complexity of sustaining
yourself in space or on another world is daunting, and the
—how you say?—payoff, the insertion into Master System, is going to be under less than ideal conditions, if I
guess right. You could steal them but not use them, and, I,
for one, would not wish to be in the position of risking all
to get the ring only to give it up and trust it to some, let us

face it, alien kind of person who can offer only a promise of some ill-defined reward. If I were Master System it would be the logical thing to do."

Hawks nodded, thinking furiously. "Unless—unless there aren't five worlds where it would be safely done. I wish we had an analysis of any one of the rings rather than just a hologram of Chen's. These things only *look* like rings, and they were designed by Earth-humans for Earth conditions using existing technology of the period. Below and in the setting are complex computer circuitry and instructions that, when combined with the other four at the correct interface, give access to the Master System core and override any existing instructions. What could they be made of? I think the gold is just that—gold. I have seen Chen's and it looked like gold to me. The setting, which looks like stone, must be some sort of synthetic to contain and protect the electronics. Hence we can, for example, rule out any atmosphere where gold would be corroded or in any way deformed or broken down."

Savaphoong nodded excitedly. "*Si! Si!* It is logical! If the rings contained anything active, they would be shorted out in water, for example, ruling that out."

"They are most certainly passive," Star Eagle commented. "It is asking too much to expect anything to hold a charge nine hundred-plus years, let alone indefinitely. They may be powered up when connected, but not individually and self-contained."

"Water is looking better and better," Hawks noted. "Gold is safe in water. It will tarnish, but it is easily restored even after centuries. The synthetic holding the electronics would certainly be watertight and airtight. And if they were water *breathers*, they would have virtually no contact with the freebooters. I would say we have a job and that is to check all the water breathers first. If we strike no gold, as it were, then we can begin to check the small number with deadly atmospheres."

"I believe I can correlate the master files from the various ships and come up with most if not all the possible worlds for this," Star Eagle told them. "However, it will not be easy to check on them all. Most will never have seen another kind of human before, and will consider us all, even Takya, as monsters."

Hawks sighed. "These are the kind of problems we expected to have to solve, and we must solve them one way or another. It is the job of you all to work out methods and a system for doing so and then implement it when we approve. If Raven and Chen are correct in their interpretation of the ore commands, then it only must be *possible*. I do not believe there is any requirement that it be easy or guaranteed."

Vulture had been down on Janipur for seven weeks when the *Thunder* finally heard from him again. The new voice was male, very highly accented, and occasionally difficult to understand, but the message came through.

"I have rigged up a repeater device to the fighter, then the relay. I hope it works," Vulture said. "I also do not know how long this is safe to use, so I will be brief. This is a far different world from any I have ever known, but there is a cultural undercurrent that shows a human origin. Much of the world is primitive, pretechnological, and ignorant, as expected. The population is dense in the desirable areas —very dense, and very poor, by most standards. They are administered by five Centers employing a total of perhaps thirty thousand inside and in the field. As the good *Indrus* captain told us, the Centers are quite modern with full technology complexes. There is a complex and rigid caste system here, as well, which complicates matters. One cannot graduate to Center level; one must be born to it, and there are physical ways to tell."

"All right, but have you seen the ring?" Hawks asked.

"I have. It is not difficult if you are of the Brahman caste. As the captain said, it is usually on public display, during which times it would be impossible to get to. Too many people and too much split-second security. After dark it is protected by a labyrinthine set of computer and mechanical devices and switches that bewilder me, and I am many engineers and computer personnel, if you remember. To remove it even if you had all the codes and keys would require at least three people. This is long enough for now. The rest of the data is being sent serially on my subcarrier direct to Star Eagle. I will call back when I can, but not before this time tomorrow."

"Wait! No chance you can get it without us?"

"None. I am third in rank in Security here and have much power, and I have even participated in unlocking the thing, but there is simply no way to do it alone and get away with it. One last thing. You were right about the trap. At least ten percent of security forces in this Center and possibly others are ringers. There may be more outside. Master System is just waiting for us to try for it. Good bye for now."

"He has broken connections," Star Eagle said. "I have the rest of his information under analysis now. It appears that the actual system is nearly identical to Earth's, but the people there do not look anything like any of us, and the

culture is a rather strange form of Hinduism. I believe with
the help of the *Indrus* personnel we could create an effective linguistic mindprinter recording, but unlike Vulture,
the rest of us would require a great deal of study to change.
Culture aside, this will not be body or life style to easily
get comfortable with."

"But what about the ring defenses itself?" Hawks asked.
"What are we facing?"

"Everything conventional, apparently nothing new.
These people have very poor night vision, making for a
daylight culture, and their regular visual range is even
more restricted than yours. That works in our favor since
their light-beam traps are invisible to them but not to us.
The outer doors are locked with a large key, but the door
has its own sensors and visual remote monitors as well.
There is a secondary vaultlike door inside the first, with an
open area that is monitored visually and with sensors. The
second door is computer-operated by coded remote from
the master console in Security. No one individual has the
whole code, which is changed periodically."

"I see. Go on."

"The inner display museum is covered by light sensors
and is also visually and aurally monitored. The display
cases appear to have weight sensors under tiles around
them, so we will have to find out what sort of weight will
set them off. The display case itself is thick but transparent, most certainly bulletproof, and perhaps cutter resistant
to anything but a laser torch. Cutting or breaking through
would not work, however, since fine alarm wires run
through it like thin mesh. The only way to open the case is
with two conventional keys, one worn by the chief administrator himself and the other by the chief of Security.

Turning both simultaneously opens the case and sounds an alarm in Security. If it is legitimate, the alarm is simply ignored, but it cannot be turned off until the case is closed again and locked."

"All right. Anything nasty waiting if you get that far and remove something?"

"No. It is a good alarm system, but not a spectacular one. You pick it up, close the case, and if you also miss the alarms on the way out and relock all the doors you have it."

"I'd hate to see what you call a spectacular system, then. This sounds mean."

"The alarms and locks are all conventional, which means traditional and essentially antique. The same sort is used at Earth Centers. The Vatican Center museum, for example, is far better defended."

"Hmmm . . . I wonder if there's any chance of Vulture being alone on duty in Center Security?"

"Not likely. If they follow the standard procedure there will probably be a duty officer and three or four others. You know the procedure, although if Master System has added personnel it is a good bet that one or more of those on duty down there will be its people. The area also has regular watchmen rounds, and the doors are checked. Bet on all the watchmen being Master System personnel. You won't be able to bribe them or turn them, Hawks."

"Dealing with the people is Vulture's job, and I'm sure he can do a good enough cover to get help. It's a sure bet that most of the regulars down there, and particularly the bureaucrats, are really going nuts under a near-occupation by Master System. Some of them might well cherish the idea of really helping embarrass the bastards—if they didn't know the theft was for real. Any chance of doing it the easy way? Cutting in the C.A., for example?"

"Dubious. Any chance we might have had left when Master System placed its own personnel down there. The chief administrator is first and foremost a survivor with self-interest paramount. No, we will have to steal it, and that brings up the first and certainly not the last of the nasty problems we will face."

Hawks sighed. "You have a plan and personnel in mind?"

"I have both, but let me work on it further. I will also need supplementary information for Vulture. Make no mistake, though. There is no getting around the fact that we will require at least some of our people as Janipurians if we are to get close enough to this to even have a crack at it. Others, with their own innate abilities, might not need anything drastic, but will require more than Vulture's help to get where they are needed. It appears clear now that the late Arnold Nagy provided us with the ones best equipped for this particular job. I am merely building off his obvious intent with others he did not anticipate."

"I know. Damn it, it shouldn't be now, not for *them*. Later, perhaps—you are sure that full transmutation is the *only* way?"

"Hawks, think of it from the basis of what you know. Back at North American Center, what would be the chance of, say, the *Kaotan* crew sneaking in, looking over and examining Security areas in detail, inside and out, while they were open, then breaking in, stealing something, and getting out and away? Even if they had a senior Security official on their side? Now add ten precent Master System forces—and you can bet a Val is somewhere around to call the shots—and you see the problem."

The leader of the pirate band sighed again and nodded. "You're right. And in that case some excuse could be made for an open colonial visit—and they still wouldn't be able to do it because they would be watched like, well, hawks around the chickens."

"We are stuck. They were obviously provided to help solve this particular problem. We may try it without them, but we would be crippled if we did."

"I agree. I'll start easing into discussing it with them. In the meantime, do you have anything visual on what these Janipurians look like? I think I'd better know what I'm asking before I ask it."

"Come up to the bridge. I haven't any such data from Vulture, but I have some recordings from *Indrus*'s files."

He went on up and found several members of the various crews there working at some of the consoles, and Raven, cigar stuck in the side of his mouth, trying to look as if he were busy too. But when Star Eagle put up a picture of a Janipurian, all turned and stared.

"What the hell is that?" Raven asked.

The creature was more animal than human, yet it had some very human gestures. The face, light tan in coloration, was large and humanoid, although the nose had flap-covered nostrils, was too large and wide, and its porous skin glistened with dampness like many animal noses; the mouth seemed too wide and the chin too small, giving the face a blocky shape. The pointed ears were upright and seemed to be on a swivellike socket, able to turn in any direction. Most inhuman were the eyes, which were large, round bulges.

The whole body was covered in very short but thick hair. The torso was tapered, thinner near the thick neck than at the rear and shaped more like that of a four-footed animal than a bipedal human. The arms, too, were more like forelegs, and the hands, on incredibly thick wrists, were enormous, the fingers and thumb long and pointed and looking deceptively boneless. And from the back of each hand grew an enormous, thick prominence that looked hard as steel. The creature was standing more or less erect on its two feet, although it gave the appearance of being slightly bent over, as if ready to launch into a four-footed run. Arms and legs looked to be of equal length, and the feet had huge, splayed toes with deep, curved nails that seemed to dig into the ground. Again, on the back of the ankles there was that same steellike growth. Some kind of brief protective bit of clothing was draped above the thick, animalistic thighs, but there was no hiding the fact that the creature was a male.

"If that thing can walk like that, I'll eat it," Raven mumbled.

A young woman, one of the crew from the *Indrus*, laughed. "They do not walk like that, you are right," she said. "The hands and balancing feet curl up, leaving the hooves for moving and running. They are quite fast, in fact. They do get around upright when inside, though, if they have something to hold on to or the distance to go is very short. Do not let it fool you, though. The hands are quite dexterous, and the people are excellent artisans. Those claws can also rip someone open with one try, and they can wield weapons with deadly accuracy. They do not see very well at all at night, but always their sense of smell and their hearing is far better than ours."

Hawks shivered. *What am I asking someone to do?* he couldn't help thinking. *Do I have the right to even ask?*

"You said 'weapons,'" Raven noted, not encumbered by such a duty. "Do they hunt or have prey?"

"Oh, no. They are vegetarians, strictly. Their mouths move more side to side, and their teeth are flat and big. Their design is based primarily on the fact that they came from a culture that was highly vegetarian to begin with—although not all—and this world developed warm as mostly grasslands, desert, and mountains. The grasslands can support a large population, but there are limits, so the system added some rather nasty predators once native to their old region—such as tigers—to maintain a balance in the early days. Today, however, most of the predators are strictly controlled and only occasionally escape from royal preserves. Much of the central grasslands is intensively farmed now, you see—those claws can also till soil. They have some domestic animals to aid them, but their tools are basically wood and stone. Useful metal is rare and prized there, and we traded a fair amount of it."

Hawks tried to put his more personal concerns from his mind and concentrate on the problem at hand. If Cochin Center was anything like North American Center, and he thought it probably was, its floors would be of smooth, hard synthetics. Those hooves would make quite a lot of noise on them. The aural sensors would be a real problem. On the other hand, if those long, pointed fingers were really all that dexterous, then they would be an advantage when it came time to deal quietly with the locks.

"This is a male," he noted. "What do the females look like?"

"Slightly smaller, with firm breasts that hang down when she is on all fours," the woman told him. "The children are born as four-footed creatures with only flaps where the hands and feet will be. These do not begin to really grow out and develop until they are about seven, and are not really useful until they're ten or eleven. The standing, walking upright, and the developed use of the hands is something they must be taught. This was thought to be a protective innovation when the world was more dangerous, as they are still essentially self-sufficient from the age of two and can walk on all fours in a matter of hours or days after birth. But it is the hands that make them truly human, that allow them to manipulate and create and build. The hands and the mastery of them are the mark of being human there. Also, you note the coloring?"

"You mean the light tan, almost white hair?"

She nodded. "That indicates that this man is a Brahman. High caste, probably either a major religious leader or from a Center, as this one was. The castes are known by their coloring. A darker tan, a light brown, would be below this one and probably a professional or a politician or regional leader. Dark, reddish brown would be working class—farmers and laborers, mainly. Black is, well, untouchable. Unclean. They roam wild and are something of a danger to the others."

"Wonderful," Raven grumbled. "So what happens if two castes marry?"

"The effect is interesting, as they take on multiple rather than mixed or blended coloration. The half castes or less have the rights and duties of the lowest caste their coloration shows. Such mixing is rare, but it happens often enough to be noticeable even in a small village such as the one we used for our dealings."

Hawks was thoughtful. "And you say only the light tan get into the Centers? Nobody else?"

"That is what we were told, and it is logical in a society where you wear your class and your social potential on your body."

"Then it's another complication. Finding enough of these light tans to copy will be a problem."

"No big deal, Chief," Raven replied. "They got to come out. If Vulture says they follow the standard procedures, then they all got to go on leave for a period—and that means some are always on leave, right? No, that ain't the problem. The problem is that everybody on that level will have everything on record, birth to death, whatever they use for prints, you name it. The odds are if they don't all know each other—them tans I mean—they know mutual friends and family. It's gonna be pretty damned tough to fake."

Hawks sat back in his chair and sighed. "Oh, I don't know. If ten percent are Master System plants, who knows whom down there these days or can take things for granted?" He leaned forward again. "No, we can make some of those factors work for us. We might even get Master System and its friends to take the fall for the robbery, which will nicely aid our getaway. No, the two big ifs we have to face aren't there. We can work all those out. The first is—is it possible to lift that ring? Can we do it under all their noses and get away with it?"

"Yeah," Raven agreed, chomping on his cigar. "And who's gonna hav'ta become one of *them* for life to spring the damned locks while Vulture covers?"

The ultimate price . . . And this was only the first time.

The Chows seemed more alive than he remembered them, and happier, too. He wished this situation could have arisen under more miserable circumstances. The girls were certainly curious, particularly when they were summoned to Hawks's private office and found him there alone with one of the women from the *Indrus*.

"Sit down," he invited. "Make yourself comfortable. So far you've played a background role in all this. You've been very helpful, but I know both of you felt that you just happened to attach yourself to this group by sheer chance. Would you be surprised if I told you that you had been included all along? That much of what happened to you was deliberaté and designed to make sure you came with us?"

That startled them. "We—just happened to be on the same ship as China," Chow Dai noted.

"Uh uh. A ship taking you to Melchior, so you could be handled and strictly controlled until it was time to move. You were not there by accident. They needed someone with very specific skills and they ran those skills through their computer and you came out, having been caught at China Center going through doors that expert technicians couldn't crack. Tell me, do you know how you do it?"

They both shrugged. "How do you sing or dance? You do not think about it—it is clear in the mind. You know our uncle was a magician, an illusionist he called himself, who loved to escape from the impossible. He taught us many of his tricks because we were good at them. There are only so many ways locks work, and there is always a weak spot."

"Huh! And does this explain how you can crack elaborate electronic combinations of numbers and even coded badge and fingerprint and eyeprint locks?"

"There are some secrets we must keep," Chow Dai replied coyly, "because we swore an oath to our uncle, but there are always ways of getting the right numbers for finding how to fake what is needed."

"Some of those locks at Melchior matched a minutely detailed hologram. You walked through them like they weren't there."

They both grinned. "There is always an alternate way to spring a lock. Anyone who needs a lock that complicated must first be very afraid that someone will get in. After they install it, and after a few times when it does not work and *they* cannot get in, they always have an equal or greater fear that this might happen all the time. The more complicated the lock the easier it is to figure out the emergency bypass, since it must work without triggering the other, more ordinary, way in."

"Have you ever seen a lock or security system you couldn't beat?"

They looked at each other and shrugged. "Yes and no," Chow Dai responded. "We have never seen one we could not beat, but we have been caught because we did not have any easy way to look over the system and take the time to find out all about it. We were ignorant peasant girls. At the time, we did not even know what a visual monitor was."

"But you do now."

"Oh, yes. We have spent much time aboard here learning more and more. Star Eagle has been very kind and has read us details of the most *incredible* security systems, and shown us moving cartoon pictures of them. We know *much* more now."

Hawks wondered who put Star Eagle up to *that* useful activity. The crazy thing was, the Chows were exactly what they said they were—simple peasants taken in as domestic servants by a spoiled China Center official's wife. Neither of them could read or write or showed much inclination to learn; neither had any formal education at all. Their good speech in English was due to a mindprinter program and extensive practice aboard the *Thunder*. They were certainly geniuses, but their genius was limited to certain areas.

"You know what this is all about? You understand what we're doing out here, don't you?"

"Oh, yes. You are trying to find the five magic rings that will bring down the machine that plays god. It is a noble thing that might free our people one day."

Here it is. "One of the rings is in a Center on a planet called Janipur. It is guarded by a complicated security system that is mechanical, electronic, and personally guarded, and is considered impregnable. This was known to the people who set up our little pirate band. They felt you could crack that system, steal the ring, and get away. That is why you are here, why you have been here all along. To steal that ring."

"Then we will do it. We have not had a good challenge like that in a very long time."

"There is—a problem. A hitch. The problem is that the people down there are not human like we are human. They are another kind of human—different from us but no more different than some of the others we have aboard this ship right now. We might, under very risky conditions, get humans to the Center, but they would be useless. They couldn't walk around, get in any visual monitor, be seen by anyone there, since there are no Earth-humans anywhere on that world. Master System also has people who look like those other kind of humans down there just waiting for anyone not of that race to even be glimpsed. All our information, all our experts and computers, say that no one could get near enough to that ring to even pick the locks who was not of their race. You understand?"

"You wish us to teach them how to do it?"

He sighed. This was even harder than he thought. "No. We can't allow any of them in on this. Not right now. They are decent people down there, mostly, but Master System is standing over them and telling them what to do and they can't fight it, so they're not going to do the job for us. We have to do it ourselves."

"But you just said—"

He held up his hand. "You remember Song Ching who became China Nightingale? You know how they did it?"

They looked at each other, then at him. "They—used some kind of machine. One that changes you."

"Yes. We have the same kind of machine, and Star Eagle knows how to run it. This ship was designed to do that, to change one kind of human into another. But we don't have any mindprinter program, or a good means of getting one, that would teach anyone changed into the kind of people down there how to use that body. It would have to be learned after someone was changed into one of their kind. It would be very, very hard."

"China," Chow Mai whispered. "They cannot change her back."

"No. People are the most complicated of all living things. We know a lot about how people work, how they're put together and why they are the way they are, and we can change much of it, but it's not just one part we're talking about here—it's the whole thing, body, brain, blood, you name it. More cells than anyone can count, all of which have to work perfectly together. Once always seems to work, but try it again and it just doesn't come back together right. It can kill or cripple or form a horrible kind of monster that's one of a kind—and maybe not make the brain work, either."

The twins were silent for a moment, then Chow Dai spoke. "You want us to be changed into these—others. Learn how to be these others. Then go in and steal the ring. And, after—we are these others forever?"

"Yes. It's the first time this has been asked of anyone, but it will not be the last. Many of us, maybe even me, will have to do the same thing. We have three more rings to get before we can head home."

"May we—see what these people look like?"

He got out a holographic still Star Eagle had run off and handed it to them. It was of the same male he'd seen. They just stared at it, not revealing their emotions, although Chow Dai breathed "Oh" very softly.

"I know what I'm asking and don't think it's easy. I expect to have to give this speech again a few more times. We may *all* need to do it just to sneak past Master System to get to its home, but we might not. It's not fair, but that's the way it's set up. I wouldn't ask if I didn't think it could be done. We have Vulture—you remember the one who was Koll, then Sabatini, very well, I think—down there now, as one of them. He's in their security system at the Center but he can't do the job, only provide information and training and cover in and out. We *will* get you out."

"As—them," Chow Dai said quietly. "And then what?"

"Huh? What do you mean?"

"I mean, suppose we can do it. All of it. We get your ring and then we come back here. What happens to us then?"

"You will still be human beings, damn it. You'll still be the same inside, too. You're both good pilots and we can use good pilots. We might also need you to train others to pick other, different locks. You will be no different from the woman with scales and her nose in the back of her head, or the Cantonese-speaking crew with their bones on the outside. Still people, still a part of the team." He thought about the missing fourth ring and Captain Sukotae's theory. "Someone, perhaps many, might have to become far more limited sorts than these. We believe one ring may be deep on a world of water breathers."

The woman from the *Indrus* cleared her throat.

"I'm sorry," Hawks apologized. "This is Sabira of the *Indrus*. She has dealt with these people and knows them well."

"They are good people," she told them, "and their bodies may look strange, but they are actually better than ours in many ways. They are tough and versatile. And, where it counts, they are quite human. They love their children, are generally good to one another, like luxuries and try to enjoy life as best they can. Most are peasants much like the sort of people yours are. If we are to win, this must be done."

The girls were not properly enthused. "If we did not to this, then what would happen?" Chow Mai asked.

Hawks sighed. "I will not order someone to do this. I could, but it is not in my nature. Too many bad things were done to too many people aboard this ship now because someone or something ordered it done. If you refuse, then we will find volunteers. You will be expected to teach them all that you can about the problem, and then they will go and make the attempt. They will not have as good a chance as you would, but we will try and we will keep trying until we are down to no one here and we cannot win. We must. If we don't get that ring then the rest doesn't matter."

They nodded. "This vault. You have information on it? Yes? Can we know what it is?"

Hawks gave them as detailed a description of the situation as he could. They listened attentively.

"That is not a difficult sequence but it is very tricky," Chow Dai said. "No amateur, particularly in an unfamiliar body, could do it. It is worse because it is mostly mechanical. The mechanisms are not all that different from one big illusion in our uncle's show. His wife would get into a coffin, and then they would fill it with water, seal it with many chains and locks, and my uncle would have to pick them all and open the coffin before she drowned. She was a Buddhist who had studied with some mystics in the high mountains and could remain under for several minutes, more than most people, but it was still a matter of speed and skill. As little girls, we knew just how it was done, and we would often practice with the coffin empty against an hourglass timer. Many long times it took us up to an hour —far too long. Now we could do it, perhaps faster than Uncle Li could. This is a very complicated version of the same problem. No one aboard here could be taught to do it fast and perfect the first time in just a few days or weeks or even months, and we cannot exactly duplicate it here because we have not seen it and its hidden surprises."

"Nonetheless, we must try," he told them.

Sabira spoke. "You would not be going in alone, as you might have had to do under other circumstances. We—the Indrus crew and some of the others—have talked it over. We know the land, the people, the customs. It was decided that one of us at least should go as well, take the same route as you are asked to take, to help teach you the subtler ways of those people. We also have a mindprinter program for the language, which is basically a very distorted version of Hindi, which is my first language. The omens of the gods brought us to you, as the minds behind the attack on the great computer demon brought you here. With all these things on our side, we cannot fail. Compared to what we might face with the others, this is readymade for us."

They gaped at her. "*You* would become one of *them*, as well? Forever?"

"It is my duty. I will not tell you that I am excited by the prospect, but I do not fear it, either."

The twins looked at Hawks. "How long before this would happen?"

He shrugged. "The Vulture has a lot more to set up, and we have to coordinate things. We don't think that getting you in will be a problem. We've been running *Pirate One* in and out at regular intervals for months now, so that it appears to be a new but regular run. It isn't even challenged anymore. Vulture can arrange a much easier and more convenient arrival than we arranged for him. We've manage to get his old ship out and put in one with a transmuting station—the same one we used on the island world. We can send directly from *Pirate One* to that transmuter now, if Vulture is there and we time it right. In fact, first we have to find prospects for Star Eagle to copy and study, and get them to *Pirate One*, where we now have a transmuter and some storage. Covers must be arranged, and no one, least of all Master System and its personnel, must suspect. We are pretty sure that down there at Cochin Center someplace is a Val. You will have to go in and be accepted there before you pull the job. Then we have to get you all out and away under their noses. It's going to be very tricky and very dangerous. Even Vulture can't become a Val."

"Very well, then," Chow Dai said almost matter-of-factly. "Then we will do it."

He was surprised. "Just like that? Don't want to talk it over or think about it?"

"There is no need to do so. We would both be dead at the hands of the security guards at China Center had this not been arranged as you say. You have given the reason we have never understood, which was why we were taken from there and sent to where only important people are sent. The ones who chose us did not make us break into the Center apartments and offices or steal. We did that ourselves, and we were caught for our ignorance. Our lives and our bodies were forfeit because we were caught. They belong to the ones who saved us. You cannot know what it is like to be so helpless as we were, to be beaten and raped not by one but by many brutish men, again and again. Neither of us has really been able to get close to a man since then, nor really trust another. When this—Vulture—creature saved us from Sabatini, we owed still more. We will do it"

"Nobody *owns* anyone's bodies or lives here. That's what this is all about." He looked at Chow Mai. "And you? You agree?"

"We do not need to speak. We know each other's minds," the other said.

Hawks sighed. "All right then. We'll set it up."

PASSAGE: TWO CHARACTERS MEET IN HELL

THE ENORMOUS CREATURE ENTERED THE SMALL DOMED enclave easily, pressing the passwords as if it had set them up, which it had. No one was present to greet it, which mildly irritated it, but it stalked down the entry corridor and into the main room where it found a lone Earth-human sitting with a glass and a bottle.

"You're late," the man said. "I'd offer you some, but I know it would be a waste."

"You should lay off that stuff," the creature admonished. "Those substances that dull the mind are dangerous."

The man chuckled. "And you should know, right? So I lay off the drinking and the smoking and maybe an occasional pleasure pill and I won't die young? I'm already dead, remember? I sure as hell do. Scared the living *shit* out of me, too. Damn it, if you can't even sin in hell then what's the use of living *any* kind of life?"

The creature let that pass. "You have been monitoring the progress of our friends?" it asked.

"Naturally. That's what this floating mausoleum was designed to do, wasn't it? After all, *we* reprogrammed Star

Eagle back on Earth. You know, I wonder when Hawks is gonna think of that? He's a pretty clever fellow."

"Perhaps too clever for his own survival. The real question is what are their chances of success?

The man sighed and took another sip of his drink. "This stuff's good. Like the old country. Not like that synthetic crap we've endured all these years. Anyway, what can I say? We front-loaded Janipur as much as we could, even lucked out in spotting the *Indrus* just ahead of the troopers and sending it a divert message to the rest of that refugee fleet. Stroke of luck. Makes me think even God is on our side, if I only could figure out who God was and what He, She, or It wanted."

"Then you rate their success as probable?"

The man shrugged. "Hey! We did all we could, but short of going in and getting it ourselves and handing it to them on a silver platter, there is no way in *hell* we can do more now. For the first time, and not the last, they are now truly on their own. We couldn't interfere if we wanted to. You know the rules that bind us. Even with everything, this one's not gonna be any snap, although I think they came up with some real original touches in their planning. Now they got two ignorant girls soon to be in very strange clothing whose only gift to the universe is that they can pick any lock ever imagined by machine and man, one girl who knows the route but is gonna still hav'ta learn to be a hoofer, and one creature—whatever the hell that thing is—against maybe sixty troops, the entire Center security system and its personnel and computers, and a shipload more troops lurking around under the command of a Val. How can they lose?

"You are not amusing."

"I do not intend to be. And if they somehow manage to pull this one off, the next one has its own real problems, and the third's a dilly and a half. And we won't mention number four, considering even we aren't real sure where it is, but they got some clues and bright ideas. Did your people bring in this Ikira girl? She's a real asset."

"We had no knowledge of her or her ship being involved in this. I am pleased to hear it, though. The more they depend upon themselves and the less they need us, the more—comfortable—I am. This is no easy thing for any of us, as you should know."

"You really don't believe they're gonna do it, do you?"

The creature paused a moment. "No. I cannot see how they can, with or without our help. Each victory will make defeat more certain down the road as Master System redoubles its efforts."

"Yeah, well, we know well how infallible Master Systems is. Scratch one Val, build a pirate fleet, and maybe snatch one big fat ring to stick in Master System's guts."

"Perhaps. I do not like to hear you say that. I find this whole thing most distasteful, as you know. It is a logic loop of gigantic proportions. If *it* is mad, then am I not also mad by definition? And if I am mad, then am I abetting a mad thing by aiding this attempt at Master System's destruction?"

"Beats the hell out of me, pal," Arnold Nagy said, lighting a cigarette.

"You are no help at all, Nagy," the Val responded.

The Rings of the Master
continues with
Warriors of the Storm
by
Jack L. Chalker
from Del Rey Books

About the Author

JACK L. CHALKER was born in Norfolk, Virginia, on December 17, 1944, but was raised and has spent most of his life in Baltimore, Maryland. He learned to read almost from the moment of entering school, and by working odd jobs amassed a large book collection by the time he was in junior high school, a collection now too large for containment in his quarters. Science fiction, history, and geography all fascinated him early on, interests that continue.

Chalker joined the Washington Science Fiction Association in 1958 and began publishing an amateur SF journal, *Mirage*, in 1960. After high school he decided to be a trial lawyer, but money problems and the lack of a firm caused him to switch to teaching. He holds bachelor degrees in history and English, and an M.L.A. from Johns Hopkins University. He taught history and geography in the Baltimore public schools between 1966 and 1978 and now makes his living as a freelance writer. Additionally, out of the amateur journals he founded a publishing house, The Mirage Press, Ltd., devoted to nonfiction and bibliographic works on science fiction and fantasy. This company has produced more than twenty books in the last nine years. His hobbies include esoteric audio, travel, working science-fiction convention committees, and guest lecturing on SF to institutions such as the Smithsonian. He is an active conservationist and National Parks supporter, and he has an intense love of ferryboats, with the avowed goal of riding every ferry in the world. In 1978 he was married to Eva Whitley on an ancient ferryboat in midriver. They live in the Catoctin Mountain region of western Maryland with their son, David.